# *Sensuality*

## Also by Zane

*Zane's Sex Chronicles*
*Dear G-Spot: Straight Talk about Sex and Love*
*Love Is Never Painless*
*Afterburn*
*The Sisters of APF: The Indoctrination of Soror Ride Dick*
*Nervous*
*Skyscraper*
*The Heat Seekers*
*Gettin' Buck Wild: Sex Chronicles II*
*The Sex Chronicles: Shattering the Myth*
*Shame on It All*
*Addicted*

## Edited by Zane

*Honey Flava: The Eroticanoir.com Anthology*
*Succulent: Chocolate Flava II*
*The Eroticanoir.com Anthology*
*Caramel Flava: The Eroticanoir.com Anthology*
*Chocolate Flava: The Eroticanoir.com Anthology*
*Breaking the Cycle*
*Blackgentlemen.com*
*Sistergirls.com*
*Purple Panties*

Zane Presents

# Sensuality

## Caramel Flava II

The Eroticanoir.com
Anthology

**ATRIA** PAPERBACK
New York   London   Toronto   Sydney

**ATRIA** PAPERBACK

A Division of Simon & Schuster, Inc.
1230 Avenue of the Americas
New York, NY 10020

First Atria Paperback edition June 2009

**ATRIA** PAPERBACK and colophon are trademarks of Simon & Schuster, Inc.

For information about special discounts for bulk purchases,
please contact Simon & Schuster Special Sales at
1-866-506-1949 or business@simonandschuster.com.

The Simon & Schuster Speakers Bureau can bring authors to your live event.
For more information or to book an event contact the Simon & Schuster Speakers
Bureau at 1-866-248-3049 or visit our website at www.simonspeakers.com.

Manufactured in the United States of America

10   9   8   7   6   5   4   3   2   1

Library of Congress Cataloging-in-Publication Data

Sensuality : caramel flava II / edited by Zane.
    p.   cm.
   1. Hispanic Americans—Fiction.   2. African Americans—Fiction.   I. Zane
PS648.E7S46 2008
808.8'03538—dc22

2008017522

ISBN 978-1-4165-4884-3

# Copyright Notices

*To Pamela Crockett Fish,*
*for being a great attorney and an even greater friend*

# Contents

# Introduction

Sensuality, in my opinion, is more important and totally different than sexuality. When a person is sensual, the experience of sex is taken to another level. More than mere private parts are involved; every part of the mind and body becomes a part of the act. These stories in this collection definitely examine that fact with vivid details of what the various characters are thinking and how they feel.

I cannot stress enough that there is nothing wrong with a person expressing themselves to their lovers. We live in a world where lack of communication causes so many issues in relationships that people often look elsewhere for their needs, or never truly experience all that lovemaking can be.

I hope that you enjoy the stories of *sensualidad,* which means *sensuality* in Spanish. Once again I have found some of the most talented erotica writers on the planet to participate in this collection. A lot of people still have trouble distinguishing between erotica and porn. Allow me to clear that up for you. Porn is all about sex. Erotica is about feelings. All of the stories contained in this collection would still be complete stories, even if there was not any intense sex in them. Therein lies the difference.

Make sure that you check out *Zane's Sex Chronicles* on Cinemax and look out for *Addicted* in theaters. Please visit me on MySpace at www.myspace.com/zaneland and join my email list by sending a blank email to eroticanoir-subscribe@topica.com.

Blessings,
Zane

# Therapy

## Patt Mihailoff

## PART ONE

It was the same as always, or so it seemed. She sat in her overly large, tufted-leather chair that made her look small when, in fact, she wasn't. Her hair was pulled back in a chignon, tucked loosely under itself and secured by a Celtic-style barrette.

He knew her lashes were long and feathery, even through her unattractive, serviceable eyeglasses. He wanted to believe she only wore them to enhance her professionalism. He liked to think she wore contacts when she wasn't working.

Her deep honey skin was clear except for the small mole on her left cheek. She had the barest hint of a dimple when she smiled. She wore no makeup except for a pale mauve lipstick that she didn't, in fact, need. Her large gold hoop earrings were typically Hispanic, but weren't the only things that gave away her Latin heritage. Her lips looked succulent and had a puckering movement that had intrigued him from the beginning. She always did it when he said something that had a sexual connotation. No one really would notice it, unless really looking for it, and he'd been looking at her a long time now.

Her dress was a deep purple matte jersey, with a pointed collar that came to a V and exposed the depth of her round breasts.

It had been a hot summer, but when her office cooled sufficiently, he'd seen her nipples pop and jut through anything she'd been wearing at the time. She'd never caught him looking—at least he thought she hadn't.

"How are you today?" she asked in that husky voice a little higher than Kathleen Turner's in *Body Heat*.

It was the same question each time, and he answered the same way all the time.

"I'm good."

Had she caught his double meaning?

"Then let's begin."

She crossed her right leg over her left and perched the writing pad securely on her knee. The dress was long but the jersey hugged her legs in such a way that it was impossible to miss the length of them or the change in shape where her leg met her thigh.

Her shoes were plain, black with a thick heel, and would not have been sexy on anyone else, but the high, sensual curve of her arch would make any man want to caress it against his hardening cock.

He talked, she listened. Every now and again she jotted down a note or two.

"And what do you think the dream means?" she asked, after he'd spent twenty minutes explaining his slumber reveries.

"Isn't that what I pay you to tell me?"

Her brow arched. She always did that when he answered *her* question with one of his own.

"You pay me to help you sort through your confusion, to help you to understand the why's, and to try and fix what might be broken," she answered evenly.

He grinned. He liked her answers. They were never really here nor there. His mind wandered for a moment as he daydreamed of her hair being loose and spiraling around her head, with one of her errant curls coiled lazily around his finger.

"So this woman that you run after, the woman with no face, is there anything recognizable about her?"

"I'm not sure."

"Why are you chasing her?"

"I don't think I want to know." His eyes didn't leave her when he'd said it.

She wrote on her little pad.

"Perhaps," she began, "your dream is about something you need to face, and are just afraid to, which is why you can't catch her. Maybe the *her* is you." Her demeanor was triumphant, as though she'd been the only one to answer the final *Jeopardy* question.

He threw his head back and laughed, his small locks hugging his head gently.

"I assure you, I am not chasing myself. It's a woman, and even though I've never caught her, I wake up with an erection so hard it's painful."

"Perhaps she's a woman out of your reach."

"I'm almost sure of that."

"If this is true, then you must do one of two things."

"Yes?" His gaze was deeper than his low-pitched voice.

"You should try and forget her. Or, maybe surmise what you *think* would happen if she stopped running and confronted you."

"She wouldn't."

"How do you know? After all, it's only a dream." She had not meant for her slight laugh to be condescending.

"Maybe it's not *my* dream?" he offered.

Her brow knitted. "People do not dream for others," she said patiently.

"If the need is great, even a dream can transcend space and time."

She put down her pen. "You've been reading too many science fiction novels."

"No, I've been living with a yearning desire for too long."

"How so?"

He got up, the material of his pants falling into perfect lines against his legs. He walked to the window, his voice reverberating off the pane like silent thunder.

"I'm not sure how to approach this woman, even though I think I know how she wants to be approached."

"Meaning?"

"She wants . . ."

"She wants what?"

"To have control, and then to give it over."

"What makes you think that?

"Because on the outside she is professional and stiff, but inside she is screaming for release." He looked over and thought he saw the slight motion of her legs squeeze together.

"So, then, you think this woman has a sexual desire for you?"

"I didn't say that."

"Not in so many words."

"You, of all people, should know by now that I always say just what I mean."

"All right, then. Do you feel you must help this woman in some way?"

He moved almost silently on the thick carpet and ended up behind her chair. She remained motionless.

"She can help herself."

"Why doesn't she?"

*Now who was the therapist and who was the patient?*

She heard the rustle of his jacket and surmised that he'd shrugged.

"Fear, betrayal—it could be a myriad of reasons."

"Then how is it that you think you know what she wants and needs?"

"Because I can see inside her when she's not looking. Like when she's writing something down."

She shifted uneasily, but remained impassive.

He came back around and sat back down in front of her, his legs wide apart, his fingers interlocked in front of him. "Some people expect a person to be a certain way," he said, with even control. "And, sometimes, that same person can only dream about what they want. They want it badly but rather than act on it, they remain in a safe zone and send their desires off in a miasmic cloud that seeks a place to settle where it can offer itself."

"To what end?" The question was as soft as a whisper.

"To know."

"To know what?" she asked with a tinge of impatience.

"To know what it would be like to be naked underneath, or over, the man she thinks she is helping."

"So, *then,* it is sexual."

He grinned and shook his head.

"For anyone else it would be sexual; for her it would be animalistic fucking."

She cleared her throat and pushed her glasses up on her nose, even though they hadn't slipped an inch.

"Well, it looks like our time is up." She rose and walked to her desk.

He watched her ass, which was round and tight even though her dress tried to hide it from him.

She looked at her date planner. "I see you won't be available next week, so I've scheduled a session a week from next Friday. Is that suitable?"

He nodded.

"I'll see you then," she said. Her face hardened into its professional mode, her lips, which had been so soft before, were now strict and straight as a slide rule.

"Yeah, I'll see you then." He shoved his hands in his pockets and left her office.


When he was gone, she allowed her body to relax. She went to the narrow floor-length mirror on the side wall and snapped open the barrette. Her hair fell in loose curls to her neck and she ran her hands through them to allow for maximum airy freedom.

In the mirror she lowered her eyes to her neck, her chest,

and finally on her breasts. Her nipples were hard and pout-
ing through the material of her dress. They were large and
round—and perfect. She reached up and ran a long-nailed
finger over one. She flinched—it was sensitive and a shudder shot through her.

It was always like that after he left her office. Now in the
confines of her own privacy, she was able to recall their earlier sessions. He had been freer then, with his offerings
about what he considered to be "a problem," and it had been
sexual.

Her professionalism had remained intact as she queried
him, then listened as he told her with the relish of a bawdy
sixteenth-century monarch how much he needed it, craved
it, and desired it. Outwardly, she'd remained unfazed when
he used words like *pussy*, or phrases like, "I sucked her dry. I
tongued her so deep I felt her baby room."

Inside she was jelly.

But it had been that one particular time he'd told her
how he'd placed his woman on all fours and talked the cum
out of her, then made her wait patiently while he teased her
with his tongue. It was with little tingly, flickering movements at first, something akin to a butterfly kiss. He explained how the woman had moaned and moved backward,
trying to get more of his teasing tongue.

Her office had grown warm when he told her how hard
his cock had gotten, and how he let the woman see it, touch
it, but not lick it—something *she* wanted so desperately to
do. He explained how he'd spread the woman wide and blew
against her proud puffy lips and talked to her. Deep, dirty,
nasty things about what he intended to do. How he was

going to drink her, taste her, own her pussy. Then he explained how the woman had loved *every* second of *everything* he did.

She closed her eyes as she thought of that session, and her hand that had been teasing her nipple wandered down over her waist, then her thigh. She pulled her long matte jersey dress slowly up into a knotted bunch. She smiled as she thought of the garter belt she wore with no panties, her own naughty little secret that no one would ever suspect.

Her fingers moved over her trimmed vee, then down to her fleshy lips that had begun to dampen the second he'd walked into her office. Her body milk had seeped twice when he told her of his recent dream, and now she was squishy wet as she searched for her clit. It was so sensitive that she was about to burst. She found the hood and exposed the hardened satiny nub and rubbed her index finger over it. Slowly at first, feeling the tough little bun soften and become pliable under her caress. Rubbing it faster, her breath became rapid as she closed her eyes and threw her head back. She saw *his* eyes, *his* face, and her finger became his tongue lapping her like a maniacal demon of the flesh.

She felt it race through her. Her secret orgasm that no one knew she could have. It fluttered through her, from her chest, over her belly, down into the bucket of her release. Her eyes were shut tight as she allowed her free hand to balance against the wall, her finger now accompanied by another working furiously against herself. Gritting her teeth, she stiffened as the satiny milk of her body creamed out of her in waves. It slithered and slathered over her working fingers, and she smiled as she finished, her nose imagining the subtle odor of his expensive cologne.

Breathing heavily, she removed her hand and let her dress fall. Taking a deep breath, she composed herself and turned to go back to her desk.

He stood there looking at her. His nostrils flared as though inhaling the high scent of her sex.

"I forgot my attaché case," his deep voice said.

A blush crept up her face as her eyes followed his to the deep brown leather case that leaned unassumingly against the side of her therapist's couch.

## THERAPY—PART TWO

It was a good thing that he was going to be away for a week. It would give things a chance to cool down—to be forgotten. She was going to a medical seminar herself in a few weeks, and it would do her good. It would keep her mind occupied and she wouldn't have to think about him. It was medically unethical, and although tired of the rules, she didn't dare break them.

The best thing was to go on as though nothing had happened. But could she do that? Could it be professional, and business as usual, after he'd seen her pleasuring herself? Thank goodness he couldn't read her mind or he would have known that he was the object of her masturbatory fantasy.

She decided she wouldn't say a word about it; after all, she was the psychologist. He was paying *her* to help *him* work through *his* problems, not analyze hers. But just what were her problems? The men who chased her but she didn't want? Or was it men she'd made love to but who could never reach the part of her where passion was aching to be freed? She wanted someone to break the rules for her.

Somehow he might have guessed that about her, and it made her nervous knowing that.

He leaned against the window, sipping a snifter of fifty-year-old cognac. It slid over his tongue with a warmth much like what he thought she would taste like. His psychologist, his doctor, his medical advisor, with her professional icy demeanor.

He knew the effect he had on women. Hell! His voice alone made more panties wet than he'd wanted to count. How he remembered that day when he went back to her office for his briefcase. He watched as she had fingered herself, then leaned against the wall for support when she released her juices.

How he wanted to taste it, but not the way she would have thought.

It was the dream. He chased her in his mind, knowing that she really wanted to be caught. Somehow he knew, without really knowing, what she needed and how she needed it.

But he also knew it could never be, not now, when they were so wrapped in the neat little package of professionalism. Not as long as there was a line of doctor-patient ethic that she would never cross. The strain of his yearning was becoming too much. There was only one thing to do. . . .

> *Dear Dr. . . .*
> *I regret to inform you that I feel I am no longer*
> *making the progress I should and, therefore, feel it is*

*best to sever our therapeutic sessions. I trust your
decision, so please feel free to recommend, and
transfer my records, to any of your esteemed colleagues you deem worthy.*

He signed it with just a single initial—J.

She had returned from her business trip and was still on
West Coast time and unable to sleep. It was 1:00 A.M. and
she was wide awake. *Maybe I should go to the office,* she
thought. Why not get a jump on all the unopened mail that
she knew would be waiting on Monday?

She put on a long gauzy dress and flat shoes. No one
would be around to know that she wore nothing but bare,
soft skin underneath. She liked the way her nipples felt
against the material, scraping against them just enough to
make them harden and stay erect.

Twenty minutes later she sat sorting through her mail.
She saw the expensive beige envelope and the neat, hand-
written return address. She opened it and her eyes blazed
with anger long before she reached the end.

*Not progressing . . . esteemed colleagues,* of all the . . .

She paced. She had invested a great deal of time on him,
trying to get him to understand his emotions, his feelings—
trying to work him through why he did and said the things
he did. True, he'd paid her a lot for her services, but she'd
thought they'd made wonderful progress.

She threw the letter on the desk and began to read her
other mail. But no matter how she tried, her eyes kept going
back to the note. There was no concentrating now, and she

was even more awake than ever. *Just go home. Go home and lie down.*

She grabbed the note, stuffed it into her bag, and left the office. She gunned the motor of her Mercedes and pulled away from the curb. She was ten minutes from her three-bedroom luxury condo, waiting at a red light, her fingers drumming on the steering wheel impatiently. When the light turned green, she abruptly turned the wheel and made a screeching U-turn and headed back up the street. She fumbled through her purse until she found the crumpled envelope. Scanning the return address, she drove five more blocks and found his building. When she was about to ring the doorbell, a laughing couple exited, leaving the door to close on its own. She slipped inside and rode the elevator up to his floor. Exiting, she followed the apartment numbers until she came to his door. Without hesitation she rang the bell. *What if he wasn't home?* After all, it was Saturday night— or worse, he might not be alone. She pushed the bell again. Then again. And yet again.

There was no telltale click of the peephole cover being raised, just the swish of the door as it was flung open. He stood before her, his face an angry scowl, and wearing nothing except a pair of striped silk pajama bottoms. His chest and belly were finely chiseled, with the slightest hint of paunch if he didn't watch it. His nipples, which seemed to catch her gaze and not let go, were as hard and erect as her own.

"Doctor . . ." he said. "Don't you think it's a little late for a house call?"

"What's the meaning of this?" She waved the note under his nose.

He moved back a scant inch and lowered his gaze to the paper.

They both heard one or two peephole latches being raised.

"Won't you come in, Doctor? No need letting my neighbors know all my business."

She stepped in. Immediately the aura of the medium-sized living room caught and held her like it was his arms.

"We were making progress. Good progress. You opened up, and now you want to see another therapist?"

"I think it would be best," he said with his arms folded across his broad chest.

"Why? I've been able to help you. I'm a good doctor."

"You don't have to sell yourself to me."

"Then why?" Her voice had raised a tiny bit.

He walked to the window and looked out onto the gorgeous view of the dark city below, then turned back to her. "I'd just prefer a doctor I didn't want to fuck."

He knew she would be shaken by his statement, but he also knew she would allow her professionalism to prevail.

"You see? That's what I mean," she said. "You've opened up. That's progress."

"Well, Doctor, how about *you* opening up? How about a little honesty from *you*?"

"Me?"

"Yes, you. What are your desires? Your needs? What are your ghosts?"

"Look," she said with a slight smile. "If this is about what you saw that day——" she began in her doctor-to-patient explanatory tone.

"It's not about that day. It's about every day I sit opposite you, which I prefer, incidentally, when you draw detail after detail out of me about who I am. Or maybe who you want me to be."

"That's insane. I don't think there's been any impropriety on my part."

"No." He laughed. "And there wouldn't be. Not with you, and you know why?"

She waited a full minute before answering, wishing his dark eyes weren't boring into hers the way they were. "Well, since you have all the answers, why?"

"Because you don't want to be responsible."

"Excuse me?"

"That's right. You don't want to be responsible for what you want, for doing the things you desire. You don't want to be responsible for *wanting* to get fucked."

Her eyes grew wide with incredulity. "That's crazy."

"Oh really? I bet you can't even say it. You want to, but you can't, and there's never been anyone to make you *want* to say it."

"I can see this has been a mistake." She sighed, fumbling with her purse. "Maybe another therapist *will* suit you better."

"Good! And now that we've detached our medical relationship, I think you should know there is no way you're leaving this apartment until I have tasted your pussy."

She stared at him, her adrenaline pumping wildly. She was beginning to feel trapped and her eyes widened to the size of nickels.

"Don't worry. I've never raped a woman in my life, and I won't begin now. You'll give it to me. You'll give it all to me because you want to, and you'll like it."

As much as she wanted to leave, his words had titillated her. He was right—no one had ever spoken to her the way he had.

He went to her and gently took her purse and laid it on the side table.

"Whatcha got under that dress?" he asked, circling her.

Surely he didn't expect her to answer.

She felt him lean in, but not touch her. Her mouth opened a tiny bit when she felt him grab the hem of the gauzy frock and begin to wind it up slowly. His other hand slid up her bare, tan thigh, all the way to her firm runner's ass, round and smooth as a new pearl. He allowed his hand to wander over the expanse of one butt cheek, then the other, caressing each gently.

Spikes of chilled hairs rose and moved, making it feel like a thousand million tentacles undulating over her skin.

If he could do this with just a touch of her ass, further musing of the effect of his future actions was unthinkable.

His hands moved up to the buttons on her dress and, one by one, with agonizing slowness, he undid them. She felt the heat of his breath against her ear as he brushed her hair away from it.

"You're not used to what's going to happen," he said.

"You think I've never made love?" Her voice was a hoarse whisper.

"I'm sure you have, but I'll bet a year's salary you've never been fucked, and I mean a heavy, low-down jungle fuck with all the nastiness that goes with it."

Her legs were weak, and she thought she was going to slide to the floor.

The dress undone, he slid it off her shoulders and let it

fall to the floor. He came around to her front and smiled appreciatively. Her breasts were much fuller, heavier than they appeared in her bra and work clothes, her hips curvy and round. Her vee was nicely trimmed, and he longed to find that treasure nub that he knew nestled somewhere deep under a hood of delicate skin.

He leaned in and whispered, "I can smell you."

Her face crimsoned, and even in the dim light, he saw it.

"It's okay. It's the most powerful aphrodisiac in the world. It means you're wet, it means you're ready."

Her eyes closed, not from embarrassment, but because his words were true. Even now she could feel a droplet oozing down her leg.

He circled her again. "Have you any idea how much I've wanted to suck you? To ram and circle my tongue so far up into your pussy that you'd scream out my name for hours?"

She shifted.

"I've wanted to invade your love hole, with one, two, then three of my fingers, readying you for the cock you desperately need."

She bit her lip, wondering why his dirty talk excited her so.

"I know you. I know what you want. You like me talking to you this way. It allows you *not* to be in control. But this isn't about regulations for me. It's about giving you what you desire. And so that we may be clear, it's not all about just your needs; it's also about what I want from you."

*"And what's that?"* she asked, just above a whisper.

"I want you nasty. I don't want the nice, prim and proper doctor. I want that nasty woman inside you. The woman who is going to squat over me and let me lick her from her ass to her pussy. The one who is going to slide her slippery, cummy pussy down my face and allow me to eat her raw."

This time she did waver and he caught her. His strong, steely arm, perfect for keeping her erect, felt like a smooth, wooden log.

"I want you to lie back, wind your long legs around my face, and hold it prisoner to your sweet hot, wet, clit. I like that word, don't you? It's just so wanton, so nasty. I want you on all fours while I eat you from the back so hard that you'll try and scamper away. But I'll be right behind you, tonguing my way inside every part of you."

"And what would you want in return for this little erotic escapade?" She tried to sound amused.

"Don't be flip; it doesn't suit you. What I want, I'll get, and that will be because you won't be able to keep yourself from *giving it to me*."

The room was quiet as he gave her a moment to absorb everything he'd said. "But first, I want you to get used to me. To seeing me, before touching me."

He loosed the string on his pajama bottoms and they slid to the floor. He stepped out of them and kicked them away. Her eyes were trained on a place just beyond his shoulder.

"Look at me."

She didn't.

*"Look at me!"* His words weren't loud, but authoritative, like he was a man not used to having to repeat himself.

She looked at his face, his chest, and then slowly downward. He stood with his legs apart, his resplendent cock, thick and heavy, his balls full. She knew that by the way they hung. His hand came up and cupped his dick. He rubbed it back and forth slowly.

"Touch your wetness for me. Like that day in your office."

Like a machine, her hands, guided by his words, not her mind, slowly moved to her front, sliding over the hairs of her trimmed mound. Her long, slender, well-manicured middle finger disappeared as the lips of her pussy surrounded it. She always liked the way she felt—soft, wet, and slippery. But with him watching her, it was different; it was more.

"Squat a little."

She did and the change of motion allowed her finger to slide inside. She bit back a moan.

"Give me some of it."

He waited while she removed her long, thin, wet finger and offered it to him. He leaned down and took her whole finger to the last knuckle into his mouth. His fat, thick tongue wrapped around it like a snake, devouring off the cum juice.

The feeling of his mouth sucking on her finger was hot and exciting. Her chest rose and fell like she'd just worked up to a fast three-mile run.

"It's as I knew it would be, tangy, with a hint of acidic sweetness."

She waited. For what? She had no idea.

He touched her thighs. "They're strong. That's good. You'll need their strength." He looked at her pert little mouth, her lips full and yearning. How he wanted to shove himself between them, to make her take him. All of him, at once, choking her with his cock.

He stared at her. With all her book learning, all her doctoral prowess, she stood before him, ignorant of her own need.

He would teach her. But to ask her to touch him now, to taste him now, wasn't the right time. He had to make her *want* to do all those things herself. If she wanted it, she would have to be the one to take it.

He lay down on the floor, not far from the couch. *She'll need that for support,* he surmised.

"Come to me."

She moved to him and he gently took hold of one leg and lifted it so that she straddled him. "Move upward to my face and squat."

As though in some state of hypnosis, she lowered her body over him, but not touching.

The high musk of her drove him near to madness, but he had long ago learned to control the sex demons inside himself and willed them back to where they waited like rabid beasts ready to pounce. He sniffed the air around them, taking in more of her scent. He looked up into her and saw her fleshy lips parted and her crack open a mere inch. He scanned her pubis. In there, hidden behind a hood of flesh, was her clit. He couldn't wait to own it. He couldn't wait to nibble and suck it until she begged for him to stop. But now was not the time.

He raised his hands and grabbed her ass cheeks, allowing several of his fingers to cup inside the crack a nanoinch deep. He pulled her down until his nose rested against the place where her clit lived. His tongue sprang out like that of a serpent and whipped along her lips. He heard her gasp and felt her ass muscles tighten. He nuzzled his nose more and pushed his tongue deeper as he lapped. She was wet, but he knew she was going to get a lot wetter. Turning his head a little to the left, he circled his long, fat tongue inside her. He heard the moan and pushed in deeper until his own lips were pressed against hers. He tongue-fucked her as he kneaded her ass cheeks. She was still, but he knew that was not what she wanted to be. He stopped and moved her back a little to see her face.

"You want some more, don't you?" he whispered.

Her answer was the ever-so-slight movement of her hips as they undulated back and forth. The oral dance request, without words. He knew it well and went to work.

He pushed his tongue back in her and flicked it in and out and around and around so hard that he actually felt her grip it to keep it in. He liked that. She was strong and that was how he liked his women.

Lost in the sensual erotic moment, she felt his tongue attack the inside of her and, to her own dismay, felt her hips undulate and grind on his face. He was exquisite in this; no one had ever brought her such pleasure so quickly. He ate her like he had been hungry for a year.

She felt his hands move from her ass to her pussy and splay her apart.

"I want to eat the pink of you," he whispered hoarsely.

She was open and exposed, but in a moment his mouth was on her, in her. His lips sucked out the juice she couldn't stop making. He drank her like a thirsty man in a desert. He kept eating her but let a hard, manly finger begin to rub her clit nub. He circled it until he heard the telltale sounds of squishy wetness. It was the only way to coax the little female nub from its lair. He felt it grow and harden beneath his touch. In a moment all he had to do was suck away the skin-hood and expose the sensitive female protuberance. She was moaning louder now, monotone, but building. Goodness! She was juicy!

He moved his hands down and licked her hood. It fell away like a curtain, and there it was, a pink fleshy pearl of delight. He blew cool air on it and felt her shudder. He flicked his tongue at it and she whimpered. He sucked it once, then twice, and a small scream escaped her. He took it between his lips, and with the barest tightness of his teeth, he began to work it. He felt her weaken as he raped her clit with his mouth.

"No . . . no . . ." she said, but her body was saying yes.

She tried to get away, but he held her fast as he feasted on her. A finger slipped inside her wet, hot pussy and again, she tried to scamper away from him.

"Please . . . please," she breathed at him.

He held her with his teeth but spoke. "What? You want me to stop eating this clitty? You want me to stop sucking?"

"Yes, please, I can't take anymore."

"Oh, but you can. You haven't splashed that sweet cum on me yet."

"I . . . I . . . can't."

"You can and you will." He fingered her deeper, and she wanted it.

She felt an orgasm race to her face and she couldn't stop it, and still fought to get away, and finally she did, falling sideways onto the rug. He had her leg and splayed it apart and pulled her up on all fours.

"Nooo, I can't," she moaned.

He knew she was a second from exploding, and he wanted it.

From the back, he shoved his face against her pussy while his hand captured her clit and rubbed it between his fingers. She was so slurpy and tangy sweet he couldn't get enough and intended to eat her raw.

She scampered away as he had predicted and he was right with her, his tongue attacking her hole like it was his enemy. Spreading her ass cheeks, he licked up her and she screeched with horrific pleasure. Down and up, in and out he went, all the time keeping her clit a prisoner between his fingers. Her hands clawed into the deep pile carpet as she tried to not want to accept the gift of his oral pleasuring.

Her body was on fire. Every nerve ending was stretched to the limit. Everything in her head was a jumble of sexual images. In her mind's eye she could see what he was doing to her, like she was outside herself. She also saw what she wanted to do to him.

She was raw, and his lips and tongue helped to ease the irritating little stinging caused by his sucking. She felt the rush of another orgasm speeding through her. She felt him press against her pubis and then shove his tongue so far in her that she couldn't help but ride it like it was a pony. Then, it slithered from her, streams of silky, sticky cum, pouring from her like syrup from a warmed, spouted jar. She felt him nuzzle his face in it and begin to lap at it . . . cleaning it off her.

She was so weak her stomach ached, and she fell over to her side, turning slightly to look at him. He lay with his back against the couch, his chest rising and falling heavily. His face was shiny from her bodily expulsion, and he licked his lips again, to show her that he much appreciated her taste.

Her eyes lowered and she saw him, large, erect, and

curved. The head of his cock was shiny, and a small bit of pre-cum sat at the top like a glistening gemstone. She crawled forward—not exactly sure why she was doing it, but knowing that nothing could stop her.

Her eyes were glued to his thick member. There was no preamble as she rubbed up his lithe, strong legs until her face was an inch above his cock's head. Opening her mouth, she took him in. Not gentle little sucks, but a wide, mouth-opening draw. She heard him moan when her mouth closed around him, and began to lower down the veiny shaft. Sliding her lips down, she let her tongue dance around him, offering as much pleasure as she could. She withdrew and took him in her fist and sucked the head of his cock . . . then tongued her way down one side of his shaft, then up the other. She kneaded his ball sac, careful not to apply too much pressure to that special spot that would make him shoot his load instantly. The sound that came from him was a mixture of moans and groans as he pushed himself up against her mouth. He knew what she was doing; she was taking her pleasure but she was being the doctor, too. She was trying to keep that perfect professional control she always had with him. He willed the tickle of his orgasm back again, and pulled himself out of her mouth.

Under different circumstances it might have been comical to see her mouth poised in that perfect O shape, but now it was exquisite.

Her eyes showed her dismay at the interruption of oral pleasuring, and he wanted to ease her confusion by sliding himself back into her mouth. But it was time he stopped riding steerage and took his place in the captain's chair.

He sat on the couch, and pulled her up to him, leaning

back so that the angle of his perfectly shaped cock was pointing upward. He pulled her legs over him. Reaching down, he opened her lips. She was so wet, just the way he had always wanted her.

"You want it?"

Of course she did, but surely he wouldn't expect her to say it. She began to lower herself, but his strong hands held her up and off him. The urge to push down was strong, almost as though her hungry pussy knew it was inches away from being fed.

"Do you want it?" he asked again.

She shook her head, but it was the beautiful word of acquiescence he wanted to hear from her own lips.

He didn't speak again, but waited, holding her up and away from the prize.

She stared into his eyes. He wasn't battling with her, but he was a man that wanted certain things and he was not giving in until he got them.

"Yessss!" The word came out as an angry hiss rather than the raspy beseech he preferred, but he had to make it be enough because he wanted her more than he had wanted any other woman in his entire life. He loosened his grip, but didn't remove his hands from her slim waist. Rather, he eased her down toward him.

The heat of his cock's head touched her lips. He moved her back and forth, hoping to have some of her juices ease his entrance. She moved down and he closed his eyes from the sheer heat of her inner lips. She slid down his shaft and the tightness of her threatened to have him shoot his load. Down she moved, and he leaned his head back as she fit around him like a tight racing glove. The juiciness helped only a little and he knew that there was a small amount of discomfort for her. Inch by sexy inch, she eased down onto him with agonizingly slow precision. Finally her firm but womanly soft ass rested on his thighs.

*He's in,* she thought to herself, trying to ignore the pain that was not exactly hurting in a bad way. He filled her and she wondered how long she'd be able to hold him inside her. She felt his hand reach up and gently push her hair away from her face, revealing a gentleness, letting go of all the boundaries of her proficient daily attitude. He leaned forward and kissed her softly, taking her lips and moving his own over them gently. Only when she answered back with a slight pressure of her own did he allow his tongue to dart out and seek the warmth of her mouth.

A white heat shot through her and she pushed her face more into his. She didn't know when it started, only that they were moving together—she pressing down and he pushing up into her. He held onto her hips, pulling her forward, deepening into her with every thrust. He let go of her lips and let her breathe.

"I can hear your juiciness as you ride me."

She looked away.

"No! Don't do that. Look at me and accept what you want and how you want it. How I want it."

"I don't know how—"

"Yes, you do. Say it and make it so. If you want my cock, say you want my cock. If you want me to fuck your hot, wet pussy, then say it. Just like that."

"I can't."

"You can't?" He pushed so hard up into her that she screamed with agonizing pleasure and dug into his shoulders.

When she said nothing, he slammed up inside her again. He lifted her up and laid her down while he was still inside of her. Pulling her legs up, he pounded himself down into her—once, twice, and then again and again. If she was going to make him work for what he wanted to hear, then he'd work her for as long as it took.

It was an assault on her pussy, but she needed it and he wanted it. Her arms were around his neck and her moans were louder. He wanted it nasty and he intended to get it just that way.

"Tell me," he rasped. He circled in her, and the second he hit her G-spot, she screeched up at him.

"I want it. Your cock—all of it. I want your dick so deep in me that it'll make me cry."

She was coming, deep thick waves of silky juice, yet still she pumped against his hard cock. Sheets of it dripped out of her and ran down between them, but he wasn't stopping if she wasn't, so the dance stayed strong.

It was forty minutes later and he was still pumping into her. She was calling him by name and scratching down the length of his back.

He loved her nails digging into him. It meant she wanted more.

Another twenty minutes as the sweat rolled off him onto her, causing the sucking sounds to become more pronounced. It was no longer a battle, but he just couldn't pull himself out of her and she wouldn't let him.

She was tiring, he knew it, but he drove on. It was the only way. He had to show her that she wasn't the one that had to be in charge all the time. He had to let her know that he could take over, and take care of *any* need she had.

"Enough?" he asked.

She could hardly breathe out her answer, but he heard it as *enough*. But still he pounded at her. She lay lax under him, a rubbery mass of delicious flesh. He had long ago stopped counting her orgasms and knew she was spent.

Her muscles gave a last grabbing twitch and it pulled the cum through his body like it was on a string. A flood of his baby juice splashed up into her and there wouldn't be a single inch of her that wouldn't contain a part of his seed. Mixing with her secretions, it melded together like their bodies—a heavy, breathing mass of pulpy skin.

He was too tired to move off her and she wasn't strong enough to move him. Together they slept with him still inside her, and her holding him there.

In his slumber, he smiled. He knew when they awoke, he'd have her again. She would be so swollen that she would never be able to take his growing cock but would want it forever. And that's when he'd know she was his.

# The Ache

## ("O Ache")

### Kaia Danielle

"I'm gonna cuff your wrists, *mulher*." Zumbi's deep Brazilian accent clung to the smooth verbal game flowing out of his mouth. Kendra caught her breath and the phone slipped from her ear at his suggestion that her bound wrists be hung from the door.

*You can do this,* she told herself. Yes, in the privacy of her home. Kendra tightened her grip on the phone and returned it to her ear. She closed her eyes and let his words become images in her mind's eye.

Kendra changed her position on the bed, sinking into submission.

Zumbi went on to describe how he would slide his soccer-sculpted, chocolate-dipped legs between her parted caramel knees. From her semisquat position, she could visualize his fingerlike toes stopping around her midtorso and fondling her erect nipples. Kendra shivered at the imagined contact. She loved it when he touched her sensitive nubs. It didn't matter if he stroked her with his fingers, his toes, or his words.

She reached out for the metal bars on the headboard with her free hand, making her chest slide against the soft, petal-like sheets. She could almost feel the weight of his palm pushing into the small of her back, forcing her ass up higher while lowering her shoulders closer to the pillows.

Zumbi paused. She heard him slurp liquid into his mouth. Hot chocolate, no doubt.

Her now exposed labia, swollen with desire, pulsed as the cool draft wafting through the room warmed. She pretended that the heated air had originated from between Zumbi's barely parted lips. Kendra wiggled her ass to receive the increased temperature that embraced her body.

On the phone, Zumbi continued to describe how his thumb would wander down her back until it was gently nestled in the pucker of her hole. Then, he would begin to swirl it deeper into her twitching, sensitive flesh. She could feel the tip of his thumb slide in so easily that it must have been slathered in cacao oil. For the first time, Kendra welcomed this invasion and leaned her hips back further.

Following his direction, she removed the ice from the glass of cachaça and held the ice just below where his fingertip would have been. Kendra shuddered as cold shot through her hot flesh. The temperature contrast stirred something within her, something that she could only describe as need. A desperate, soul-stirring need for Zumbi's thick pipe of a dick inside her. She guided the ice along the crease where her ass turned into pussy.

She nearly dropped the ice as she finished with a circle around her berry-ripe clitoris. Kendra's eyes rolled back up into her head as ecstasy made her oblivious to the ice-cold water that now streaked down her inner thighs.

She stroked herself with the ice like it was a pendulum, just as Zumbi promised he would stroke her in several hours, back and forth until her plump pussy turned numb to the stinging sensation. Another blast of heat from the vent pushed its way between her folds. The insatiable need expanded, caressing everything below her waist. Kendra's tightened jaw clenched the pillow until her teeth broke through the fabric. It was now essential that she ride Zumbi's dick tonight.

As the ice slipped through her fingers, Zumbi's words pulled her hips back and eased them down on his phantom shaft. The rounded tip would graze the most sensitive spot in her pussy first, sending a tingle as far south as the webbing between her first two toes and as far north as her molars. Kendra gasped at how real his imagined dick felt in her empty pussy. She, now in a deeper squat, rocked on her ankles as she longed for the stiff dick that was not there yet.

*"Ah, mulher, você 'tá pronta para mim ainda?"* Zumbi growled into the phone like a silver-gray puma stalking his prey in the Amazon rain forest. His lapse into Portuguese told her just how close he was to losing it himself. But she had picked up enough of the language to understand what he'd said: *Woman, are you ready for me yet?*

Was she? He had spent the better part of their last three phone calls describing in detail each and every thing he was going to do to her when he returned from this trip to Brazil. Kendra had better be ready.

Kendra almost lost her grip on the phone as her body reconstructed its memories of how Zumbi's dick felt sliding into her. Her vaginal muscles instinctively slackened to accommodate his thickened inches. But there was no meat to satisfy the hunger. Her body's lingering tingle intensified. Kendra pulled in a deep, ragged breath. *"Eu não sei,"* she confessed. *I don't know.*

"You better be ready, woman." Zumbi paused again. "Now, Kendra, remember the rule."

"I know, I know." Kendra knew he was going to repeat the rule. She wished he wouldn't. It had become a mantra in her head. But she knew it was coming. She tried to beat him to the punch, but they wound up saying it together.

*"Você melhora não o toque você mesmo."*

*You better not touch.*

Silence followed. Kendra could hear Zumbi gathering his breath to say something else, but he stopped.

"Shit, I gotta go. They're boarding my flight."

Click.

She threw the phone across the room.

That's when the ache began.

Kendra picked up the phone with a heavy huff. Then she rolled over on the bed and examined the face of her watch.

Zumbi's flight wouldn't land at Newark International Airport for another three hours. They had not seen each other in two weeks. And she had never before felt like such a gushy mess below the waist. It was going to be one hell of a wait.

Before Zumbi, Kendra always got what she wanted, when she wanted it. But Zumbi returned home to Brazil quarterly to check on his family's cocoa plantation in southern Bahia. During these separations, Kendra was forced to deny her own pleasure, her pleasure being fucking Zumbi. Now she hated herself for letting him throw away her vibrator, her second favorite pleasure. Thank goodness he'd been calling from his layover in Atlanta and not from Rio de Janeiro. A journey starting from Rio could take over sixteen hours, even when the airplane and all his connecting flights were on time.

This last conversation had her hot pussy throbbing at an all new high. Unconsciously, she slid her fingers down the darkened line that extended below her waist. A jolt went through her as she held the slippery ball of flesh between her fingers. Her eyes widened when she felt its flushed size— almost the width of a raspberry. Kendra touched all around it to further investigate its size. Tremors began to violently shake her body.

Damn, that felt good. It felt so good that she teetered on the edge of cumming.

No. She withdrew her hand because she promised Zumbi that she would wait for him to get her off. Kendra could wait a few more hours. Maybe.

Their reunions seemed to gain in intensity with every separation. Last time they came dangerously close to injuring themselves. Zumbi had surprised Kendra with a bondage kit he had picked up during a brief stop in Rio de Janeiro. He bound her wrists and ankles to the four corners of their bed—good and tight so she couldn't move. Zumbi then proceeded to slurp, nibble, and suck her pussy while stroking her inner thighs with a purple feather.

Unable to move, all she could do was scream so loudly that she had been hoarse for a week. Her body quakes became so violent that her bound leg yanked off one of the bedposts and broke the bed. The tumble had left Zumbi woozy. Kendra had feared that he had a concussion.

Zumbi had promised a special secret something in addition to the ice to top even the broken bed. Kendra couldn't imagine what.

Three hours was a lot of time to kill, especially when you're horny as hell and can't do anything about it. Kendra decided to pass the time by making her pussy "pretty." It was her special ritual that involved her favorite jasmine and ylang-ylang-scented shower gel, a similarly scented massage oil, and gold-plated scissors. She went into her bathroom closet and retrieved her pretty-pussy kit.

However, between the aphrodisiacs mixed into the cleanser and the cool metal against her already aroused skin, Kendra's hand became too shaky to finish trimming the few stray hairs on her already shaved snatch without nicking herself. Further agitated, she cleaned everything off and put the kit away.

Kendra tried to think of something that she could do that did not have anything to do with sex. But with Zumbi in her life that had become a near-impossible task. She tried cleaning the bathroom, again. But when she pushed the toilet bowl brush into the cave of the commode, she flashbacked on the time that Zumbi plunged his dick into her cave from behind and they wound up breaking the seat off the toilet in her parents' guest bathroom.

No, that definitely wasn't going to work.

Kendra thought she might find relief in the homemade chocolates they kept so readily stocked in the kitchen. After all, chocolate was the ultimate comfort food.

She realized her mistake with her first bite. As the cara-mel filling and bits of broken chocolate shell swirled around her tongue, Zumbi's scent and the taste of his cum over-whelmed her. Zumbi, having been raised on a Brazilian cocoa farm and now spending his days crafting his signature candies, had become a walking, talking, and cumming version of his famous chocolate caramel treats.

The real Zumbi hid behind the persona who had turned his father's humble plot of land into a world-class cocoa plantation. Zumbi was really a freak who enjoyed the challenge of coaxing out pleasure from Kendra's stiff veneer. He was always telling her, "You are not enjoying life. You must let go. I will show you how, yes." He then began to show her just how incompetent all her previous lovers had been. Zumbi drew out her first real orgasm with just a kiss.

And now she was hooked, strung out. Kendra was willing to do whatever he said. Well, almost.

She was willing to do anything but let Zumbi hit it in public. Kendra was the Middlesex County district attorney, after all. The bloodthirsty press already had a problem with a sista running things at the courthouse. They'd be all too happy to slap a picture of her bent-over, naked ass on the front page.

Kendra slipped her favorite satin nightie over her head and lay in bed on her side, curled in a semifetal position. She wasn't sleepy but she knew some "rest time" would be wise, given how abundantly and generously blessed Zumbi was between his legs. The study that reported the average Brazilian penis was bigger than the average American one hadn't surprised her a bit.

She had no idea how Zumbi showed enough restraint to prevent tearing her or causing permanent damage of some sort down there. Half the time she could barely give him head without her jaw catching a cramp. But Kendra thrived on the tension that Zumbi's dick created inside her.

After about ten seconds, she flopped onto her other side. No matter how she lay, Zumbi's words still echoed back to her. His promises continued to linger in her imagination every time the air cooled, causing the central heat to kick back on. It made her antsy. The impatience made her rub her thighs together.

She let out another loud sigh. Then she crammed the heel of her hand up between her thighs. The throbbing only intensified and the restlessness remained coiled tight within every joint. There was no way she was able to lie still. Kendra wanted that dick now!

She flipped through the endless choices that digital cable provided. Kendra had to laugh as she settled for an adult channel. Zumbi was the first guy she'd brought home that her straightlaced bourgeois parents actually liked. Little did they know that he was the freakiest boyfriend she'd ever brought to the house.

Mere hours after meeting them, she'd allowed Zumbi to damn near penetrate her in her parents' hallway. Kendra's mother had poked her pink-roller-and-night-capped head out of the bedroom to check on the noise. Her mother never said a word about it to her, then or since. She had just thrown Kendra one of those secret "go get yours, girlfriend" smiles. Kendra never knew the old girl had it in her.

Kendra squeezed her eyes and prayed that Delta didn't play their usual delayed flight shit tonight. Outside, distant thunder rumbled. Thick, dark clouds began to cover the early evening sky. She whispered, *"Santa Barbara."*

Fuck. She already knew his plane was gonna be late.

• • •

"Where are you?" Zumbi's words had pulled her from her lingering slumber. Thank goodness he had called when he did. She'd been about to drift into so hard a sleep that she wouldn't have woken until morning. Kendra had scrambled off the bed and stopped only to snatch her raincoat, flip-flops, and car keys before running out to the garage.

Now the rain pounded on the roof of the car so hard that it sounded like someone was beating it. Kendra took her foot off the gas pedal to keep the car from going too fast. This part of Interstate 78 was not a place to crash. The drive through the Watchung Hills barely had any lights. She never saw cops cruise this area. And traffic was light through this area even when the weather was clear. She glanced at the clock on her dashboard—11:15 P.M. Yep, she definitely didn't need to do anything that would crash the car.

She continued driving down the darkened highway. Suddenly the lightning lit up the sky. Kendra saw the crumbled concrete and other construction materials blown onto the road ahead. It was too close for her to swerve. Slamming the brake would cause the car to fishtail out of control. She braced herself as she passed over the spot. The car coasted to a slower speed as it rumbled over the debris.

The rain danced sideways across the windshield. She hoped the water would pound down on her and Zumbi's bodies with the same intensity when they would take a shower together later. He would love the new massage showerhead she'd installed that week. That good hurt between her legs screamed for relief.

Light flashed through the sky, bright as sunlight. A loud rumble shook everything that touched the ground.

"*Santa Barbara!*" Kendra swerved the car to barely miss a

large tree limb that fell. The Quiet Storm radio announcer warned, "Don't go out on the roads unless you absolutely have to."

"Yeah, now you tell me," Kendra threw back to the radio sarcastically. She couldn't help feeling that it was her own fault that she was still out there. Had she not overslept, she'd be pulling back into the driveway with Zumbi beside her by now.

The cool satin negligee brushed against her sensitive nipples, bringing Kendra back to the present. She had no control over her body's response to Zumbi's favorite fabric against her skin. Suppressing the tactile memory of Zumbi's satin hands stroking her breasts required more concentration than she could afford to divert from the road. The reason why she was out on the road during this storm came to the forefront of her mind—Zumbi was waiting for her.

She couldn't believe she was going out in public wearing only her lingerie underneath her raincoat. It was a big step for her. However, she did have her panties stuffed into the glove compartment, in case she lost her nerve.

Zumbi was always trying to get her to experience the thrill of public sex. Hell, she had just overcome the public-displays-of-affection hurdle. But Kendra had never been in a relationship this serious before, so she had never felt moved to do it. And her parents had never been overly affectionate in front of her. Was it possible that she might not be able to hold out until they returned to the house? The thought dampened her inner thighs with a force that rivaled the intensity of the storm outside.

Images of the position they discussed flashed through her mind. Thoughts of wanton abandon remained during the rest of her cautious trip to the airport.

The reassurance that she'd soon be in Zumbi's embrace made Kendra feel like she'd turned to liquid. She inhaled the earthy scent that was all Zumbi.

An airplane rumbled overhead. The road glowed orange as the streetlights became more abundant. The sign to the side read NEWARK AIRPORT, 2 MILES. With a renewed sense of purpose, Kendra turned her attention back to the storm-beaten highway.

"I hope you're not too tired. You have promises to keep, *O Senhor Oliveira*," Kendra purred into his collar. She looked around before sucking his plump earlobe. " 'Cause I'll ride you in your sleep if you try to break them."

"Keep talking like that and I'll fuck you right on the baggage-claim carousel over there." Zumbi reached inside her open raincoat and yanked her hips to his and ground his hard length against her mound. Kendra wrapped one ankle around his thigh before she gained any semblance of control over herself. All he had to do was drop his fly and he could stuff himself into her dripping wet nakedness right there.

Kendra shuddered out of pure need. His touch reactivated the good hurt pounding inside her body and caused it to rush to her nipples, even to her fingertips. Zumbi knew her spots well. Loud whispers assaulted her ears and the heat of intense stares burned into the back of her neck. It took an incredible force of will for Kendra to push her hand against Zumbi's rock-hard chest. Kendra unwound her leg and smoothed down her raincoat. "Not here, Zu. Save it for when we have some privacy."

"*Ah, mulher*, we'll have plenty of privacy when we reach

the car." Zumbi chuckled, causing the dimples to deepen in his dark chocolate cheeks. He shook his head as he bent to pick up his suitcase. Zumbi made sure his juicy ass brushed her front while he did it. He whispered, "Ah, Kendra. Always the Goody Two–shoes. One day I'll get you so hot you'll do whatever I say, while we're out in the open for all to see."

The lights overhead gleamed off his bald head. The sight made Kendra lick her lips. He grabbed a handful of her ass as she bent over to pick up his small carry-on bag.

"Hey!" Zumbi grabbed her booty while trying to blink away the lustful shine in her eyes. "I said not now."

Her tight-lipped frown did not prevent the blush that stained her cinnamon-freckled face. She was embarrassed because the urge to grind her ass into his hand almost over-powered her sense of propriety.

"What'd I do?" Zumbi's accented words were laced with lust. He held up his hands in innocence. He couldn't hide his amusement, though. Zumbi's silver-gray eyes sparkled with mischief. They both knew good and well how sensitive Kendra's backside was and how much she enjoyed Zumbi grabbing it. "Tsk, tsk. It's not like you to wear so short a skirt in public."

Kendra turned and winked before stepping into the re-volving doors to the outdoor parking deck. "Who said it was a skirt?"

Kendra had just placed Zumbi's carry-on bag onto the floor behind the driver's seat. She turned to step away and close the door but wound up turning into Zumbi's chest. Before she could blink, Kendra was laid out on the backseat and he was hovering over her. Her legs had landed spread open. The only hair on her body lay in a wispy mess over her face. Zumbi's cocoa-brown eyes gleamed as he gazed upon her naked, bare secret. She wore no underwear.

"*Meu Deus*, it is so wet!" Zumbi never looked away as he deftly loosened his belt and lowered his pants. His anaconda, born and bred straight out of the Amazon, flopped out at a perfect ninety degree angle. Her cunt winked in response. Zumbi stroked his length once. Kendra swore she heard the thing hiss as Zumbi aimed for his target. Her back arched like a woman possessed when he plunged balls deep into her hot, humid rain forest. Kendra groaned as Zumbi fed her desire.

It was on now. Zumbi got into his groove as he rocked his hips in a figure eight motion. Kendra pressed her hands against the closed door to keep from banging her head. She felt like the lower half of her body had liquefied. She leaned her head back and briefly opened her eyes. That's when she saw the security camera scanning the parking lot from the ceiling.

"Stop, they can see us." Kendra slid her hips away and then pointed toward the camera. She could feel her pussy scream in protest.

"Fuck them. Let them watch." Zumbi rubbed his dick-head against her swollen pussy lips. "I don't care."

Kendra pushed him away again as her opening trembled. "But I do."

She pushed herself out of the car and stood. Zumbi slammed the door shut. He stomped away but not before kicking the front tire as hard as he could. Kendra flinched but her pussy wept and shuddered at Zumbi's violent action.

The motion further energized her libido. The throb between her legs pulsed worse than before.

"Don't *ever* do that again!" Zumbi's heated anger rippled off his body. "I should fuck your pussy raw next time."

"Well, shit. Then I need to get your ass home!" Kendra started the car and backed it out of the parking space. But once they were past the cashier's booth, Kendra couldn't stop her hands from trembling. She didn't know how she would make it home.

Even with the rain still pounding, the ride home was too quiet. Kendra snapped the radio on. Sade's "No Ordinary Love" crooned out of the speakers. Her nipples perked up and stood at attention. It was the ultimate song for fucking, just the thing she didn't need to hear right then.

Kendra was just about to snap it off when her side of the car suddenly slouched and the car violently rumbled. She took her foot off the accelerator and steered the car onto the left-hand shoulder.

"Dammit! Now we'll never get home!" she cried.

"Baby, chill. You didn't crash or get stuck out here alone," Zumbi assured her through clenched teeth. "It's all gonna be alright."

"Is it? All I wanted to do was make tonight special. My hormones are driving me crazy. I've been horny since you called me from Atlanta. Even cleaning the toilet makes me want to fuck you." Kendra began to gulp for air. Her rib cage constricted and she felt like she couldn't breathe. "Never knew my pussy could throb this hard."

"And you had the nerve to stop me because of some stupid security camera?" It didn't help that Zumbi began to laugh at her embarrassing outburst. Her frustration made the sides of the car seem like they were closing in on her.

"I gotta get outta here." The rain drenched her bare leg the instant she opened the door. By this point, Kendra didn't care. She wanted to be free from the car. She'd been stuck inside it all evening, holding her in, keeping her from relieving the diabolical ache that had been tormenting her for hours. She got out of the car and pressed her palms against the concrete highway divider. Kendra lowered her head and took a deep breath.

"You don't understand how bad I want you!" she screamed back toward the car. Water cascaded down, plastering her hair to her face. The ache had her skin so sensitized that the very feel of satin now irritated her. She ripped the gown from her body in one motion.

The empty highway had no streetlights, no passing car headlights to illuminate the way. The pitch-black darkness hid Zumbi's approach. He reached out his hand at the same moment lightning flashed through the sky. Startled by the sight of the approaching hand in her peripheral vision, Kendra screamed again.

Zumbi enveloped Kendra in his arms. "Shh, baby. It's just me. It's just me." Zumbi breathed into her ear, holding her tight. "Calm down. It's alright."

Zumbi's arm rested on her already alert breasts. Kendra's unsatisfied lust drove her backside into Zumbi's snug groin. She clutched the arms holding her with one hand, the other providing support against the concrete. She rubbed herself against him like an affection-starved cat. Kendra felt him stiffen as he backed away a step.

She understood his hesitation, especially after the stunt

she pulled in the parking garage. Suddenly it didn't matter anymore that they were stranded on the empty road. The ache had taken over every part of her body from the cup of her ears, to the tip of her nose, and even to her toenails.

The moment had come. The ache ravishing Kendra's crotch had won. "Do it, baby. Fuck me now."

Kendra clutched her torn garment to her front, protecting her skin from the highway divider's rough concrete exterior. She spread her legs wider and lifted the back of her raincoat, guiding his hand between her legs.

Zumbi, recognizing what the invitation meant, quickly lowered his still unfastened pants and released his equally aching, solid member. He teased the thick sensitive head across her slick ass cheek. It felt good, causing her labia to spasm, greedily reaching out for more.

"Don't play with me, Zu. Put it in now!" Kendra demanded.

Zumbi's belly laugh shook the air between them. "Woman, I always knew you'd beg like this one day."

Seconds later Zumbi was once again balls-deep inside her. Kendra's flowing juices mixed with the downpour of rain facilitated his entry. His penetration jolted through her body like electricity. Tears welled in the inner corners of Kendra's eyes. A jagged sob ripped from her throat.

Zumbi's furious stroke rhythm rammed Kendra's hips against the highway divider. Her breasts bobbed against the highway divider's resistance. The drenched, crumbled satin caressed her nipples, creating a tingle that cupped both breasts. The Sade song continued to blare out of the open car doors. Kendra pushed out a long moan that originated deep from within the core of her being.

She braced herself against Zumbi's forceful thrusts that threatened to catapult her headfirst over the divider. Kendra's moan coincided with the drawn-out, agonizing pleasure of her release. What started out as sporadic twitches quickly transformed into full-blown convulsions.

The torrential rain showed the couple mercy by quickly easing its fury. Her body continued to spasm until she felt the ache no more.

Zumbi gently pulled himself out of her spent canal. Kendra clutched her raincoat closed as she began to shiver. The chill air threatened to ruin her afterglow. Kendra pushed her wet, plastered hair away from her face. Then she returned to the car.

"You should relax while I deal with this blowout." Zumbi popped the trunk open with his key and retrieved the spare tire. "I still have to punish you for teasing me in the parking garage."

Kendra shivered again, but out of anticipation this time. She leaned back in the driver's seat and closed her eyes. Zumbi jacked up the car and began removing the blown tire.

Kendra's mind ran rampant with imaginings of Zumbi's threatened discipline. She wound up not getting the rest she needed. For, once again, her insides began to ache.

# The Sweetest Revenge

KD King

Marisela's muscles clenched Quinton's dick. Her wetness saturated the sheets as he stroked in and out of her. The smell of sweat, sex, and strawberry-scented candles filled the bedroom. She looked into his gray eyes and watched his face contort with effort and pleasure. An Isley Brothers' slow song drowned out the loud smacking of his balls against her slippery wet pussy. She felt light-headed as he banged into her. The champagne she had consumed at the New Year's Eve party had nothing to do with it. She met him thrust for thrust, in tune with the music.

Quinton moved his hands down her body to massage her clitoris. The sensation of his hand and his shaft pleasuring her was too much. She bit her tongue in an attempt to suppress her screams. She had her best friend, Francine, who was visiting from out of town in the next room.

Quinton bent his head down to suckle her Hershey's Kisses nipples. His cool tongue licked her areola. Then his teeth scraped her already hard peak. The contact sent rippling sensations throughout her body. She pierced his back with her nails. He shoved deeper inside of her. Her back arched in response. This time she could not contain herself.

"Quinton! Quinton!" she panted frantically, chanting his name. "Don't stop!" she breathed.

Her lips became dry from all the panting. She licked her lips. Quinton's salty pre-cum still lingered.

Francine stood in the doorway, peering inside the partially closed door. She should have been quietly sleeping off her alcohol consumption. Although Marisela and Quinton tried to be quiet, the seductive music was a dead giveaway to their "activities." Francine couldn't lie still in the bed, knowing what was happening in the next room. She wanted to watch. Actually, she really wanted to join them. She sauntered from her guestroom and opened Marisela's door. She moved it just a crack, enough to enjoy the free sex show.

Francine had met Marisela's boyfriend earlier that week. He was tall, muscular, and handsome, with a smooth coffee complexion. He was exactly the kind of guy Francine liked. She and Marisela had always had the same taste in men.

Quinton seemed like a nice guy. Francine had only met him that week. However, Marisela talked about him all the time. From what Francine had observed, he was an attentive boyfriend. He listened, opened the doors, and made love to Marisela like he cared first about her enjoyment, then his own.

Marisela seemed to like him. That was all she could talk about lately. Francine was happy Marisela had found happiness. She was also a little jealous that Marisela could attract such a good-looking, nice guy. There was no real difference between her and Marisela. They looked similar enough.

Francine thought she looked better, even more exotic, with her mixed heritage.

Francine continued to watch them fuck. They did not have the gentleness of "making love." Her nipples hardened, her breathing became shallow, and her pussy wept with neglect. She reached down to touch herself. She simply wore her normal bedtime attire—panties and bra. She rubbed her hand down her belly, reached inside her panties, and let it travel to her clit. She was already drenched. She moved her hands in the same circular motion as Quinton's hips. She imagined it was her, instead of Marisela, beneath him. She slid her middle finger inside her wetness as she massaged her nub of pleasure with her thumb. She let out a slow, silent, contented breath. Though her body wanted Quinton's fingers, she massaged the need.

Quinton abruptly stopped and withdrew his still-hard member from Marisela. He flipped her over and drove into her from behind. Francine bit her lip to stifle the moan. Francine enjoyed watching Marisela's new position.

Marisela's hands clenched the sheets. Her head was buried in the pillow, muffling her screams. When Marisela turned her head, Francine saw a tear of sheer ecstasy roll down Marisela's face. Francine froze. If Marisela opened her eyes, she'd be staring dead at Francine. Thankfully Marisela's eyes remained closed.

Francine closed her eyes, imagining she was in the bed with them. She slipped another finger inside her dripping cunt. The intrusion caused her eyes to roll back and flutter open. She didn't want to miss any part of the show. From the grunting noises and the constant screams of "I'm coming . . ." Francine knew their session would soon come to an end.

Quinton and Marisela were both close to their final climax. Francine wanted to cum with them. She ferociously dug in and out of her wetness, bending her fingers, massaging the spot she knew would bring her over the edge. A tingling sensation crept through her body. She continued to watch them, but could no longer support herself. She slid along the opposite wall, until she was seated on the floor. She could still see their love play through the crack in the door. She spread her legs, giving her better access. She then took her fingers out of her slick folds, and focused solely on her sensitive spot. She couldn't help moaning, but it blended with the music. The lovebirds in the next room did not notice.

"Oh, shit!" Quinton's deep rumble vibrated throughout the room and out into the hall. She vigorously rubbed her clit. Her body shook. Her leg convulsed involuntarily. Her head bent back and she whispered their names. As Marisela and Quinton came, she felt her liquid ejaculate rush from her *punani* and onto the plush blue carpet of Marisela's apartment. This was the hardest she had cum since she had started masturbating only five years ago at the tender age of sixteen. She was too spent to get up and return to her room.

Quinton had just had the best fuck of his life. After he came, he slapped Marisela on the ass and she collapsed onto the bed. He followed suit and collapsed on top of her, careful not to put the full weight of his body on hers. Damn, she was so tight. He loved fucking her. Although she was a virgin when they first met, she was a quick learner with very few inhibitions. He liked being the first and only one inside of her. Her pussy was molded for his dick. When he gained enough energy, he moved off her. He spooned Marisela's back into his front. Quinton watched the slow rise and fall of Marisela's chest. Her light snoring sounds were the ultimate compliment to his already large male ego. He smiled.

Quinton thought he heard a whimper. He got up, careful not to wake Marisela. He padded naked across the room. Marisela had company, but he didn't care. He opened the bedroom door and saw Francine on the floor. Her hand was down her panties. She leaned her head against the wall. Seductive eyes looked up at him and she smirked. She smelled of sex. His member rose and he responded with a devilish grin. He bent down to her level, helped her up, and escorted her out of the hall.

Marisela awoke alone in the bed. She heard the shower running. Immediately she knew Quinton was in there. Already her body craved him again. She decided she would join him. She picked up his discarded polo shirt off the floor. She put it on and walked to the bathroom. When Marisela opened the door, she was torn between vomiting and committing acts of extreme violence.

The shower muffled the sounds of Francine and Quinton's panting. Francine's long slender leg was hitched on top of the sink, the other planted firmly on the floor for support. She was slightly hunched over, hands bracing the wall. Quinton's hand was wrapped around her waist. He was bent over her, his chest pressed into her back. As he moved in and out of her, he licked and nibbled her neck. Only moments before, he had made love to Marisela. Now he made love to Francine with the same intensity.

"What the fuck is going on?" Marisela's voice trembled.

Quinton quickly withdrew and moved away, causing Francine to lose her balance. She stumbled.

Marisela looked down at the used razor on the shelf. She grabbed it and lunged toward them.

Quinton caught her arm. "Stop!"

Tears streamed down Marisela's face. She had just experienced the ultimate betrayal. "Get out of my house now, or I'm calling the police."

They clothed and left the house. Marisela, hurt and betrayed, swore vengeance.

*Seven years later, present day*

Though on the surface it appeared that Marisela had moved on with her life, she had not. Marisela had followed Francine's life for the past seven years, waiting for the perfect opportunity to collect on her vow of retaliation. Outside of close family Quinton and Francine were the only two people she had trusted. She had shut them out of her life and hardened her heart. How could one trust again, after an incident like that?

Getting vengeance on Quinton had been easy. A couple of years ago, she had discovered his penchant for laundering money. One tip to the FBI and his freedom was lost. As for Francine, the opportunity had yet to present itself.

In the interim, Marisela had devoted her time to her private investigation agency, Broken Hearts. She had managed to make a very good living off the lies and infidelity of men. The elite of Dallas society made up her clientele. Ninety percent of her business came from referrals. Marisela picked up a folder off of her mahogany desk. She read through the latest information on Francine.

Apparently, Francine had also become rich off the lies and infidelity of men. Francine would marry older rich men and sign a prenuptial agreement. However, in the agreement there would be an "out clause" that awarded her ten million dollars upfront and one hundred thousand dollars a month in alimony payments if the husband was found having an affair. If she cheated first, she was entitled to nothing, not even communal property or money earned during the marriage. She would leave with the clothes on her back.

Two marriages and two infidelities later, Francine was a very rich woman. Marisela wondered why the men would agree to such a deal if they knew that they were cheating. *Also,* Marisela mused, *is it possible that all the men were set up by Francine so she could take their money?* The biggest piece of the puzzle lay in front of her—a small society page announcing Francine's third marriage. She'd had a very un-Francine-like, small ceremony. She had married a Panamanian professor, Javier Dominguez. They met while she was vacationing in Panama. A year later they married.

*What was her motive?* Marisela deliberated. Javier was not a rich Columbian *hombre de negocios* (businessman), or an upper-class American from the Canal Zone. He was not famous, nor was he part of high society. He did not fit the mold. Like a thunderous boom hitting on a stormy night, the answer suddenly came to Marisela. *Love!* She had actually married for love.

The time had finally come for vengeance. According to her sources, Francine had moved to Panama City, Panama. Francine also had a trip planned to visit her family in New

York that upcoming fall. That gave Marisela three months to brush up on her Spanish, and contact her favorite *prima*, Carmen. Her cousin Carmen also taught at the University of Panama. Hopefully, Carmen would help her figure out a way to get close to Javier.

Marisela flipped through the file on Javier. It was important to study all of her subjects. She examined his pictures, stopping at the one taken on a beach. He was beyond handsome and very photogenic. Standing on the shores of a white pristine beach, in blue swim trunks that clung to the contours of his body, he reminded Marisela of a Hershey's chocolate Adonis. Chocolate was Marisela's favorite flavor. She wondered what kind of treat lay underneath his blue swim briefs. She couldn't wait to taste it. The photograph froze the tiny droplets of water that outlined his lean muscular physique.

His almost bald head made him sexier. From his stats, she knew he stood an even six feet. His large pecan-brown eyes captivated her. He appeared to be looking directly at her. She felt the temperature in the room rise, especially in between her legs. His face was perfectly angular with a neatly trimmed goatee.

*Scrumptious.* Marisela's erect nipples strained against the satin fabric of her bra as she stared at Javier's picture. She grew wet as her mind filled with images of revenge. Her instant sexual attraction to his picture was alarming. She was being silly, it was only a picture. Her palpitating pussy told another story. However, she convinced herself that she would not lose focus. She would lick him, suck him, and fuck Javier's brains out. Then she would make sure Francine knew about it.

She gave Javier's picture another glance. She debated on pulling out her emergency office "toy" to douse the flames that burned between her legs. She knew that she shouldn't. She had business to handle and a seduction to arrange.

*Fuck it!* She reached for her key chain and unlocked the bottom drawer of her desk and pulled out a pink vibrator. She turned it on and propped her left leg on her desk, exposing her nether regions to the cool office air. She stared at Javier's picture and put the pink pleasure pole in her panties and massaged her throbbing nub. The pulsing sensations on her clit caused shivers to run up her spine. Her head rolled back and her eyelids drifted shut. Gently, she directed the vibrator in between her slick folds and nudged it inside. She imagined it was *El Profesor* inside of her. The pulsing beat of the pink intrusion matched the pulsing of her sex. Her liquid seeped out and she gasped for air. She came quick, shuddering and shaking in her leather chair.

She took a moment to collect herself before returning Javier's picture to his file. She wiped her pink pleasurer, placed it back in the drawer, and locked it. She picked up her office phone and began making calls.

*"A man can only take so much temptation before he says to hell with it and succumbs."* The excuse that Quinton had given for sleeping with Francine echoed in her mind. She would make sure that was the same excuse Javier gave to Francine.

## Three months later

Marisela sat in the oversized seat afforded to the first-class passengers, drafting a fake résumé on her laptop. The final step before arriving in Panama was to have a résumé with a list of references. Thanks to Carmen she had found a way to not only get close to Javier, but live with him while Francine was in New York. As it turned out, he needed a live-in cook. Francine had fired the old one before she left. Marisela, co-incidentally, enjoyed gourmet cooking as a hobby. With a lovely recommendation from Javier's colleague—Carmen— she was set to start work in a week.

Marisela arrived at the massive electric, black iron gates that surrounded the Dominguez estate. After speaking to the silver intercom box located outside the perimeter, the gates opened. She drove up the cobblestone driveway and let out a low whistle as she admired the large, five-story, yellow stucco mansion. Javier stood outside on the veranda, watching her slow approach.

He appeared taller and more defined than he did in his picture. His pictures were an insult. He was downright gorgeous in person. He wore a white linen outfit. Too bad he wore boxer briefs underneath. Marisela really wanted to know what she would later be working with . . . not that it mattered, of course. Vengeance was vengeance. Big or small, he was hers.

*"Buenos días, Señor Dominguez."* Marisela extended her hand in greeting. He accepted. *"Soy Marisela."*

*"¡No! ¡Por favor, Javier!"* His voice was deep. She had been around Spanish speakers all her life, but his sounded different. His was the only one to set her body aflame. His cologne emanated the scents of sandalwood and musk. It only added to her already blossoming attraction. He oozed sex with every word. She would call him Javier as he requested, and later, when he begged, she would call him *"Papi Chulo."*

*"Aquí."* She shoved the résumé in his face. She knew the job was guaranteed because Carmen gave her a rave recommendation, but it never hurt to be extra-prepared.

Javier stood there flipping through the papers, not really seeing what was on the page. He needed something to distract him from staring at the new cook. She was tall, about five feet eight inches, and thick in all the right places—hips, legs, and breasts. A gentle breeze passed, carrying the sweet smell of her perfume. Her smooth, flawless honey-brown skin enticed him. He wondered if she tasted like honey. Her hazel eyes held secrets, ones he wanted to explore intimately. His dick leapt at the thought. *"¡Está muy caliente afuera!"* Though he was accustomed to the stifling Panama heat, he needed to explain the sudden perspiration on his forehead. He turned to go toward the house, shielding his growing erection. He peered over his shoulder. *"¡Vamos!"* She followed him inside.

*Hot outside, my ass!* She saw the slight bulge in his pants. She knew it was more than humidity that had him hot. She was sweltering for the exact same reasons. That, and she wasn't used to the sultry weather. She felt like she was going to melt into a puddle on his veranda.

As she entered his home, a cool breeze welcomed her. Her nipples automatically tightened. From the hooded look in Javier's eyes, she knew he noticed. He showed her to her room, which was on a different floor than his. It didn't matter. She would be sure to be caught by Javier with a towel around her dripping wet, naked body while she was roaming the halls.

The first time she pulled that trick, he had appeared flushed and quickly pointed her in the right direction. The second time, he had been understanding. He had even relayed tales of his getting turned around when he had first moved there. The third time, Marisela noticed, he had simply stared. His pupils dilated and he had definitely noticed she was an attractive woman, naked in his home while his wife was away.

*Trouble!* This new cook was nothing but trouble with a capital *T.* He didn't have the heart to fire her. Her rice and peas rivaled his mother's. He would lick his lips, imagining it was Marisela he was eating. She made no move to leave now, but just watched him watch her.

*Damn, he's fine!* He was definitely interested in her. Marisela realized that it was now time to make her move. She pretended to leave, by partially turning her body toward the staircase. She "accidentally" dropped her plush red terry-cloth towel on the white marble floor in the process. She gasped and tried to look mortified. Javier closed the distance between them and bent down. He picked up the towel and slowly rose to give it to her.

*"¡Gracias!"* she mumbled and turned around to leave, only partially covering her body with the towel. Javier had no way of knowing, because her back was now to him, but Marisela had a huge grin on her face.

*Danger* better described Marisela. Danger with a capital *D.* Javier didn't know what he was thinking. He was a recently married man who should only desire his wife. But Marisela was an attractive woman who always managed to be naked or half naked around him. He knew he should have turned away in modesty, but he couldn't turn down the chance to see her up close. He grabbed his opportunity when the towel fell. It was like a gift from heaven. He took his time returning it. He bent down, only a breath away from her naked skin, to pick up the fallen covering. As he slowly rose, he took his time perusing her body, admiring everything about it. Her perfectly manicured feet, sexy long legs, ripe pussy, slightly rounded belly, and large coconut breasts. He caught the scent of her desire. His cock got harder. He knew he couldn't give her what she wanted. He was married and she was the help. He returned the towel and watched her walk away. He decided to scurry away to his office.

The smell of vanilla and honey brought him out of the confines of his office. He knew he should stay away, let her fix his plate, and come down to get it when she left the kitchen. But he couldn't. The sweet scents beckoned to him. He followed his nose. He walked into the kitchen and froze.

She was reaching for a jar from the upper shelf, humming a soca tune, swaying her hips to the beat. She was wearing a short blue shirt and nothing else. Her luscious folds were on full display, yet again. She seemed oblivious to his presence, humming and reaching for dinnerware. She then bent down to check on the food in the oven. Javier couldn't help it. The view, the sensuous smell of vanilla made him excited. He began to rub his hardening manhood. He massaged it through his khaki linen pants. He wore no underwear. He rubbed his manhood, imagining he was deep inside Marisela. He could almost feel her tightness. He moaned. She jumped up and turned around to face him. He snatched his hand away and nervously cleared his throat.

"Smells good. What are you cooking?" he inquired in his heavy Caribbean accent.

She peered down at his blatant erection, visible through the pants. She looked back up at him with passion-laden eyes.

"*Tentación.*" Temptation.

Time stood still. The air around them crackled and heated with their mutual desires.

"*¡Venga!*" One simple command and she followed, slowly and seductively crossing the short distance to him.

He didn't need to give any more instruction. Once she reached him, she dropped to her knees and released his steel rod from its khaki prison. Before he could utter another command, she took all of him into her mouth.

"*¡Ah mierda!*" he grumbled. *Oh Shit!*

After a few slurps, she withdrew. She then licked his crown. She wanted to take time to enjoy the taste and feel of his penis. Her tongue massaged the slit, licking his pre-cum. She tasted salt and traces of vanilla. Knowing that vanilla increased lust, Marisela added the aphrodisiac in all of his meals. Now she tasted it in his essence. She gently traced the length of his penis with the tip of her tongue, before bending down further to suckle his sac.

As she sucked his balls, she rubbed his dick with her right hand. She moaned. His responsive tremor excited her.

Her tongue was magic. The vibrations of her moan caused tickling sensations that traveled from the base of his feet to the top of his head. Javier felt like he was going to explode. He refused to do so before finding out if she tasted like honey. He stopped, grabbing her thick curly hair. His hands moved to her shoulders and yanked her up off her knees. She stood before him. He grabbed her ample bottom and groaned at the soft supple feel of it. He lifted and carried her to the kitchen island. He placed her on the edge in a sitting position. He then moved between her thighs and buried his face in between her legs.

"Oh, my God!" she couldn't contain her shout. Her English came out loud and clear. He didn't seem to notice. She had expected to have him shouting and begging, not the other way around. He teased the outline of her labia with his tongue. He alternately sucked and licked her clit until she was bucking on the counter, begging for mercy. He didn't give her any; instead, he inserted two fingers inside her vagina and bent them in a come-hither motion. She fell against the counter and rubbed her pussy deeper into his face.

She tasted like honey. He couldn't get enough of it. He could feel her muscles clenching around his fingers, and he knew she was on the edge of cumming. He thought he would come from merely tasting her. He continued his oral assault of her clit until her body shook and the last of her tremors subsided. He lifted himself from her and licked his glistening lips.

*"Estoy listo para la cena ahora." I'm ready for dinner now!*

*Two weeks later*

Javier was one disciplined man. After the incident two weeks prior in the kitchen, he had avoided Marisela like the plague. She could tell that he wanted her. The lust was still in his eyes, but his control had come back with a vengeance.

Marisela watched as the handymen finished the last installations of the new huge chandelier in the foyer. She stared in amazement and with a bit of fear.

When the last of the men descended the ladder, she voiced her fear. "I hope that doesn't fall," she said in Spanish.

"Don't worry," the handyman replied. "It has a steel support beam and extra support. The house would have to collapse before it fell. Plus, the chandelier is made of iron. You could get three people on that chandelier and it wouldn't even splinter." He pointed to the ladder. "Go up there and sit on it. See for yourself."

At first, Marisela looked at him like he'd lost his mind, but then decided what the heck. The man followed close behind her. She knew he was getting a nice look at her bare derriere, underneath her floral skirt. She wore no panties in her ongoing attempt to entice Javier. But with this man looking, it was just creepy. She hurried up the steps until she reached the chandelier.

"See!"

He joined her up on one of the chandelier posts. The clearing of someone's throat made them both look down. It was Javier. The handyman got nervous, descended the steps, and Javier escorted him out of the house.

After shutting the double doors, Javier looked up at Marisela perched on the chandelier. He could not stand to see her huddled next to another man in *his* house. Her short, low-cut floral dress sent him over the edge. The predator in him was released. He knew she wore no panties; she never did. She looked so small, fragile, and fuckable. *To hell with it.* He could no longer take it. He had to have her more than his next breath. He stalked up the long ladder like a jaguar seeking his prey. His gaze never wavered from hers. When he reached the final step, he joined her on the chandelier. He said nothing, simply pulled his steel rod out of his pants, grabbed her waist, and settled her on top of him. They both let out a contented sigh.

Damn, she was tight. He held his arm around her waist,

supporting her on his lap. He pumped into her three times before deciding to take full advantage of their surroundings and change positions. He turned and straddled her body on the chandelier posts, face toward the floor, which was very far below. It was a large, hanging chandelier that spread out, so there was plenty of room to lie. He then adjusted his position, so he could easily grab her ass and smack it into his pulsing member. Once comfortable, the journey began. He leaned his body over her, supporting most of his weight on the chandelier stems, and lifted both of their midsections for deeper penetration. He had to touch her. He took one hand and massaged her breasts. Her head rolled back toward him. He bent to suckle her ear. His balls smacked against her sex, coating them with her wetness.

"Ooh, right there! Don't stop!"

Her command took him over the edge. He dove into her hard and fast, trying to keep balance and not look down.

He was huge. She already knew it from when she had taken him into her mouth. From his back-entry penetration, she could feel all of him deep inside her. There was no beginning or end. They were one. His rigid shaft moved in and out of her, massaging her inner walls, touching her pleasure spots. The chandelier began to sway gently with the force of their copulation. Marisela held on to the chandelier bars for support. Her head rolled down. She noticed how far up they were. Her heartbeat sped up. The fear of falling only intensified the sweet torture Javier created in her body. The air brushed her clit, tickled her pussy, and plumped her already swollen lips. All of her senses were alive. The dick that massaged her insides gave her the most explosive orgasm she had ever experienced. She screamed, "Oh God!"

and her cum slid down her leg, and journeyed toward the floor.

*What the fuck was that?* Francine wondered as something wet hit her smack in the face. She wiped the drop of moisture from her cheek and bent her head upward to see from where the noise and the moisture originated. What she saw brought bile to her throat, tears to her eyes, and caused her heart to ache. Her husband was swinging on a chandelier, banging into Marisela, and grunting, "I'm coming."

Francine yelled, "What the hell is going on?"

Javier came, Marisela laughed, and Francine cried. Vengeance had been served.

# Alibi

CB Potts

"I'm sorry, Mrs. Alvarez. Our school district is too small. We're simply not prepared to take on a student that doesn't speak English." Donald Altari rubbed the side of his temple with one aching hand. "It's not that we don't want to. Christian would be more than welcome. It's that we can't provide the education that the state says we must."

Luisa smiled. "But you must understand my position, Mr. Altari. Christian must go to school somewhere. If he cannot go here, and he can't go to Willsboro, and he can't go to Lake Placid, where can he go?" She shook her head, her short black curls fanning over her shoulders. "Plattsburgh is over an hour and a half away by bus. That is unacceptable."

"That is a long ride." Donald tapped a few computer keys. "Maybe we could find a Spanish-speaking tutor who could homeschool Christian."

"I'm not sure that's a good idea. He is a very social boy, and I think a year of being isolated from all the other children would not be in his best interests." Luisa leaned forward.

"Maybe if the tutor could come with him to the classroom, and translate—"

"You wanted to see me, Mr. Altari?" Glenn Rabideau, a short, stocky man leaned into the office. He handled language arts for the campus—largely French.

"Yes," Donald replied. "Glenn, this is Mrs. Alvarez. Mrs. Alvarez, Glenn Rabideau. He turned toward the teacher, thankful for once that the man was not reeking of aftershave. "Mrs. Alvarez's son doesn't speak English, and we're trying to come up with some way to teach him."

Glenn smiled. It was a thin, narrow grimace, the type you see on well-fed weasels. "Well, maybe she should have him swim back to wherever they came from. I bet they speak plenty of good Spanish there."

Donald's jaw dropped so hard his cheeks hurt.

"Mr. Rabideau," Luisa said, whirling to face Glenn in one fluid motion. "Let me assure you that while my son speaks no English, my command of the language is more than adequate. Your presence at this meeting is no longer required."

Face flaming, Glenn looked to Donald. Hurriedly, Donald shut his gaping mouth, and nodded.

He'd barely left when Luisa continued. "Is this the attitude I am to expect from your school? Is this the environment I should send my child into? I think not!" She grabbed her purse from the floor and headed to the door.

Donald scrambled after her. "Mrs. Alvarez! Please, stop!" He caught her above the elbow, and found himself facing furious black eyes. "I apologize from the bottom of my heart. Mr. Rabideau will be reprimanded. I do not allow, nor do I tolerate, that kind of behavior on my campus."

Time froze for a moment. Luisa held perfectly still, not moving for the space of a dozen heartbeats. Her eyes never left Donald's. And then she smiled.

"Well, then, Mr. Altari, perhaps we can discuss how we will arrange Christian's class schedule."

Two hours had elapsed since Luisa Alvarez had left Donald's office. A thin folder of neatly completed paperwork sat before him, filled with Christian's health and educational records. He'd only skimmed them. It didn't take much to see the boy's grades were excellent.

A tutor had been hired to accompany Christian throughout the day and provide English instruction. It wasn't easy to find a qualified teacher on such short notice, but Donald's mortification had been a powerful motivator. And when Luisa had suggested that it would be a good gesture for the school district to pick up the tab for the special tutor, he couldn't help agreeing.

There were almost four months of the school year left. That was almost three thousand dollars of tutoring he had to pay for, three thousand dollars that were nowhere in his budget.

Donald Altari was not a happy man.

"Shirley?" he said, barking into his intercom. "I want Glenn in here. Yesterday."

A few minutes later, Glenn entered his office. "Don, I—"

"Just stop." Donald cut him off. "I really don't want to hear it." He picked up his pen, sprawled on the notepad in front of him. "Just tell me what you were thinking."

"How was I supposed to know she spoke English?" Glenn

exploded. "You bring me in here, tell me her kid *no habla anglais*. What the hell was I supposed to think?"

"I'm not sure where I led you to believe it was the time to make inappropriate racist comments." Don's eyes screamed *asshole!* But too many years of dealing with the teachers union kept his mouth from following suit.

"So, once again, some athlete moves up here from some banana republic, and we're supposed to jump through hoops providing services for their family?"

"Well, Glenn, we are not only jumping through hoops. Because of your smooth talking, we're paying to provide tutoring for Christian. Full-time, five days a week, for the rest of the school year."

Glenn sputtered.

"Do you know how much that costs, Glenn?" Don glared at his subordinate. "Three grand. Do you know how much it costs to insure the hockey team, Glenn? Three grand. That's a telling coincidence. Don't you think?"

Glenn's face turned purple. He coached the hockey team, the same team his son had played on, that his grandson played on now.

"You . . . you can't—"

"Don't tell me what I can't do!" Don roared, planting both hands on his desk and jumping to his feet. "You're in no position to do that."

He clenched his teeth together. When his tongue finally stopped dancing against his incisors, he spoke.

"I haven't made any decisions, yet. But you should know I'm not happy. Not happy at all. Is that understood?"

Glenn's shoulders collapsed into his collarbone. "Yes, sir."

"Dismissed."

• • •

The Candyman Chocolate Shop was not on Donald's way home, not by any stretch of the imagination. Yet he found himself there anyway, picking out a box of mixed truffles.

"*¡Mamá!*" the dark-haired sprite yelled from the doorway, staring suspiciously up into Donald's eyes. "*¡Mamá!*"

"*¿Qué?*" Luisa came from the back of the apartment. "Oh! Mr. Altari." She murmured something to Christian, who took off running. "This is a surprise."

"I wanted to apologize for earlier." He looked around the empty apartment, and noticed the skate bag lying on the couch. "I hope I'm not interrupting."

She smiled. "No, no, this is fine. Won't you please come in?" She led the way to the kitchen. "I've just now got the dinner on, but maybe you would like some coffee?"

"Coffee would be fine."

There were three chairs at the kitchen table. Donald sat down and deposited the chocolates carefully onto the table. "I can't tell you how sorry I am about Glenn Rabideau."

Luisa set a steaming mug of coffee in front of him. "You are not the one who needs to be sorry, Mr. Altari—"

"Donald."

She smiled. "You're not the one who needs to be sorry, Donald. It is Glenn Rabideau who needs to be sorry."

"I'm sure he is, too." Don gave her an edited version of his conversation with the teacher.

Luisa frowned. "And now these hockey players will be after my Christian?"

"No," he assured her. "They won't even know Christian exists. They're in the high school now. More important, they'll never know this conversation happened."

"They'll know," Luisa said blackly. "And they will have brothers."

"I promise it will be o——" He rose from his chair.

Standing before him was the smallest woman he'd ever seen, with perfect mocha skin and twinkling eyes. "Hello, I'm Donald Altari."

Giggling aloud, she held out her hand and said, "I am pleased to meet you, Mr. Altari."

Luisa beamed. "*Mi hermana,* María." She nodded toward the younger woman. "She is practicing her English when she is not skating."

"*Mi hermana,*" Donald repeated. "I should be practicing my Spanish. She is your daughter?" He looked at both women. "Can't be." They looked the same age.

"Well, it could be, but it's not," Luisa replied. "She is my sister, come here to skate in the World Championships next month."

"That's why you wound up in our neck of the woods," Donald said, recalling Glenn's words about banana republic athletes. "I was wondering."

"We were told the New York training facilities were the best," Luisa said. "But we did not know that Lake Placid was so . . . remote." She looked out the window. A red squirrel was hanging precariously from the bird feeder, snatching sunflower seeds even as it fell.

"We are that," Donald agreed.

"It is too bad our mother did not come," Luisa said. "This, she would have enjoyed. She stayed home because she was afraid of the city, with the taxis everywhere and the subway and the gangs . . ."

María rattled off something, talking faster than Donald could think, much less comprehend. Luisa burst out laughing, only to catch herself a moment later, covering her mouth with her hand.

"What's so funny?" Donald asked.

"My sister said our mother stayed home because she was afraid of leaving her boyfriend alone. He will be visiting all the other ladies in the village if she's not there to keep an eye on him." Her eyes were flashing. Donald felt himself drawn to their light, to the deep well of joy he sensed inside Luisa. "And she is probably right."

"What about your husband?" Donald blurted out, reddening at his own boldness, but compelled to ask. "Won't he be visiting all the other ladies as well?"

A look passed between Luisa and María, one that spoke volumes of which Donald wasn't equipped to read.

"We are from El Salvador, Mr. Altari. Wherever my husband may be, I am sure women are not one of his problems."

*Stupid, stupid, stupid*, Donald thought, resting his head against the steering wheel. *So much for making a good impression with this family.*

Christian's first day of classes went well. The tutor blended seamlessly into the school's routine, allowing the boy to try his own hand at the unfamiliar language when appropriate, stepping in when necessary.

He made friends easily, which helped. Donald watched through his office window as Christian slid effortlessly into a recess pickup soccer game, passing and kicking and laughing in the universal language of competition.

Maybe things were going to turn out well after all.

It must have been coincidence that brought Donald to the Olympic oval that Saturday—the same time María just happened to be practicing with the other Championship hopefuls.

Donald eased into the stands beside Luisa.

"Hi!" he said. "I come bearing hot chocolate."

"You are a big one for chocolate, aren't you?" Luisa asked, taking the steaming cup. Their fingers touched for one split second, long enough to send her black eyes flickering to meet his blue ones.

"Guilty as charged," Donald replied. "I've an incurable sweet tooth."

They stood side by side, watching María work through her routine. Triple axels were followed by sit spins, alternating with dizzying footwork.

"So how did a girl from El Salvador decide she wants to become an ice skater?" Donald asked, resting his arms on the thick barrier wall separating spectators from the ice. "It doesn't seem the most natural choice."

Luisa laughed. "There's not much natural about María." She nodded her head toward the giant screen centered over the rink. Black and silent now, it provided close-up coverage during hockey games and high-profile skating events. "I blame the television. Too much *Wide World of Sports,* and here we are."

"She must be incredibly determined."

"All of the women in my family are," Luisa replied. She eyed Donald sideways. "We decide we want something; we don't stop until we get it."

Donald smiled. "I'll consider myself warned."

Friday afternoon, half past two. Donald had the Alvarez phone number written on a Post-it note on his desk. Maybe it would be alright to call Luisa, invite her to dinner.

His office door flew open. His unflappable secretary, Shirley, with two dozen years' experience, was in a panic.

"Mr. Altari! You've got to come quick! There's big trouble!"

The hockey players did have brothers. Six of them, in fact. Six tall, chunky fifth-grade boys, nearly the size of men. They surrounded Christian in the boys' bathroom and beat the living hell out of him.

It was over by the time Donald arrived. Two teachers had wrestled the boys out into the hallway and had them sitting against the wall. They stood over the culprits—two puffing, red-faced, oversized banty hens.

Christian lay on the bathroom floor. He looked very small, very red, and very still.

*This can't be happening,* Donald thought, as he knelt to feel for a pulse. At the same time he was barking orders—for the nurse, for an ambulance, for the police.

His arm bent at a particularly ugly angle. Donald felt a slight pulse, faintly thudding in the boy's thin wrist.

"How could this happen?" Luisa raged. She glared at Donald. "You told me he'd be safe in your school!"

Through the hospital window, they could see Christian

sleeping. Doctors had set the multiple broken bones, stitched close the four-inch gash above his eye. No internal organs had been damaged, but the doctors still wanted to keep the boy for observation.

"He took quite a beating," the doctor said to Donald and Luisa. "Luckily, it didn't go much longer or he wouldn't be here now."

"I am going to find out what happened."

"He could have died!" Luisa's reply shot back like a rocket through Donald's head.

"I know," he said softly. Luisa fell into his arms sobbing. He held her tight, rocking back and forth. "I know," he said, lips soft against her black hair. "I will make this better."

Easier said than done. Christian's recovery was slow, but not nearly as slow as the investigation into the school beating. The half-dozen boys had come from five of the town's most prominent families, with fathers in law enforcement, medicine, and the media. And, of course, on the school board.

"What happened was unfortunate," one of the fathers said at a meeting. "It shouldn't have happened. But boys will be boys. Things got out of hand so fast they didn't realize what was happening."

"Not even when they heard the bones break?" Donald looked from one father to the next. "Not when they saw the blood spurting out of Christian's head?"

They had the good grace to look ashamed.

"We need to have a policy in place," another father said.

"To deal with these transient type of students. They're not part of the community. They're merely passing through. It's not realistic to expect that to happen without problems."

"Baloney." Donald snorted. "We're a tourist community. We depend on people passing through here, for our livelihoods. Do you really want to put it out there, that it's not a safe area to visit?"

"The right kind of people know that it's a safe area already."

"The right kind? Would that be the rich, white kind?" Donald shook his head. "That's definitely the message we want to spread. Anglos only."

"Get over yourself. Just 'cause you've gone soft on the kid's mother is no reason to turn on your own."

"That's it!" Donald's hand hit the table. "From what I'm hearing right now, it seems to me that you all are at least partially culpable in the beating of Christian Alvarez. If this is the kind of talk your kids hear at home, no wonder they don't even hesitate before attempting to kill someone who looks a little different!"

"Someone different who threatened their hockey program."

"If that hockey program was in danger, that was due to Glenn Rabideau—and me. Are you going to send your kids after us next?" Donald had difficulty speaking clearly, he was so angry. "I know you're not going to bother Glenn, so I guess I need to watch my back."

A rumble of protest started, but Donald cut it off.

"I am going to recommend that all six boys be suspended for the remainder of the academic year. Whether that recommendation is put into place or not is up to the discretion of the school board, as you well know. But I urge you to take it." He eyed each father in turn, forcing them to meet his eyes. "A stiff academic penalty may mitigate the charges the boys are facing in court. Maybe."

"I can't believe them," Donald said. Luisa was leaning against him on the couch. "I've known them all my life, and never in a million years would I have expected this reaction out of them."

"They're defending their children." Her words were soft, almost conciliatory. "You never know what you're capable of until you believe your child is in danger."

"I guess." Donald shook his head. "But what about personal responsibility? What about doing what's right?"

Luisa turned toward Donald, sliding her arms up around his neck. "You are such an idealist. Do you know what we call such men in my country?"

"No," Donald whispered, lips inches from hers. "What?"

"We call them dead men."

Her kiss was magical, warm and melting under his mouth. Her mouth tasted of strong coffee and stronger spices. Donald drowned in it, reeling in the taste of her, the scent of her, the silky tumbling ebony length of her hair curling round his hand.

"Jesus, Luisa," he whispered. "Should we be doing this? Are you okay with . . ." Words trailed away as he stared at her lush, full lips, the need to taste them again thudding loud inside his skull.

"There will be sorrow enough tomorrow," she replied, running her fingertips over Donald's cheek. "Let us grab joy where we may."

And with that, she was on him. The buttons on his shirt parted at her touch, and she slid it off his shoulders. She pulled off her blouse, its silk fluttering to the ground without a sound, revealing perfect round, bulging breasts, barely contained in a black bra.

He cupped one in his hand, marveling at the firm weight of it, the way the thumb-thick nub of a nipple stiffened against his palm.

"Mmmm, Don . . . ," she moaned, encouraging further exploration by letting her bra strap slip further down her shoulder, revealing dark raisin-colored areolas capped with even darker nipples.

The sight was so foreign, so exotic, so real, that it sent a jolt directly to his cock. He stared, transfixed for a moment, and then lowered his head to suckle at the tempting treat, flicking his tongue over and around the sensitive spot.

Luisa replied with a string of words he didn't understand, and some physical actions he did. Gentle pressure directed his head from one breast to the other, then down the soft plane of her belly until he reached her waistband.

She looked down at him and smiled. "I'm not sure if American men do this the same . . ."

He tugged her zipper down. "Let's find out." Her jeans and black panties fell easily down her slender hips.

Experience had led Donald to expect a thicket of curls, heady and rich with musk. Instead, he got a smooth, shaved mound, topped with a trimmed thatch of close-cropped black hairs, shaped into a narrow band.

Just below, dusky pink lips held the first drops of arousal, glistening and tempting.

The first touch of Donald's tongue had Luisa writhing, moaning louder with each lick. With growing confidence, he got bolder, plowing his tongue along well-oiled folds, stopping to slurp from her molten core every few minutes.

Long, caramel-colored legs folded round his head, pillowing his ears between surprisingly strong thighs.

He pointed his tongue, like a miniature cock, thrusting deeper and deeper inside her. His nose rubbing against her clit made Luisa shudder.

"*¡Madre de Dios!*" she gasped, squeezing his head tight as she climaxed. Donald held on, staying in place and licking until her passion passed.

Then she fell back on the couch, letting her legs fall limp. The sudden return of oxygen was almost as welcome as the sight of her blissful smile.

He was so hard that his cock was slapping against his stomach, something that hadn't happened since he was a teenager.

"Can I?" he asked, panting with need. Drops of sweat were plummeting from his forehead, puddling just above her belly button.

She smiled. "Of course."

It was like coming home—tight and wet and challenging. A tad lethargic a moment before, Luisa came alive once Donald was in her. Each of his strokes was met by an answering thrust of her hips, powerful and welcoming.

One arm wrapped round his torso, pulling them together. He could feel her nails on his back, skittering.

"God, Luisa, I can't . . . if you . . . not long . . ." he
panted.

She smiled, and flexed some internal muscles. Suddenly
his cock was being squeezed, tugged, and twisted all at the
same time.

"Garrrrh!" he groaned, losing his heat deep inside her.
They collapsed together, a tangle of sweaty arms and legs
and silly, teenage grins.

Then they heard tires crunching on the gravel driveway.
Don grabbed his clothes and booked for the bathroom,
while Luisa hurriedly put herself together.

In burst María, rattling off an excited round of chatter to
Luisa. Even through the bathroom door, Donald could hear
her gasp of shock.

"What's the matter?" he asked, buttoning his shirt as he
walked back into the living room.

María did a triple take, swallowing before holding out
her hand. "Pleased to meet you, Mr. Altari."

Luisa shook her head and batted down María's hand.
"Not now, you dingbat! Donald, there's been a horrible accident. Glenn Rabideau's car exploded!"

"My God! Is he hurt?" Donald looked around for his
jacket.

"Not badly. But his grandson Mikey was with him, and
they say the boy has some burns—"

"I've got to get to the hospital. I'm sorry to leave like
this, Luisa, but he's one of my teachers and—"

"I'm going with you." Luisa tucked her purse under her
arm. "They're never going to believe I didn't have anything

to do with this, unless people see us together." She chuckled, an old and bitter sound. "I guess you are my alibi."

Rocketing down the twisting back roads to the hospital, Donald had to wonder. What had he become? Luisa's lover—or her alibi?

# Leap of Faith

## Gracie C. McKeever

Sonja Delgado felt Homeboy watching her from the moment she'd entered the store, surreptitiously following her from a distance as she wove in and out of aisles, browsing the rack of sports and athletic wear.

If he hadn't been surrounded by his small posse, stage-whispering fresh remarks like "tight body" and "*¡Mami caliente!*" under immature, Similac breaths, she might have thought his interest in her strictly of the watching-the-minorities-for-The-Man variety.

Sonja had a time wondering exactly which was more alarming: that a barely twenty-something was eyeballing the mother of both a twenty- and a nineteen-year-old, or that he thought the Latina in the elegant designer outfit was in the store to shoplift.

The young brothah was fine. She may have been a mother and a widow, but *she* wasn't dead or blind. However, he was off limits. End of story.

Her pussy had other ideas—inner muscles clenching,

labia applauding beneath her thong as if in approval when the infant stalker broke away from his boys to approach her.

It had been a long time since she'd played the game. Too long. The last time when she'd been single and unattached and was at the same age as this young brothah. Eighteen? Nineteen?

Damn, by twenty she'd been married with one toddler and another baby on the way.

Sonja missed her *papi,* missed the cozy nights they'd spend together talking, or watching one of her sappy chick flicks on cable, or just sitting serenely in the same room— her reading a trade magazine, him doing the *New York Times* crossword puzzle after a long day of taking care of business at the interior design firm they co-owned.

She missed the quiet moments, the arguments, the romantic weekend getaways, seeing his face every day at work. She never tired of him the way her girlfriends thought she should have since they worked and lived together.

She especially missed his hard cock.

Carlos had been the epitome of the hot Latin lover. He liked to fuck often, had the staying power to back up his incredible libido, and knew how to use his big *bicho* with maximum effectiveness.

He'd died too young. Much too young.

Hence, Sonja's trip to the sporting goods store.

She wanted to stay healthy and in shape, was already watching what she ate, had stepped up her aerobic activity, and now was planning to add weight training to her workouts.

She'd tried months and months before his death to convince her husband to do the same, but hadn't been able to

get past the machismo attitude about his burritos. *Pastelillos*
and *pernil* being good enough for his mother and father, he
didn't see why he had to settle for tofu or fish.

Half of their arguments had been about his bad eating
habits. She tried to convince him to take better care of himself. If not for *himself,* then at least for her and the kids.

Sonja had to own up to at least half the blame since she
loved to throw down in the kitchen, liked her fried dishes as
much as the next *boricua,* so she found it hard to deny her
hardworking man his treats.

She angrily gulped down the tears she felt climbing from
her chest. The man still had the ability to upset and piss her
off almost two years after his death.

*Ay, Dios,* she couldn't believe it had been that long. The
funeral seemed liked yesterday.

Then sometimes it felt a lifetime ago.

"You look like you need some help."

*You have no idea.* "Sure your boys can spare you?" Sonja
instantly pasted on a saucy smile, surprised at her flippancy,
surprised when Homeboy had the decency to blush.

In this day and age, especially from a young b-boy, his
reaction was refreshing.

"Actually, you can help me. I'm interested in buying a
pair of ankle weights and handball gloves." Her eyes drifted
down for a brief second, long enough to take in the fact that
he was harboring a nice package.

"Sure, come this way." He led her to the aisle where the
weights were located, and she stayed far enough behind him
to get a good view of his tight, round brothah's ass. Carlos
had had one, too, had gotten it from his African-American
father.

She was glad Homeboy wasn't sporting the no-belt, too-baggy-jeans look. She couldn't stand it on her son and his friends, and definitely wouldn't stand for it in her man.

*My man? Jumping the gun a little aren't you,* chica?

Sonja stopped herself from salivating over his ass right before he turned and pointed to a lower shelf that held a selection of ankle weights that she might be interested in.

She glanced at the name tag pinned to his navy polo shirt—Kaj Reynolds—and wondered what his muscled chest would feel like beneath her hands, or how his hard cock tasted.

*Down* chica! *Down!*

But it didn't matter how much she reminded herself that he was close to her son's age and forbidden fruit. The fact was, he wasn't her son, and she wanted him.

For the next five minutes, Mr. Reynolds held her en-thralled as he extolled the benefits of the adjustable ten-pound weights as opposed to the nonadjustable, heavier variety. For the handball gloves, he told her a pair of all-around weightlifting gloves would suit her purpose.

He sounded so conscientious and earnest, Sonja was beginning to wonder if she had misheard the lascivious dialogue of his homeboys earlier, had misinterpreted Mr. Reynolds's interest.

Was she *that* out of practice?

Sonja listened to his spiel, more mesmerized, however, by the young brothah's full lips, the sound of his deep voice, and the way she had to crane her neck to look at his face when he talked, than she was in the health benefits of work-ing out with weights.

She'd been respectfully silent during his pitch, peppering

the air with the appropriate "ahs" and "hmms." But now Sonja wanted to get down to business, or at least find out whether Mr. Reynolds was as interested as her. Or had her assumptions been the wishful thinking and overactive imagination of an in-heat almost-forty-year-old?

"How old are you?" she blurted.

He shot back the expected, "Old enough."

"Don't get insulted. I'm just curious."

"I'm not insulted." He smiled, straight white teeth briefly gleaming against his new-penny brown complexion before he slowly licked his lips, LL Cool J–style. "But I am interested."

"Is that a fact?"

"And I think someone like you will be interested, too." He pulled a business card out of his back pocket and handed it to her.

Sonja stopped herself from smirking as she took it, expecting to see the standard DJ-for-hire services, or a blurb about handmade hip-hop gear. But then she glanced at the embossed, fancy and official lettering, and her eyes popped wide when she saw the business it advertised. "Bungee jumping?" she sputtered.

"Yes, brothahs and Latinos do it, too." He chuckled.

Not any brothahs or Latinos she knew. Was she that old, or just that chickenhearted?

"You said someone like me? That would mean . . . ?"

He licked his lips again, looked her up and down, and there was no mistaking his intent now. "A fine Latina who likes to stay in shape. A woman not afraid to take risks."

Obviously, since she was talking to him with lust in her heart and pussy juices already spilling into her thong.

*¡Ay, Dios mío!* She hadn't realized she was so *bellaca* until she'd laid hazel eyes on him. Horny *and* hot to trot.

Sonja crossed her legs and squeezed them together, hoping to stem the tide and her already swollen clit, but trying to restrain it only made things worse. "So, are you inviting me on an excursion?" she asked.

Bungee jumping? There had to be better ways to get with a man, even a young one, than—

"Are you game?"

She was game; she just didn't think she was for leaping off a bridge with her life in the strands of a few cords. "I'm game," she said.

FIVE . . . Sonja stood at the edge of the bridge, sheer canyon walls rising around her, mouth dry, palms perspiring as she grasped the rail, all trussed up in the requisite gear and harnesses, and feeling like a turkey on Thanksgiving Day for more reasons than one.

FOUR . . . She stepped out onto the platform mounted on the catwalk railing, glanced at the churning waters at least fifteen stories below, barely heard the encouragement of the other prospective jumpers behind her as they counted down.

THREE . . . Warm spring air rifled her wavy brown hair flowing loose beyond her shoulders under the helmet—like a helmet would do any damn good if that three-quarter-inch cord broke!—sunlight reflected off of the surrounding mountains and the surface of the lake below, almost blinding her.

TWO . . . For the life of her, she couldn't remember now why she'd chosen the swan dive. She wasn't exactly scared of heights, but she wasn't too crazy about looking down from them either. When she did something, she had to do it up, go all out, especially now.

ONE . . . Her heart drummed and Sonja had a second to wonder whether it was only the male hormone that triggered the need to show off for the opposite sex, before she quickly discounted the theory altogether.

JUMP . . . She leaped off the platform, arms outstretched, plunging into nothingness, an enormous charge of adrenaline surging through her body as she free-fell and accelerated from zero to seventy miles an hour in less than five seconds.

*I better get some* bicho *out of this!*

Sonja survived, her fellow jumpers throwing down a rope and pulling her back up to the bridge so that she could do another solo jump with the body harness.

She had several moments after her second jump to take a breather and prepare for her next and final jump.

A tandem jump. Connected with ankle harnesses. To Kaj.

He murmured in her ear as he stepped to her and wrapped his arms around her. "You're already a pro, *Mami.* I'm proud of you."

Her pussy responded immediately as cream flowed out of her cunt—a testament to his flattery.

She thought a solo jump was gut-wrenching, but standing belly to rigid hard cock, the adrenaline doing double-time through her veins—now that was a rush!

The countdown behind them started again.

Kaj squeezed her tight against him. She wondered what

it would feel like to be in his arms, naked, moist heated skin to moist heated skin, his spicy male scent heavy in her lungs, long thick cock heavy between her copper-tone thighs.

"I'm twenty-four," he said.

Not as bad as she'd thought, but still so young. "You know I'm not."

"I know. It doesn't matter."

Sonja's heart sped with anticipation, pulse pounding in her ears. She wasn't sure whether it was Kaj's declaration, his tall, broad-shouldered proximity, or the approaching jump causing the erratic rhythm.

They stepped out onto the platform as one, ready and willing to throw themselves into the vast ravine below.

Sonja closed her eyes and took a deep breath, filling her lungs with his sexy-ass musk, all the appropriate sexual metaphors and innuendoes shuddering through her brain. Her pussy muscles clenched as they jumped off the bridge clamped in each other's arms, tight as two dogs fucking.

Before she could get out a full-bodied scream—there was something so much more dangerous and out-of-control about falling upside down, suspended by the ankles—they splashed into the water headfirst, to their breasts and chest.

The quintessential bungee jump, she'd been told.

Like she wasn't wet enough already.


They reached the top of the bridge several minutes later.

Everything that needed to be said had been said on the way down, body language taking over like a mothah now as he caught her by a hand and led her back to his tent, about fifty yards away from the bridge, on the edge of the impressive Angeles National Forest.

The sun had already dipped low on the horizon, leaving a salmon-hued trail across the sky, and Sonja had a moment to admire the view before Kaj guided her inside his tent ahead of him and zipped the flap closed behind him.

"I suppose now I have to put out, since you paid for this extremely death-defying package," Sonja teased, trying to take the edge off when she knew there was no possible way she could until she had his dick firmly nestled inside her hot, wet depths, gloving him until he cried, *¡Ay, Mamí!* "Don't you think I've paid enough already in three near heart attacks?"

"Not nearly enough." He chuckled, and approached her carrying two big white terry towels. He handed one to her, then peeled off his soggy T-shirt and leisurely began drying his hair with the other, dark eyes traveling the length of her five-foot-four frame, lingering on her titties and making her nipples stand at attention more than the cool dip in the lake had. "At least not yet, anyway," he murmured.

She'd worn a white T-shirt and no bra, small enough to get away with it, but generous enough—and now wet enough—to draw horny-dog attention to her erect brown nipples beneath.

*Palm-sized,* she thought, then reconsidered when she looked at his big mahogany hands clutching the towel and imagined them swallowing her titties.

Sonja followed his lead, slowly drying her hair as she returned the favor and gave his lean-muscled, six-foot-one physique the once-over.

She licked her lips and Kaj dropped his towel, closed the couple of feet separating them to retrieve hers. She gladly relinquished it, watched him discard it with his.

Sonja reached for the hard bulge in his jeans, fondled, then firmly cupped him.

Kaj stood still, staring at her with his sloe-eyed gaze, biting his bottom lip as if to hold back a groan. "I've been waiting to tear that pussy up since I met you."

"When you put it that way . . ." She expertly unbuckled his belt, unbuttoned and unzipped his jeans in short order. Young or old, things never changed and she was well acquainted with the steps to the horizontal Lambada, hadn't forgotten *como hacerlo.*

Sonja pulled his jeans down his lean hips, and he reached out to pull her T-shirt up and off before haphazardly tossing it over his shoulder.

He bent his head to suckle one of her already moist, extremely sensitized titties and she arched her back, feeding it to him with one hand while she massaged her jeans-clad cunt with the other. Wet heat pooled in her thong as he licked, bit, rolled, and sucked her nipples until they glistened and pebbled.

"I want to taste you," Kaj whispered against her skin, stepping back to impatiently toe off his sneakers and peel off his jeans and boxer briefs.

Sonja quickly stripped, too, faced him in only her black lace thong, daring him to come get what was underneath.

She knew she looked good, tantalizing, and knew her body was "tight" for an almost forty-year-old.

But would someone fifteen years her junior think so?

She only needed to look down at the hard cock jutting at

her—at least nine inches, long and thick, just the way she liked—to get her answer.

She had a flash of herself calling Carlos "Zeus" at the sight of his godlike hard-ons, pointed at her like a compass needle at North, and giggled.

Kaj frowned. "Something funny?"

"Not at all," Sonja said, stepping into his arms and caressing his hard pecs, rushing to reassure him. "I was just thinking how much I want to *devour* you."

"You'll have to wait, baby."

"Not too long, I hope."

"As long as it takes me to make a meal out of this . . ."

She chuckled, laughing with him as he ran his hand between her legs, teasing her slit on the way up and brushing her engorged clit on the way down. He pushed the miniscule front of her thong aside, a gush of her sweet pussy juices his reward when he slipped two fingers inside.

He took the waistband of her thong in each hand, slowly sliding it down her endless thighs as he got down on his knees in front of her to explore more thoroughly.

Sonja stepped out of her thong, opened her legs, and planted her feet as Kaj spread her pussy lips with his thumbs, covered her with his mouth, and thrust his tongue into her cunt, slow and deep, hitting her from the front to the back and all corners in between.

She threw back her head and moaned, hands buried in his short red-brown locs, and shamelessly pitched her hips into his face, grinding her pussy against his mouth. "That's it, baby . . . do me just like that. *¡Ay, Dios,* Car—Kaj! That feels so damn good!"

She'd almost said her dead husband's name, felt the heat

of a blush rushing up to her face from more than just what Kaj was doing to her, didn't know how she'd kept her head enough not to totally slip.

Would he have understood? Young brothah like him with his entire life of sweet young things to look forward to? Would he understand what it was like to lose someone so close, so significant to him?

Kaj retreated suddenly, pushed her roughly toward the air mattress.

Luckily it was soft and well-padded, since she landed on her ass against the bouncy material.

"I want inside your pussy *now,* baby."

She wanted him inside, too, but, damn, he'd ruined her groove—she'd been about to come!

Sonja watched now as he fumbled in his jeans' pocket for a Trojan, deftly opening the noisy foil pack and quickly rolling its content down over his erect penis.

He was back in a blink, crawling up the mattress between her legs like a big jungle cat, heavy cock teasing the crease between her thigh and pussy.

He straddled her hips, leaned in to greedily attack her mouth, his tongue invading, tangling with hers, pushing past it and down her throat, sharing the intimate taste of her.

Kaj bracketed her face with both hands, sliding his palms back to the base of her skull where he fisted her hair and held her in place against his probing mouth.

Sonja bucked her hips, reached down to catch and steer his dick where she wanted it.

Kaj followed willingly, poised above her for a brief moment before burying himself balls-deep in her snatch.

They groaned together as he slowly rolled his hips and

she wrapped her legs around his waist and dug her heels into his back.

"Damn, your shit is tight! Squeeze me, baby. Squeeze me hard . . . yeah like that . . . shit!"

She would squeeze the shit out of him if he wanted her to, just . . . as . . . long . . . as . . . he made her come hard!

Kaj drove into her, alternately pistoning and rotating his hips. The friction was so fierce, Sonja thought he would start a fire inside her pussy and she'd combust.

She matched his moves, tightening her twat around him, pumping her hips in a hard, steady rhythm before he stiffened above her and growled, "Fuck, I'm cumming!" Right before he did, Sonja's pussy spasmed and she came herself.

He rested his weight on his palms in a push-up pose, sweat dripping down his face as he looked down at her with those dark, intense eyes.

*Old man eyes,* Sonja thought. "You're not finished yet, are you?" she whispered.

"Not by a long shot."

The eyes may have been old, but the body was young and willing. Ah, the joys of fucking a young man.

She'd missed some of that staying power with Carlos.

After nineteen years, the sex had still been good, and made most of her married and unmarried girlfriends envious. But toward the end, Carlos's moves had been nowhere near the athleticism of Kaj's moves, nowhere as raw.

She'd needed this badly.

Kaj groaned, slowly pulled out of her as if he really didn't want to leave her hot pussy. He peeled the condom off his semi-erect cock.

Sonja leaned up on an elbow and eyed it hungrily, licking her lips.

"Damn baby, you're scaring me." Kaj chuckled, showing her that lopsided, dimpled grin she'd first seen in the sporting goods store. "You really meant that shit about devouring me, huh?"

"I always say what I mean, and mean what I say."

"I like that in a woman."

"Do you?"

"Mmm . . ." He reached for her and pulled her close.

Sonja imagined getting cuddly and lovey-dovey with him before she remembered her mission and that "cuddly" and any variation of "love" were probably not in Homeboy's vocabulary, and might scare him away if used in the same sentence.

Nonetheless, she rested her head against his chest for a long moment. She listened to his strong, young heart and watched his cock rise from the nest of red-brown hair at his crotch.

Sonja massaged his smooth chest. Sliding down his body, she left a moist trail of nips and kisses in her wake before she reached the Promised Land.

He caught a fistful of her hair, steering her down further.

But Sonja didn't need prompting. She dipped her tongue into the slit at the head of his penis, lapped at the pearl of pre-cum gathered there, reveling in the sweet-salty taste of him—all earthy male, all Kaj Reynolds.

He shifted beneath her and she took more of him in her mouth. Down, down, down until she reached the base of his cock.

She reached for his balls with one hand and fondled them for a long while before moving on, sliding her hand back and under him to tease the edge of his asshole with a finger.

Although he'd loathed to admit it, Carlos had loved this maneuver, but Sonja waited for Kaj's inevitable shock and withdrawal—it never came. He only moaned deep in his throat, holding her head in place as he mindlessly pumped his hips.

She pushed her middle finger into his ass, felt him bear down on the digit, automatically pulling it in as she sucked his dick like a thick chocolate shake was at the other end. She searched with her finger until she found that male G-spot and stroked it.

Kaj released a guttural shout and spurted into her mouth.

Sonja drank him down, every last drop, licking her lips like a proud, sated lioness as she crawled back up the mattress to rest her head against Kaj's chest.

"I think I just died and went to heaven."

"You aren't getting away from this old lady that easily."

He laughed and pulled her against him with one arm. "Ain't nothin' old about you, Ma."

Sonja just barely winced at the designation, turned her back to spoon, nestled her ass against his finally limp penis and, as she drifted off to sleep, wondered how she would tell her children about him.

Seven months later, Sonja and Kaj were still going strong, still doing the nasty—usually at his house. Her children hadn't yet met him. They had only heard so many good and exciting things about this mystery man that their mother had taken up with.

"Well, when are we going to meet this paragon?" This had been from April, her grounded and curious nineteen-year-old, over the phone a few months ago.

Until then, Sonja hadn't realized how much and how glowingly she had talked about Kaj.

Her twenty-year-old, awe-inspired Ricky, had later added his two cents with, "Yo, he took you bungee jumping on your first date! That's fierce."

If her son only knew how fierce.

But he soon would, Sonja thought as she pulled a *pernil* out of the oven and placed it on the stove with some of her other cooked holiday fare.

Home from college for Thanksgiving, Ricky bopped into the kitchen, leaned over her shoulder, and took a whiff. "You got things slammin' up in here, Ma."

"Don't I always?"

"No doubt." He peeked over her shoulder again. "Can I get a taste before dinner?"

The boy was a human garbage disposal, looking and sounding more and more like his *papi* every day.

Sonja reached up to ruffle his short curly fade, what her Cuban mother and Carlos's Puerto Rican mother called "good" hair.

She wondered what they would think of Kaj and his locs, and whether his hairstyle would matter as much to them as her lover's tender years.

Sonja shrugged as she took off her apron and moved away from the stove to give her son access to the roast.

She watched him wash his hands, get a carving knife, and

slice off a succulent chunk of meat before popping it into his mouth and giving the thumbs-up.

"Homeboy's gonna appreciate this."

"You think?"

"He'd bettah." Ricky came over and gave her a hug. "He treatin' you right, Ma?"

"You know he does. I wouldn't be with him otherwise."

April picked that moment to sidle into the kitchen, still clad in her pajamas and bedroom slippers. "I know that's right."

"He's going to be here eventually. Think you can get dressed and make a halfway decent impression so that he'll know our mother raised us right, brat?"

"Up yours."

"Kids, watch the language."

April and Ricky both laughed, knowing their mother could get down with a vice cop when she wanted to.

The doorbell rang and Sonja took a deep breath and looked at the kitchen wall clock.

She knew it was him. Unlike some young men his age, Kaj was always prompt. Prompt, self-employed, mature, responsible . . . and a good-ass lay. What more could an almost-forty-year-old ask for?

Sonja headed through the kitchen's swinging doors, out into the living room.

FIVE . . . She wanted her kids to like Kaj, or at least understand how she felt about him. But if they did neither, she was prepared to live with it, as they would eventually learn to. She was their mother; they weren't hers.

FOUR . . . She liked Kaj, liked spending time with him. Liked fucking him.

THREE . . . It wasn't love, and they weren't getting married any time soon.

TWO . . . But for now she enjoyed having him in her life.

ONE . . . The doorbell rang again. "*¡Ay, espera!* I'm coming!"

Sonja opened the door to his wide smile, took the bottle of expensive liqueur he had in one hand, and leaned in for a deep soul kiss. "You're right on time." She caught him by a hand and led him into her house.

JUMP . . . Her kids would either accept him or they wouldn't.

Either way, *que será, será.*

# Butterfly

## Jordan Grace

"Solo, girl, you've lost your mind," I said to myself as the breathtaking beauty of Cuba came into view. I still couldn't believe I'd left my tiny, peaceful Bahamian country, home to less than five hundred thousand souls, for Cuba, home to eleven million, and a way of life so vastly different from my own. All for a man who probably didn't even want to see me. But I needed to see him. I needed to know if the connection we'd shared a year and a half earlier was still there.

He'd touched my soul the moment his dark chocolate eyes connected with my black, almond-shaped pair on a crowded bus in the Bahamas. He'd taken the seat next to me. His mango complexion, jet-black, shoulder-length curls, and rugged good looks made him pop amongst the sea of faces in varying shades of beautiful earth tones. He'd taken my breath away with a smile and a look that told me he was feeling the same butterflies that were wreaking havoc in my stomach. The heat from his body had taken me by surprise. I could feel it seeping into mine, making me moist in places that made me blush.

I'd never been so strongly attracted to a man before. It was unlike my body to be so brazen when I'd never allowed a man to get that close to me. At thirty, I was still very much the only person that I'd ever had sex with. I'd made a decision in my teens to save myself for marriage. The decision was based on the fear of getting hurt and my strict upbringing. I was always known as a good girl in my small community. Being good had become a part of my identity. Old women had smiled proudly at me in church and prayed that someone in their family would bring me home.

But when I became an adult, being the good girl became less of a virtue and more of a burden. I lived a double life, trying to please everyone and still stay true to myself. I wrote books for children, which I proudly showed my family while I wrote erotica under the safety of a pseudonym. Sometimes I felt as false as my pen name.

In my bedroom was a stash of toys and books to keep me company in the lonely hours. I knew how to love myself, even if I didn't know how to be true to myself. I lived vicariously through my spicy characters but sometimes it was just not enough. I never thought I would still be single at thirty but I was determined to stick to my principles. That is, until I met him.

"I'm Andreas," my Latin dream had introduced himself in a deep voice I knew could make a woman melt with whispered sweet nothings.

"My name is Solo. Nice meeting you."

"Unusual name," he commented.

"It suits me," I said. I'd been a loner all of my life, thanks in part to an absentee father who had made it hard for me to trust people, especially men.

Over the blare of reggae music and excited natives and tourists, I got to know Andreas a little better. He was from Cuba, traveling in the Bahamas, and a communist. The latter led to a discussion that continued long after we had gotten off the bus in the center of town. I welcomed the healthy banter. His political views were just the buffer I needed against my growing attraction to him, but Andreas soon wanted to get more personal. We spent the day talking about everything under the Caribbean sun. I was surprised how much we had in common. I felt like I'd known him forever. We watched the boats pull into and out of the harbor, transporting food, supplies, and people to twenty-nine Bahamian inhabited islands. Everywhere around us were portraits of Bahamian life in action.

I played tour guide, giving him a glimpse into the culture that I loved so much. After the sunset, Andreas took my hand in his. I could see desire in his eyes and it scared the hell out of me. I pulled away from him. There was no way that I was going to sleep with a man that I'd only known a few hours, although I now felt closer to him than some people that I'd known for years. Most of the men I'd dated saw me as cold, but Andreas had seen beyond that to the embers that just needed a caring man to ignite them into an inferno.

"I only want to kiss you," he assured me.

"I'm not ready," I told him.

Andreas nodded in understanding. He caressed my arms. My mind recoiled even as my body welcomed his touch.

"I only have a few more days here," he said. "I'd like to spend them with you."

His smile was genuinely beautiful. Everything in me longed to say yes except for that small part of me that could come up with a million reasons not to. Those reasons bothered me as I made plans to meet up with him the next day. I allowed him a soft kiss on the cheek before getting a taxi home.

He came to me in my dreams that night. I woke up with my nightdress plastered to my skin and an ache between my legs that demanded my expert touch. As I ran my hands over my heated flesh, I imagined they were Andreas's. I could write epic fantasies about him. I created our first sex scene in my mind in explicit detail. When I finally moved my hands between my legs, my crotch was soaked. I rubbed myself through the fabric. I loved the friction of cloth against flesh. My release was loud but I still felt hungry.

I saw what I was starving for the next morning when I met up with Andreas. We spent our time snorkeling until lunch. Then we headed to a local restaurant where we enjoyed Bahamian fried fish and conch salad and drank a few too many local beers.

At first glance, Nassau's colonial history is still evident. Once part of Britain's vast empire, she still retains its Old World charm and British sensibility. It wasn't unusual to see men and women in powdered wigs in front of the courthouse and government buildings. Yet, among these traditions thrived Internet cafés, five-star hotels, and elegant boutiques. Andreas loved it all.

After three days with him, I couldn't fight my attraction to him anymore. I practically attacked him as we watched the sun set during our evening picnic on the beach.

I lifted his hands from my waist and placed them on my

breasts. I looked up into his questioning eyes. My smile reassured him that I was ready. He slipped his hands under my top. My nipples were already hard. I reached under my skirt and untied one end of my string bikini. I backed further into him, rubbing up against his hard penis. I wrapped my arms around his neck. Standing on the tips of my toes, I pushed my backside further into him.

His breath was ragged against my face. He pinched my nipples and made my arm tingle with his wet, wicked tongue. Heat spiraled down my body and centralized in my pussy. My hands left his neck in search of the heat between my legs. I ran my fingers over my clean-shaven mound.

I slipped my finger inside me. I found that ultrasensitive ribbed flesh that had the power to drive me out of my natural-born mind. Slowly, I began to massage it. One of Andreas's hands moved down and cupped my behind. His fingers slipped between my cheeks. His fingers slid lower and joined mine in my pussy. As the waves of pleasure rose to wash over me, I pulled my hand away, not ready to let go of the sweet sensations building inside. I unzipped his pants and pulled his penis out. It felt wonderful in my hands. I wanted to memorize each vein, each color distinction and sensitive area.

Nervously, I placed him at the entrance to my prized pussy. He removed his finger and expertly slipped it inside of me. He felt amazing. I felt my body stretching to welcome him but there was far more pleasure than pain. He danced inside of me. Each sensation was new; each contact sent a shiver down my spine. Now I knew what all the fuss was about. A penis just wasn't a penis unless it was pulsating with pure human sensations and emotions. The idea of knowing we could be caught at any moment made our loving feel exciting and taboo. Our cries competed only with the sounds of the ocean. His hands grabbed my hips as our bodies traveled to that special place of sweet release. My chants of *yes* filled my soul as his release filled my body. When our bodies finally stilled, we held on to each other weakly. When we came back down to earth, the sun had made its lazy descent.

As my pleasure faded, the guilt set in. I couldn't believe I'd given myself to him. This was not the wedding-night fantasy I'd held on to for so many years. Did he even love me? My heart told me yes, but I couldn't trust it.

When he kissed me good-bye at my door, he thought we would spend his last day together. My heart was breaking because I knew that I would never see him again. The next morning I took a flight out of town and didn't come back until I was sure that he was back in Cuba.

That was a year and a half ago, but I'd remembered everything about him, including the name of the family-owned bed-and-breakfast he'd talked about. I found it on the Net and made reservations. I couldn't wait to look into his eyes. He had created an ache that all of my self-loving hadn't been able to satisfy. I was a master at masturbation but I'd become his slave. The wheels of the plane hitting the tarmac brought me back to the present.

Once outside the airport, I looked for a taxi. My steps faltered when I saw Andreas. The sight of him took my breath away. He was well over six feet tall and more muscular than I remembered him being. He was the kind of man that could make even a big-boned woman like me feel small in his strong arms. With the face of an angel and a body that still made me want to sin, he had only improved with time. There was something about the intensity of his brown eyes, accentuated by day-old stubble, that made my heart skip a few beats. He gave me a nervous but sexy smile.

"Solo. It's good to see you again."

My smile was so big it almost cracked my face. I couldn't believe that he was standing in front of me.

"It's good to see you, too."

"I wanted to be the first to welcome you to Cuba," he explained in beautifully accented English. We stood there staring at each other while people milled around us. I could see the questions in his eyes but I wasn't quite ready to answer them. Finally, someone bumped against him and shattered the trance we seemed to be under.

I was still tingling long after I was sitting in the passenger seat of his old pickup truck. I lapsed into another trance as the spectacular slide show that was daily life in Havana played in living color. Vintage American cars sped by us as I stared in wonder at the grand buildings in desperate need of paint but full of a regal beauty. The city had a frozen-in-time essence that any modernization would only erase.

"It's intoxicating, isn't it?"

My eyes shifted from the window to Andreas. "Yes," I answered, although I could've been saying it about Cuban life or about the Cuban beside me. Havana was alluring. Children played in the streets and sidewalks, mindless of traffic and the world outside their little oasis. Despite all of the seeming hardships, Cuba was proud and resilient. I could feel it in her tropical breeze, whispering across my face. She had a sensual joy of life; it was evident in the sway of hips and the tossing of every texture of hair over a rainbow of brown-toned shoulders. Andreas made a stop at an outdoor market to pick up a dessert pie for his mother, María. As we navigated our way among the throes of natives and tourists from almost every corner of the globe, he took my hand in his so as not to lose me.

His touch felt safe. It made me want to snuggle up to him and tell him more of the secrets he'd seen in my eyes. I hadn't touched many men in my adult life. I still had limited contact with the opposite sex. But I'd never realized how much I truly missed it until I felt Andreas's touch. I grabbed his forearm with my other hand.

He pointed out exotic produce to me. As a Caribbean girl myself, some things were familiar, like plantains, guavas, and okras, which were a favorite of mine. Every word and gesture spoke of Andreas's love for his country and their way of life. He had me laughing and still near tears as he showed such reverence for a lifestyle a lot of people would see as backward because of the U.S. embargo. Suddenly, I felt a deeper connection with him, an intangible human link stronger than anything I'd ever felt with anyone outside of my close friends and family. I held on to him tightly. I felt a tingle in my stomach that turned into a sense of regret when he released me to shop.

While he flirted with the elderly lady at the bakery, I took in the colorful array of items being sold in the marketplace. I was happy that a lot of the vendors spoke enough English to make shopping pleasant but I knew Andreas was only a few feet away if I needed help. When I rejoined him, he took my hand again and we made our way back to his truck.

"Can I buy you an espresso?" he asked.

I accepted with a smile. The coffee shop was crowded but we managed to find a table in a corner. I watched his full lips as his tongue glided across them in search of the strong, sweet brew. The simple sensuality of the act made my body tingle. I wondered how he would react if I told him how much power he had over me. Would he embrace it or had I made him wary of me after my disappearing act? I instead focused my attention on his words. Andreas told me about his writing, his paintings and sculptures.

"It is not easy to be creative in a country where so much is censored, but it forces you to be even more creative with how you express yourself," he said.

"I don't think twice about what I want to write," I admitted. "If I feel something, I write it. There's no one looking over my shoulder, except the critic in my head."

"Then why are you so afraid?" he asked softly.

I turned to look at him with troubled eyes. "I've been asking myself that very same question."

The rest of the journey passed in silence. I occupied myself by capturing the scenes playing out before me and locking them in my mind. Despite the turmoil Andreas was causing, I already knew this trip to Cuba would stick with me for a long time.

It was comforting to see so many brown faces in a foreign land. From my research, I'd learned that Cuba was one of the first countries in the Caribbean to import African slaves.

María was waiting for me in front of her three-story home and business. She greeted me as if we were kindred spirits. She threw her arms around me. "Welcome, my child," she said in almost perfect English.

She exuded confidence, from her shoulder-length, curly black hair and laughing eyes, to her summer dress and bare feet. How could someone have so much presence in a place where so much was censored? I wondered. I gravitated to her like a butterfly to a rare flower.

Andreas gave her an affectionate peck on her rosy cheek.

"Thank you, baby," she said. "Can you take the pie into the kitchen? You are staying for dinner, right?"

He smiled and nodded.

María took my hand and led me inside. Her home was spectacular. The courtyard was filled with misbehaving vines going wherever the hell they pleased while more cautious plant life was contained in pots and flower beds. The riotous colors attracted a host of insects and drew me to the plants' unique beauty. As an avid gardener, I immediately felt at peace among some of nature's most beautiful creations.

"This is so peaceful," I commented.

María sat down on a wooden bench and patted the space beside her. I dropped my bag and sat next to her.

"Is that what you came here to find, peace?" she asked softly.

I looked over at her in surprise. There was no way I could tell a lie under her intense scrutiny. "Yes," I admitted.

She gave me a kind smile. "I suspect this has something to do with Andreas. He was different after his trip to your country. Whatever you two didn't do, then I hope that you have the courage to do it now."

"I hope so, too," I said quietly.

The smell of food drew us inside the cool confines of the

large home decorated with Spanish Colonial furniture, vibrant paintings, and delicate-looking books. I heard laughter coming from the same direction as the smell. There were five people in the large kitchen/dining room.

"Everybody, I want you all to meet Solo Jakes from the Bahamas. This is my daughter, Jennifer."

The beautiful young woman watching over the steaming pot smiled at me shyly.

A woman, with skin the color of midnight, came over from the dining area and embraced me. "I am Lourdes," she said.

"Lourdes and I have been best friends since we were girls," María explained.

We sat around a beautiful old dining table. There were also three men in the room. Two, like me, were foreign guests. The other, like Andreas and María, was part of a Cuban newspaper I soon learned often published pieces that got one of them arrested.

"Castro was good for Cuba," María stated. "Before Castro, Afro-Cubans did not have as many opportunities as white Cubans. The rich had everything and all others were like dogs under their tables. What Castro did was put all of us on the same level."

Andreas picked up her thread. "But that was only the beginning. Our people are hurting and it is time to bring Cuba out of her communist past and into the democratic future of the world."

His eyes and voice were filled with passion. He'd talked about his ideas for a new Cuba when we first met but I didn't appreciate it then. I could feel myself falling deeper into those eyes. Our discussions lasted well into the night.

"I'd like to show you my studio tomorrow and a little more of Cuba," he said to me just before he left.

"I'd like that very much," I said as I walked him outside. As we stood under the light of a full moon, I brought up that fateful day. "I'm sorry that I never came to meet you," I told him. "I was just too afraid to trust what we felt could be real."

"I came to your house. You had disappeared. Even though I came back home angry, I couldn't get you out of my mind."

My heart flooded with joy. "So where do we go from here?" I asked.

"That depends on you. What do you want, Solo?"

Images flashed across the canvas of my mind. I saw myself waking up alone too many times, losing my grandfather, the only man that I'd ever allowed myself to truly love. I saw my mother, beating cancer and still enjoying life. In a year, I'd experienced enough to know that life was too short to live it in fear.

"I'm not afraid anymore," I whispered as my eyes filled with tears. "I want this enough to trust it."

He opened his arms and I went into them. I was shaking so badly for him to kiss me that when his mouth finally touched mine, I wanted to sob. He tasted like heaven. Boldly, I pressed my body into his. He moaned and grabbed my ass as my tongue slipped into his hungry mouth. He backed me up against the wall. I could feel the heat from his hard cock through the fabric of my dress and my desire soaking my lace panties. It would only take one push for me to explode. That push was his hand slipping down my dress and caressing one rock-hard, dark nipple.

My pussy started a twitch that soon ricocheted through my entire body. I held on to him and growled in a voice I didn't even recognize as my own. I didn't care about the faces I made as I came, especially as his mouth replaced his hands. As his wet tongue flicked over my nipples, I threw back my head and howled at the moon like the animal that I'd become in his arms. He held me for a long time after the tremors stopped. Then he carried me upstairs and placed me in my bed.

"Rest now," he said. "Your loving has only just begun."

When his pickup pulled out of the driveway, I floated into a blissful sleep.

The next day he took me to old Havana, home to the Plaza de la Catedral, a beautiful square featuring magnificent examples of baroque architecture, and El Templete, a small neoclassical temple established in the sixteenth century. After a long day, Andreas took me to his favorite restaurant for dinner. After three hours we dragged ourselves from the restaurant to a crowded bar where people spilled out into the streets. Women in brightly colored dresses, their hips sensual and proud, danced on air while supported by strong, masculine arms. They were so free, more so than I'd ever been. I realized that I'd been my own Vidal, a dictator trying to control every area of my life. On an impulse, I grabbed Andreas's hand and pulled him into the midst of the dancers. I didn't care that I had two left feet. I wanted to be free. I wanted to explore the feeling coursing through my veins.

Always keeping my emotions in check had become so unbearable that I'd often felt like I would explode. I wanted to explode in Andreas's arms. I laughed out loud as he swung me around. Along with the music, a quote from Omar Khayyám kept the beat in my head. "Be happy for this moment. This moment is your life." This was my life, I thought. It was time to stop putting it on hold for self-preservation.

Andreas's home and studio reflected his creative personality. They were both adorned with his paintings and sculptures. But I was more interested in the sculpture of his body. He lifted me in his arms and carried me to his bedroom. As we stood there, staring at each other and breathing heavily, Andreas started to strip off his clothes. The desire in my body intensified as each piece of his body was revealed to me. He made my mouth water. His face was strong, with a wide mouth that I knew would look wicked, even during the innocence of sleep. His broad shoulders and well-defined hairy chest tapered down to a slim waist and muscular legs. But it was the region that had yet to be unveiled that held my attention the longest. His erection was clearly defined through his shorts. I wanted to yank them down, to touch and taste the power between his legs. He put his fingers under the waistband but left the shorts in place.

"Don't tease me," I pleaded.

"Then come and get it," he told me.

By the time I was kneeling in front of him, I already had a way to turn the tables on him. Instead of removing his shorts like he wanted me to, I started to caress him through the fabric. He seemed surprised that simple cotton could feel so good against his heated flesh. I lifted the fabric slightly between my fingers and pulled it back and forth over his shaft. Andreas groaned, the sound coming from deep inside of him.

I tortured him sweetly for a while, then replaced my hands with my very wet mouth. I sucked him through the cloth.

"Holy Mother of God!" he cried out.

I nipped at him with my teeth, secure that his sensitive area was protected by his briefs. When his legs began to buckle, I pulled away from him. An instant later, he took his shorts off. His intention was to shove his naked cock into my mouth but I had other ideas. I stood up and backed away from him.

"Lie on the bed," I instructed. He stretched out on the bed. I leaned over him and tied his hands to the iron bed railings with my head scarf. His eyes registered shock that quickly turned to excitement. He allowed himself to be totally at my mercy. I walked to the foot of the bed and started to strip, my body sexy and graceful. One leg glided out in front, highlighting a well-defined calf and thick thighs. Slowly and mercilessly, I teased him, revealing my treasures to him for a few seconds before covering them up again. I closed my eyes and became lost in the fantasy of what I thought our loving would be like. I ran my hands over my breasts before undoing the center clasp of my bra. They spilled out. I could feel his hungry gaze on them. I lifted each to my mouth. I opened my eyes and, while looking directly into his, licked the large, dark areolas.

"Do you want to taste me?"

I gave him a wicked smile.

"You know I do. Stop torturing me."

I slid my panties down my legs and stepped out of them before turning around and bending low, affording Andreas a spectacular view of my assets. When his moans grew unbearable, I stepped up on the bed and placed a foot on either side of his head. I started dancing again. He stared up at my pussy. I bent low, until I was mere inches from his face. He inhaled me deeply into his lungs.

I played with him, lowering my body to his face, then standing up again and taking away the object of his desire. When he started to curse and beg for it, I sat on his face, finally giving him what he craved. His greedy mouth assaulted me. He lapped at my body. He rolled his tongue in at the sides and burrowed it deep into me.

"I want to taste you, too," I whispered.

I turned around and slid down his body and buried my fingers in his chest hairs. I grabbed one of his nipples between my teeth and pulled gently.

"Baby, that feels so good," he said. Spurred on by his pleasure, I slid further down and grabbed his mammoth penis.

He was already starting to cream. I licked up the salty liquid with the tip of my tongue. I cupped his heavy balls in one hand while I gorged myself on him. When my mouth grew tired, I caressed him with my breasts and hands. I ran his large head around one stiff nipple before placing both into my mouth. I feasted on him and myself until I felt the first tingle of release. Andreas cried out with pleasure when I finally untied his hands.

I grabbed his penis and straddled him. With his strong muscles, he pushed up into me. I moaned as my body started to tremble. Our lovemaking was raw and savage. It was animalistic, with bared teeth and Neanderthal grunts. Andreas let out a loud roar as his body finally exploded. I felt more than his semen gushing into my body. All of his strength, his life essence, flowed out of his body into mine. In that instant, I knew a part of his soul would always belong to me.

I bucked as if I was riding a wild horse. I cried out his name as I came. His warmth flooded my body, filling me with pleasure and love. In our release I found the strength to tell him that I loved him. When he whispered the same words to me, I started kissing him softly. Our bodies responded. Our loving was filled with promises.

The new dawn brought a new outlook on life. I could look to the future with a love I could trust. I still find it poetic that in a beautiful but scared country like Cuba, I've finally found freedom and true love.

# Picture Perfect

## Leni Davidson

"Please don't tell me you're seriously considering doing this. Lyd. Lyd, do you hear me?" Pilar's words fell on deaf ears as her best friend continued rummaging through her clothes, looking for the right outfit to wear.

"She's a grown woman, Pilar. Let her be, if that's what she wants to do," Simon added, ignoring Pilar's rants for sanity.

The trio had been best friends since childhood and had recently become roommates, as well as business partners, since opening the Smokescreen, an urban coffeehouse. When they were in agreement there was harmony, but when they disagreed the sounds of their high-pitched voices shrieked like an angry wind.

"Listen, Mr. Thang, I'm not trying to stop her. She's just not thinking straight," Pilar snapped back, her blood starting to boil.

The Latina was nothing if not fiery, and when it came to her friends, she often smothered them with being overprotective. Although Simon, who struggled with his bisexuality, found Pilar attractive, she was too aggressive for his own taste. He ignored her snide remarks about his lifestyle, but knew she meant well. The two of them warred constantly—a dark-skinned gay man and a Hispanic freak. Lydia always said their sexual desire for each other drove them to the brink of heated words.

"Passion is the underside of hate," she would always tell them. But this time, their argument wasn't centered on them, but their friend's unwarranted intentions.

Lydia Freeman, at thirty-five, felt attractive, sexy, and desirable. At least, she had felt those things until her latest main squeeze, Jarvis, had dumped her for another man, of all people. Simon tried to warn her that he was down with the club, but an angry Lydia had surprisingly told him to mind his own business. Ever since then, he never interfered in her life unless asked. While the breakup didn't hurt her badly, her self-esteem had taken a huge blow.

Women, by nature, gain power from their beauty. It's been that way since the days of Cleopatra. What's a woman to think when a seemingly straight man doesn't want to be with a woman who's beautiful, but with a man he thinks is more beautiful? Like most women, Lydia didn't understand the difference between the mind-set of a straight man and a gay man. She only assumed that Jarvis's lack of interest had more to do with her shortcomings. So, like most women, she wanted to do something to stroke her ego.

Most women would have found some boy toy and rode his dick for an hour or two until that feeling of domination came back, but not Ms. Lydia. Her quest for egotism went a step further. Ms. Freeman intended on taking some professional nude photographs to remind herself that she was still sexy. Not that there's anything wrong with doing that, many women do it. But Lydia was conservative. She didn't own a skirt that went above her knees. Men stared at her, but more for the mystery. Behind those dark-framed eyeglasses, cashmere sweaters, and long skirts, they knew dwelt a tiger. She just didn't know it.

So between the three friends, Pilar was the aggressive go-getter, Simon was the chic, bisexual man, and Lydia was the inexperienced tight-lip who seemed clueless about the real world.

"You shouldn't do this because of Jarvis. He's not worth it. I'll snap a Polaroid, if you're that desperate to see yourself au naturel. Why would you use Juan Cortez's services anyway? He is a professional photographer."

"You just answered your own question, Pilar. That's exactly why I want to use him and, yes, this has less and less to do with Jarvis the more I think about it."

It had taken Lydia one entire night and a bottle of their best champagne to come to that conclusion. Their sex life was lacking, to say the least, and getting his dick to stay hard had become more like a miracle that wasn't worth the effort.

"Don't you ever see those shows like *America's Next Top Model* when those supermodels are being photographed? The photographers set the mood by telling those women how beautiful they are to get the perfect shot. It's like the whole world stops for them. Every woman wants to be that picture perfect."

"I think you need a therapist," was the only response Pilar could muster as Lydia threw more of her lingerie on the floor. "This wouldn't have anything to do with the fact that Juan Cortez is soooo damn fine?"

Lydia dropped her clothes on the floor, and sat down on her bed to think about that. That was an understatement. Juan Cortez was a sexual god, or at least looked that way. He was a six-foot-two Latin stud with smooth almond skin and dimples, and a body to match. His muscles made women want to dig their fingernails into him. Not to mention that smile that could drive women wild. And then there was that Ricky Martin accent. Every word sounded so sexy. It wasn't a wonder he was one of the most requested erotic photographers around.

Since his studio was a block away, he was a regular customer of the Smokescreen and their famous café latte. On top of that, he was best friends with Simon's brother and his appearance alone brought in a lot of customers. While she was attracted to him as well, she knew it was pure fantasy.

"It's strictly professional, Pilar. Nothing else."

"Really? Then why did you tell him the pictures were for your boyfriend, Jarvis, who is now your ex-boyfriend? Surely it wouldn't matter if it was professional."

Lydia was busted on that one. Sure, she liked him and saw this as an unorthodox way of getting some alone time, but Juan was a private man who rarely committed himself. Women threw themselves at him all the time. Surely, a man that fine never noticed her. Besides, he was adamant about his work and said that photographing naked women was simply his job and not a turn-on.

With Simon's insistence, Pilar let the argument drop for the time being. Knowing that Lydia could be just as headstrong as Pilar, the last thing he wanted to do was get in the middle of an argument between two feisty best friends. Besides, despite her desires, Lydia was a wallflower and he knew that. Taking her clothes off in front of a perfect stranger was a feat she would never be able to overcome, even if it was Juan Cortez.

Lydia barged into the guestroom, looking for inspiration. Pilar followed, wanting to talk some sense into her friend. It wasn't that she thought Juan would take advantage of her. One, he was too professional for that and, two, Simon would kick his ass if he did. Although he was only five eight, their gentle roommate could slug it out with the best of them. While Lydia plopped down on her armchair in frustration over the lack of sexwear, Simon entered with a bag from an area boutique, much to the girls' amazement. "I know you're not into freakwear, so I picked up a few items for you."

Pilar couldn't resist digging into them. "Where did you get them? Your closet?"

"Actually, no. Your momma loaned them to me," he fired back.

"Oh, would you two fuck already and get it over with! DAMN!" Lydia yelled as she went into the bathroom to try on her freakwear while Pilar and Simon glared at each other. She came out ten minutes later, fully dressed, with a bewildered look.

"What's wrong, honey? Didn't they fit?"

"They do. It's just that they're so revealing."

"That's the whole point, darling. You're hanging with the big girls now, you know, the whole supermodel experience you were talking about."

Simon shot a smile at Pilar, who suddenly realized Simon's plan of using reverse psychology. He'd surmised that

Lydia would show up at Juan's studio and chicken out. At least, he hoped that she would.

The moment of truth had arrived. Lydia was standing inside of Juan's studio, waiting for their six o'clock appointment to begin. His assistant, Josette, began doing Lydia's makeup and hair. The whole point of the session was to give the customer a new experience and that often meant a new look. It got the female customers in the mood and it gave his baby-making sister something to do besides bring babies home to his retired mother. Eyeing Lydia from a distance intrigued him even more. From a distance, she looked like a schoolteacher, but there was definitely more to her than met the eye. Beneath those glasses, her shy smile, and long, straight hair stood a sensuous woman.

When Simon told him she wanted pictures made, he couldn't believe it. He had had his eye on her for months and, truthfully, that was the main reason he remained a loyal customer to the Smokescreen. While Simon was a cool cat, he kept in contact with him at the request of his brother, who happened to be Juan's best friend. Juan didn't understand bisexuality, but he didn't stand in the way of it either. It was Simon who asked him not to approach Lydia while she was still dating Jarvis, and last he had heard their relationship was still on and popping.

"Lucky fucker," he mumbled. "Doesn't matter. For at least this evening, the señorita is all mine."

Juan was amazed how different Lydia looked. She was still beautiful, but now she had a glow. For the first time, Lydia felt beautiful.

"Well, well, Lydia, you have some beautiful brown eyes hidden behind those glasses."

Before she had a chance to blush, he directed her to the changing room so the session could begin. Luckily, he didn't have any more clients tonight. He could take as long as he wanted with her. He'd have his work cut for him. Getting a woman to expose herself was often complicated. The models were no problem, because they were used to it, but the other women either felt their bodies were too fat, or they'd be cheating on their husbands, or worse. They usually wanted to sleep with him.

He saw women of all shapes and colors as beautiful. It was all a matter of how that woman felt about herself. Sometimes, they only needed a little encouragement to show that sex appeal.

The women who felt like their husbands were cheating on them usually got the pictures made in some last-ditch effort to hang on to a man who already had one foot out the door. The worst kinds were the women who wanted him. Some wanted to use him for his contacts, or had kinky fetishes that included sex right in his studio, which he didn't allow. For one, he didn't want that kind of sleazy reputation and, two, he hated women who pursued him for sex. It took away from the whole mating dance. He liked to be the tiger, not the other way around.

Besides, a woman like that had almost cost him his career. A medical student, Heather Owens, had wanted some pictures done, as well as a sexual encounter. When he said no, she went back to her boyfriend and claimed Juan had attacked her. After a police interrogation and losing some good clients, Heather's mother finally got her to admit she'd made the entire thing up. Turns out the girl had mental issues. Ever since then, and because his business was going well, Juan had decided to become very exclusive about the women he photographed. While he promised Simon that he wouldn't touch Lydia, he knew keeping that promise wasn't going to be easy.

He dimmed the lights so she wouldn't be nervous when coming out. Why women had a thing about lights was beyond him, but he humored her all the same. Cutting them back on, he noticed the lace panties and bra she wore. Juan grunted. Lace was one of his weaknesses. The photo shoot was to take place in the bedroom that was painted white with a bed that had an iron frame.

Nervous, Lydia kept pulling at her strap that kept dropping due to the weight of her 38C breasts. He gave her a glass of wine to calm her down and to settle his dick, which had started to swell the moment he saw her on that bed. Tucked firmly behind his loose black jeans, he'd hoped she hadn't noticed his lump.

"Just relax, Lydia. We're just going to take a few pictures and we'll be done."

FIRST POSE: He asked her to remove her bra and to get on the bed, on her knees with her back facing him. Juan bit his lip as she slipped on the heels and got into position. Seeing the natural pose of her breasts, he wanted to touch them so badly, but then looked at the lace panties barely covering her ass. A little bit thicker than a thong, the panties barely clung to her waistline and her muscular cheeks hung out of them. This woman was giving new meaning to the term "onion booty." On direction, she turned her head while he got the camera into position to take the first shot. With each pose, she became more and more alive while he talked to her. "You are so beautiful." [CLICK] "Stick it out for me." [CLICK] "Jarvis is such a lucky man." [CLICK]

SECOND POSE: He had Lydia remove her panties while he fumbled with the camera so he wouldn't be tempted to look. Whenever he'd felt excited, he remembered Heather and the big fiasco that had followed her bullshit. Still, the sight of Lydia naked made him weak in the knees, thinking of all the things he could do to her. He brought out a pair of high-heeled stiletto boots that went past her knees. After watching her stumble a few times, she finally got the hang of walking in them. Taking out a leather whip, he told her to hold it while he walked to where she stood in front of his bed. He was facing her, and she could feel his heavy breathing. Whether it was his cologne, his voice, or the thought that his body was so close to hers, she could feel the tension. She could also feel the wetness of her pussy starting to make its descent.

*Stop it,* she told herself. *This man looks at beautiful women every day. You can't let him see you lose control like that.*

Juan stood so close to her breasts and wanted them in his mouth. Everything about her was beautiful. Grinding his teeth, he took the whip and sat down in front. He wrapped the leather whip in a criss-cross pattern around her ass and in between her pulsating mound. The rope was tight enough to cause tension, but not tight enough to hurt. She could feel her folds wrapping around the rope and her insides getting wet again. Doing some abdominal exercises, she stopped it, but didn't know for how long. Putting what was left of the whip in her hand, he placed a black velvet cowboy hat on her head and started taking the pictures. The confidence buried inside of her came forth in seductive smiles. Untying the whip, he could see it was wet, which meant, dammit, she was, too.

She stood up and face the camera, and spread her legs, which, given the boots, wasn't an easy task. She got them pretty far apart, which meant she was enjoying the tease. With her legs spread, he could see how swollen her pussy had gotten and how excited she was just by the hazy look in her eyes.

*Damn, two more shots to go and we're through.*

THIRD POSE: Juan asked her to lie back on the bed, knowing full well he wanted to join her. He then asked her to spread her legs with her knees bent. With her pussy fully open, Lydia felt a gush of wind enter and held back a moan. Her nipples were rock hard and she was ready for a good fuck. Then he walked to her and she hoped he'd at least noticed her. Opening up a satchel, he laid rose petals at various parts of her body, except her pussy, and he placed a soft scarf over her eyes. She listed as he brought the camera closer, she knew he was preparing for a close-up.

She looked like a caramel-colored honeysuckle, waiting for him to suck her juices. As her open pussy lay there, he saw the glossiness of it and felt the hardness of his dick. He could also see her hole, which made him want to taste, or at least put his finger in it.

Would tasting it be such a crime? he thought. *Dammit, Simon!*

The more the camera clicked, the more her body quivered. Then he asked her to lick her fingers. "Lick them like you want to be licked." [CLICK] "Good. Let me see more of your big lips." [CLICK] "That's what I like to see."

Lydia was in heaven. Whatever she was doing turned her on so much that she didn't want to stop. For the first time, she felt absolutely wicked, and didn't care.

FOURTH POSE: This was the final shot, which suited Juan fine. He excused himself to get some more equipment and to give Lydia a chance to ease the dripping going on between her legs. When he returned, he had a medium-sized beach ball with him. After a few shots of her holding it over her head, he asked her to get back on the bed. Placing the ball at the head of the bed, he asked her to get on top of it. Once she did, she felt weird until Juan told her how sexy she looked.

Somehow, the image of her with that ball between her legs sent him into a tailspin. Then he had her turn around and lie on the ball, with her breasts hanging slightly over it. The lower her shoulders were, the higher her ass rode in the air, a sight that almost made him nut on himself. Before he realized what had happened, he ran out of his allotted amount of film, which meant their session was over.

On the way home, Lydia knew she had cum on her pussy. Just thinking about her session made it flow even more. She had started to cum and wanted to cum again.

Thinking again of how he had talked to her, how he had looked at her, made her wish that he had touched her. Imagining him inside her, she slid her hand inside her skirt and fingered herself into oblivion, trying not to get into any accidents on the way home.

Back at the studio, Juan scratched his head. He couldn't remember the last time a woman had made him that hard.

He looked at one of the developing pictures in the dark-room and traced the lines of her silhouette. Not that it was right, but he would definitely keep a set of pictures for himself. He called Simon to report that he had behaved himself.

Walking through Smokescreen, Lydia went upstairs to find Simon and Pilar to let them know she was okay. Not seeing anyone, she walked into her bedroom and heard nothing but screams.

"What in the hell are you two doing!" she yelled.

"Nothing. It's not what you think, Ms. Supermodel," Pilar replied.

"You're naked, in my damn bed!"

Pilar and Simon let out a giggle. Lydia had caught them knocking boots. Simon escaped downstairs.

"You couldn't find anywhere else to fuck, Pilar?" she asked.

"I'm sorry, kiddo. You know Simon and I are always fussing. We got into one of our arguments, over you, coincidentally, and then next thing you know, we're fucking. You cool with this?"

"Hey, that's between you and Simon."

"How did your session go?"

Lydia spilled the beans as the two friends laughed at all the crazy things they did.

"I guess you needed a Lydia moment."

"Yeah, that's all it was."


Later that evening, a freshly showered Lydia was still picking at Pilar until they both heard a knock on the upstairs door.

They weren't expecting anyone. Pilar opened the door to see Juan. He said that Simon said he could come over. Lydia had transformed into the conservative woman that had walked into his studio, wearing jeans and a white sweater.

"This is a surprise, Juan," she said, but was referring to the heavy satchel on his shoulder.

"Oh, I'm going to do a last-minute job for a friend, but I got the first set of pictures and I wanted to see how you liked them."

"I'm not in the mood to see myself in freak mode."

"Too bad, because they're the best I've taken in a long time."

Sitting down on the sofa, he took out the pictures as Pilar, noticing the tension, excused herself to check on Simon. Looking at the pictures brought back memories for Juan.

Standing up, he had another confession. "You know, usually I am a consummate professional. I see women every day and they never faze me. But you were different."

"Really?" she was puzzled.

"Yeah, as a matter of fact, it took all the self-control I had not to walk over to that bed today and touch, feel, and taste you."

"But you didn't."

"No, but only because I promised Simon I wouldn't touch you. I was under the impression that you were taking these pictures for Jarvis. I was hating on him big-time. But I just found out that you broke up with him."

"See, Juan. It's like—"

"Did you take those pictures just to see me?"

Lydia felt like a complete and utter idiot, or at least that's what Juan must have thought of her. How desperate he must have thought she was.

"That was one of my reasons, but not my only one."

"I see," was all he replied as he opened his satchel and began putting together his camera.

"What are you doing? I thought you had another job to go to."

"I do." He snickered. "I'm looking at her."

Quickly putting the camera and the stand together, he pulled her up to him and kissed her until she could barely breathe. Then he bathed her neck with butterfly kisses, sending her into a song of moans, doing all the things he had wanted to do to her a few hours ago. Then she heard the first [CLICK] from the camera.

"Are you snapping pictures of us?"

"Yep, it's on an automatic timer."

He pulled off her sweater, unhooked her bra, and stared longingly at the breasts that had eluded him earlier. He put one in his mouth, pulling on the nipple while his tongue flickered back and forth across them. Repeating the motion for the other breast, he pulled them both together, sucking while she held her legs together, squirming. Juan sat on the sofa while she stood in front of him. After sliding her out of her jeans, he slipped the wet thong off of her body. All he could hear were moans while she rubbed his cock's head in approval.

Spreading kisses across her body, he spread her legs just as she had done earlier. While she spread her legs for him again, he could see the milky juice sliding down the side of her thigh. Racing with his tongue, he met it on her skin and traced it back to the opening of her pussy where the rest of her sweet nectar flowed. His tongue traced her second set of lips before it massaged her opening in circular rhythms. Laying her down on the table, he stripped naked while she stared at him dreamily. His silky hair glistened in the light. Everything about her Latin lover inspired sex appeal. Pulling her legs over his shoulder, he tasted some more of her and then held her clit in his mouth, sucking on it and releasing it only to suck on it again. While his mouth fed on her clit, his fingers found their way into her pussy and fucked her wall until her body moved in rhythm with his.

Lydia couldn't concentrate on anything other than the erotic sensations, the double excitement Juan elicited in her. The moaning was so loud, she barely heard him unwrapping the condom before he entered her. Their bodies rocked back and forth on the table when Juan coaxed that wild, confident side out of her, rewarding her with passionate kisses until they both exploded together in a final climax. Their bodies shook with excitement. Reading her thoughts, he answered an obvious question.

"No, Lydia, I don't make a habit of sleeping with models, or any other clients. It's not good for business, any more than you make a habit of taking nude pictures with a whip between your legs for a photographer."

"Ouch. But you have done it before."

"Once or twice, with a lot of regret, because the women were using me either for who I knew or what they think I have."

"So, why me?" she asked although she wasn't sure if she wanted to know.

"Truth is, I've been crushing on you for months. That's

why I've been coming into the Smokescreen just about every day."

He knew that surprised her. Lydia never gave him a second look, maybe because of the way the other women flocked around him and because she was too intimidated. All he knew was that he had wanted her for a while.

"I thought you came in here because you and Simon were friends."

"I know his brother, but Simon and I are just cool. We don't go to the same parties, if you know what I mean. I would have approached you months ago, but Simon told me to back off. You were still dating Jarvis and he didn't want me interfering. I respected that and kept my distance. Simon may be quiet, but he's very protective of you and Pilar."

Both lying there in their nakedness, Juan watched his brown-skinned beauty and hoped to God that this would be something he wouldn't mess up. There had been women in and out of his life for a while, but Lydia was one he wanted to keep.

"So what happens now?"

"Now," he said, kissing her on her forehead, "we get up, take a shower, pay your roommates for the crack in that coffee table, go over to my place for a late-night snack, make plans to go a movie tomorrow, and then take it from there."

Lydia just stared at him, not quite knowing what to make of this man who had seen her well out of her box.

"Look, Lydia, for the record, I'm not here to hit it and quit it. I want to get to know you, the real you. Today was a lucky break. Maybe we shouldn't have gone there so soon, but you were looking so hot today I couldn't help myself. But let's see where this goes with us."

The camera clicked once more as they lay there, the moon shining in on their bodies.

"Now that's going to make a good picture," Juan said.

"No, picture perfect," she responded before kissing him one more time.

# The Rain

## E. Charles Smith

The drip-drop sprinkles are soothing. Right now, Marcus Jackson needs all the comfort that he can get. He can feel his right hand trembling slightly as he shifts into third gear, switching to the fast lane on I-75 headed north. He's gotta get there, gotta get there quickly before his mind changes. A tingle works its way up his lower back, toward the top of his spinal column as he reminisces on what she had just said sixty minutes ago.

"Will you come, please? I need to see you," she had said.

Those sweet words would forever caress his heart, yet haunt his soul for the rest of his natural life. He could never forget the immediate feeling of triumph and pleasure at hearing her soft voice yearn for his company.

"Will you come, please? I need to see you," she had said.

The sporadic raindrops across the windshield begin to pick up pace—sprinkles turning into light rain, calming rain, mellowing rain. Marcus's heart begins to quicken as he passes by Exit 50, Grand River, continuing northbound toward her. His brow moistens; his temples dampen. The palm of his left hand releases the steering wheel momentarily, leaving behind a wet streak. Yet he smiles, devilishly at the reflection staring back in the rearview mirror. He chuckles to himself and then speaks aloud, as if there was a passenger next to him.

"My god, what am I doing! This is insane. There's gotta be at least twenty different reasons why I should just turn around, *now,* and go home."

He waits for some spiritual response while the road ahead begins to shine with the new-fallen rain. He waits for something, anything, that would persuade him that the single greatest mistake in the history of huge mistakes is about to be committed. He waits, and as he waits, he remembers how soft and sensual her voice sounded over the phone.

"Will you come, please? I need to see you," she had said.

That phrase spoken by anyone else could have meant anything other than what it meant as the words slipped from her lips. He knew what time it was. He knew what she was asking. The time for kids' games and playful flirting had just taken the leap over that dreaded line of no return. Those spoken words had signified that. She was ready to have him. And he wanted her just as badly. The cold, hard admission of truth simultaneously sends a heat wave through his chest, down into his crotch, and a cold chill up his back and around his shoulder blades. He flinches.

"Holy shit. I'm really gonna do this! This can't be real. I'm actually gonna go through with this."

Light rain becomes steady rain. Marcus thumbs the knob for the wipers, and watches as the blades rotate back and forth. Mack Avenue exit ahead. Twenty minutes to go, still enough time to change his mind. As if by magic, his mind's eye focuses on the casual dress she'd worn today. The low-cut yet tactful trim of the box neck accenting the beautiful, natural curve of her neck, underneath the long dark locks of her silky hair. Her skin was smooth and the perfect shade of golden butter pecan. There were days when he'd imagined creeping up on her from behind, wrapping his arms around her waist, and gently kissing the nape of her neck. He could see the perfect curve of her bosom as the dress sashayed from left to right as she walked by him in the aisleway of the copy room. Marcus could feel his member pressing harder against his cotton boxers as he focused on the perfect shape of her behind, the way the dress simply slipped off the peak.

Her smile was intoxicating. He loved the look of her full lips but it was her eyes that captivated him. One stern look into her deep brown stare always seemed to make the backs of his knees lose strength. It wasn't just one feature of this woman that entrapped him, it was the entire package. Marcus was in the moment now. The point of no return had been crossed over. There would be no turning back. He was going to do what he'd never dreamt possible before this day.

"Will you come, please? I need to see you," she had said.

Behind the wheel of the speeding Mustang, Marcus replies, "I'm comin', babe. I'm comin'. I am on the way."

The rainfall picks up speed as Marcus passes by the I-94 interchange. The soothing sensation slowly takes on a raging storm effect. Visibility quickly decreases, and he downshifts for safety. That's when Mia pops up inside of his head. Goddamn if that wasn't the mind's conscience at work, as if the onslaught of rain had somehow forced him to suddenly remember the oath he'd given to his fiancée. He thought about what he'd told her right after Veronica's call.

"Emergency meeting over in Ann Arbor, baby. Some new development after the associates' meeting. I'll call as soon as I get back into town."

The words had dropped from his lips as if he was a seasoned liar. Why not, he's paid well to sell people. It's his job, and he's good at it. The majority of his clients have already made up their minds by the time Marcus is brought into dealings. His quick wit had closed many deals, changed hundreds of minds, and sold people on what they wanted to hear. Why should his fiancée be any different? She'd told him that she loved him. Ouch. Damn, that thought comes out of the dark like a blind fist, smacking him so hard upside the head that he actually lifts his foot off the gas pedal.

"This is wrong. She's gorgeous, but is she worth it?"

That's when the phone vibrates on his left hip. Startling the hell out of him, he swerves slightly. Regaining control of the 'stang, he reaches for the Bluetooth earpiece protruding from his left ear, and taps the call button. An audible, soft beep sounds off and then . . .

"Hello?"

There is a silence on the other end that seems to last a dog's age. He knows who it is. Still he plays it cool—despite the sweat forming under his arms. The rain is full throttle outside the car now, and lightning has joined nature's dance.

"Hello, is anybody—"

"Hi, *papi,*" she says timidly. It would have been hilarious, actually, considering the type of woman she carries herself as during office hours. His heart skips a beat, instantly taking him back to junior high school and his first real date behind his parents' backs.

"Hey," he replies, struggling to contain his composure. "I'm on the way, Ronnie. I should be there in—"

"Mark . . . what are we doing? Are you okay with this? At this point, there's really no need to . . . listen to me. I'm babbling like a schoolgirl on her first date," she jokes.

"Hey, that's funny, 'cause I swear I was just thinking the same thing about myself," Marcus replies.

That awkward moment of silence bridges the gap between small talk and the nitty-gritty. This time, it's Marcus who steps up. He admits to himself right here. The two of them had danced around this for months now, both secretly hoping and lusting for things to take a turn toward that forbidden place. That time was here. That time was now. Marcus takes in a deep breath. His shaking hands steady, his throbbing heart slows ever so slightly. He focuses on the road sign ahead: DAVISON FWY—not too far now.

"Veronica, I've gotta be honest with you and I expect you to be honest with me. I've wanted this for quite some time now. I've been telling myself that it's the wrong thing for me to do, for all the right reasons, and still I lie down each night clinging to whatever words were spoken between us during the course of the day. I think about the smell of your perfume as you walk by me—it lingers in the air long after you've left the room. I see the look in your eyes staring at me *that way,* when no one's around. And I have to admit, the day you brushed by me in the conference room as we moved past Mr. Jenkins—"

Veronica chimed in, "I know, Mark. I probably shouldn't have touched you, but . . . it was one of those moments,

you know? I didn't realize what I was doing until it happened. Guess that's *really* when I admitted to myself how
much I liked you."

"That was probably *the* defining moment for me, too. I
didn't want to admit it. Call it lust or whatever you wanna
call it. That was *it* for me," Marcus said.

Veronica sighs. She speaks in that sexy voice that Marcus
has come to hear in his sleep.

"Well, that makes me feel better about going out and
spending money on . . . you'll see, Mr. Jackson. I want you
to know that this isn't the norm for me, Marcus. This is
somewhat special for me. This isn't something that I regu-
larly do. Me being your boss and all, the whole situation is
damn near the perfect drama. I just wanted to make sure
that I wasn't forcing you into a situation that you really
weren't prepared for. Do you know what we're doing?"

Marcus shakes his head as he answers her question. "We
are two grown people who know exactly what we're doing.
So of course it doesn't make any sense, boss. But it feels
right, so what else can we do about it? Call it an act of nature."

"What about—" Veronica starts.

"I don't want to think about her right now. She has nothing to do with us. Can you handle that?" he says.

His confidence is building. She seems vulnerable now.
There is another long pause. Marcus watches the road; he
barrels up I-75 at ninety miles per hour, passing the I-696 interchange. His adrenaline is high. What is she wearing at this
moment? How long would it take to undress her? How much
time would they have? What is Mia thinking right now?

"No!" he yells out, shaking the last thought.

"Are you alright, Mark? What's going on?" Veronica asks.

"Nothing. Everything is as it should be. I should be there shortly. Do I need to pick up anything?" Marcus asks.

"Just yourself, hon. Just yourself. I'll leave the back door open for you. Hurry," she closes in that sultry, sensuous voice.

Marcus's member throbs so hard, it begins to ache. "My God, I'm gonna do this," he pronounces. Outside, the rain continues to punish the pavement around the Mustang as it veers off the eastbound Big Beaver ramp.

Moments later, Marcus makes a right turn onto Athena Drive, and there it is, just the way she'd described it, two houses up the block, on the left. He slowly pulls into the driveway, parking alongside the cream-colored luxury sedan he'd seen pull into the executive lot hundreds of times before. Marcus switches off the windshield wipers, turns off the headlights, and kills the ignition. The sound of the Mustang's rumbling engine is replaced by the steady pelting of the rainfall against the soft-cover roof of the black convertible. The rain, though intense, is soothing. Marcus concentrates on his breathing. His soul is alive with both fear and anticipation.

*The calm before the storm.* As he sits here listening to the rain beat against the car, he carefully looks over Veronica's abode. The redbrick home seems to call out to him, inviting him to start the walk up the pathway leading from the driveway to the back entrance. He can see faint glimmers of light flickering throughout windows of the house.

"Candles. She's ready for me. This isn't just some fling," he whispers.

He looks at his ring finger.

"Soon, Mia. Soon, but not tonight. Tonight's not about you. God help me, tonight is about me," he whispers.

Opening the door of the Mustang, he darts up the brick path, toward the rear entrance of the house, looking like a cat burglar making his way toward his next score. Somewhere inside, she's waiting to be taken.

The back door is open, just as Veronica said it would be. Marcus slips into the house, then gently closes the door behind him while shaking the rain from his soaked suede jacket. Spying the coat hooks just off the wall-mounted doorstop, he slides the dripping jacket onto one of them. This is when he catches a whiff of that sweet, warm tinged fragrance. His member, already hard, stiffens up a notch more to the point of painful throbbing. He stares at the jacket, somehow afraid to look in the direction of the flickering light beyond the kitchen. His heart is beating a mile a minute within his chest. The click of heels against the tiled kitchen floor forces his breathing to momentarily stop. The smell of her perfume is stronger than ever. Marcus clears his throat, and settles himself down.

"I'm here, Ronnie. Just getting settled in. Your home is nice." Marcus digs deep, reaching for whatever small talk he can muster.

"It reminds me of—"

"Hon, did you really come here to gibber with me, or to screw me?"

He glances up the stairs, three in all, and there she is, leaning against the wall of the adjoining foyer. Long black hair falls loosely over her left shoulder, as she tilts her head, accentuating the question. She licks her moist, luscious lips with a quick tongue flick, as she slowly strokes her thigh with the tips of her French-manicured nails. Her butter-pecan colored skin glistens in the wan candlelight, with the sheen of some flavored oil, complementing the scent of her perfume.

Veronica's caramel-colored camisole also falls loosely from her left shoulder, giving Marcus a ghost glimpse of her aroused nipples behind the thin teddy. The skimpy camisole stops just shy of her upper thighs, teasing Marcus with a peak of her honey pot. Damn . . . he can barely hold it together any longer. Veronica is drop-dead gorgeous. By the light of the distant candle, he can read the steamy look in her eyes as he gazes back at her. Outside, lightning flashes and a thunderclap rolls. The outside flash temporarily lights the kitchen, giving Marcus a silhouette view of Veronica's slim figure underneath the teddy. Fear and uncertainty are instantly replaced with lust and heat.

"I thought that we could—" she starts to say, before Marcus interrupts on his way up the three steps, in one giant leap.

In a gruff voice, he cuts her off. "Don't talk. Don't say anything to me."

He's up the steps and into the foyer in a blink. His strong arms quickly but gently wrap around her waist from both sides as he pulls her toward him. She doesn't put up a fight. Instead, she reaches out at the same time, wrapping her arms around his neck, simultaneously pulling him toward her own opening lips, and thrusts her pelvis toward his crotch. They collide violently, passionately. Her tongue darts in and out of his mouth with an uncanny speed. His hands slide down her waist, grabbing two palmfuls of rump. Her petite frame is easy to lift and Marcus does so with little effort. Their mouths never slow the dance, as he lifts her from the floor of the foyer, a caramel-colored high heel pump smacks against the wall. She wraps both legs tightly around her lover's backside. Marcus breaks off the passionate kiss, slinking the tip of his tongue down her chin, underneath her right jawline, straight for her earlobe. Veronica's breathing heaves as he twirls the tip of his tongue into her ear. Her hands fall from his neck, down his back, up to his shoulder blades, back around his neck; she's frenzied with lust. She tries to speak in between breaths.

"Ohhhhh . . . Marcus, I've wanted this for so long, baby. My God, I've wanted you for so long . . . ohh . . . unhhh . . . I need you, baby! Please give it to me!"

Marcus's brow breaks out in sweat as his tongue action trails back down to the nape of her neck. He walks into the kitchen, with her tight in his arms.

"Where's the bedroom, Ronnie?" he huffs, staring into her eyes.

"Damn the bedroom, Marcus Jackson, I can't wait! Fuck me here! NOW!" she screams into his face, and attacks his lips with passionate kisses, sucking and biting his bottom lip until it almost bleeds, all the while groping and fondling any and every inch of his body in a desperate attempt to get to flesh. Marcus plops her rump onto the marble countertop of the center kitchen island, then literally rips the camisole straps from the garment. Perking breasts with rock-hard nipples spill over the top of the fallen garment. Outside, the rainstorm continues. Mother Nature's pissed rage matches their primal rustle with every move and with the next flash of lightning, Marcus can see the crazed look of want in the eyes of his forbidden lover. The look grants him strength, but it's also enough to take him over the edge.

"Oh, shit, I can't believe this is happening! Not yet!" he yells as he concentrates on squeezing his groin.

"Wait for me baby, wait . . ." she whispers in between huffs.

Veronica's hands thrust off the marbletop counter, sending her into a sort of leap from the countertop, tackling Marcus to the ground. The impact against the vinyl flooring winds him enough to calm his lust for a second. He doesn't have time to ask what the hell's going on. He opens his eyes and glances toward his now vertical feet to see that Veronica is *on* him. She's already unlatched his belt and is pulling at his jeans. With one swift and steady tug, she manages to yank his boxers and jeans to his kneecaps. His prick bounces free of the boxers and immediately stands at full attention. She's fast. Her mouth closes around him, swallowing his prick completely. She sucks him with incredible speed, her teeth never once shaving his delicate skin, her left hand gently squeezing his scrotum sac. Marcus begins to hyperventilate; his mouth dries as she continues to give him the blow job to end all blow jobs. His hands find tangles of her silky dark hair as he focuses his sights on the patterned ceiling paper above the island. The lightning flashes, and the thunder rolls, and the rain continues to rage outside.

Flickering candles from the nearby living room offer a soft varied glow of this beautiful woman's head quickly bobbing up and down over his crotch. The whole dreamlike action proves too much for him to handle. He tries to speak up and warn her of the inevitable outcome of this wonderful head job. As she continues to move, she moans in pleasure as the rain outside continues.

"Fuck . . . oh, shit! Ronnie . . . baby! I think I'm gonna cum! Aw, God, Veronica, I'm gonna cum, baby!" he yells as his muscles tense.

She stops long enough to speak, before continuing at a faster pace. "Give it to me Mark! I want it now! I wanna taste it!!"

Marcus involuntarily grips down on her head as his prick erupts. Wave after wave, she never stops sucking and groaning in pleasure as he unloads between her lips. He cums so hard that he thinks he might shit right there on her kitchen floor, while holding the back of her head into his crotch. His breathing stops as she sucks him dry. Marcus has a brief moment to worry as he continues spewing into her open mouth; he thinks he might faint. Just when the colors around him begin to turn the dull gray of a fainting spell, he exhales deeply, and inhales just as deep.

Veronica flings her head back up into the air, wiping her luscious lips with the tips of her right hand while continuing to squeeze his balls with her left hand. She's in ecstasy, savoring the taste of his life-producing juices. Marcus raises his hands to her breasts as she straddles him, her lips wet and sticky, glowing by the light of the candle. His fingers gently circle the areolas, then pinch down on the nipples firmly. She squeals in pleasure, then begins speaking in fluent Spanish.

"I don't know what the fuck you're saying, *Mami,* but keep going," he gruffs.

Capturing a full breath, Marcus shoves her backward to the vinyl floor, her back smacking the ground smartly. Veronica giggles like a schoolgirl and taunts him playfully.

"Mr. Jackson, I didn't realize you were so robust, sir! And what do you want to do to me now, hon?" she asks coyly.

"I'm gonna suck your pussy until it hurts. It's your time to cum, Ronnie," he answers matter-of-factly, then grips the camisole at the hips and rips what's left of the now-tattered garment from her body.

Ohh, it's beautiful, trimmed to perfection and just lovely to look at. The lightning-flash dance begins to intensify and with each flash, he finds himself in awe of what's happening here, of what had just happened. Mia had never sucked him dry before! She, in fact, hates the idea of even giving oral sex. This, by comparison, is incredible! Marcus sits up on his rump, kicking his shoes off of his feet. Veronica then pulls his jeans and boxers free before lying to the floor on her back. He strips his shirt free, then lowers his lips to her right breast. As he gently sucks the nipple, she arches her back, allowing a moan to slip from her lips. His right hand grips at her left breast. Veronica's in heaven.

She pants and says, "Eat me, Marcus. Please, baby, eat *your* pussy."

"My pussy," he replies.

"*Sí, bebé*. It's all for you tonight. It's yours, Marcus. Take it," she pleads.

Marcus slowly trails down her breast with the tip of his tongue, stopping at the bottom to kiss it with his lips. His pace slows even more as he trails his tongue over her stomach, circling the button, his fingertips gently massaging and tickling her sides on the way down. She giggles and shudders at his touch. It's unfamiliar territory for the both of them. Marcus's tongue-travel finally ends at her thatch and plunges deep into the honey pot, tasting her juices. Veronica moans in bliss. Next he trails back up the thin wall of her inner lips and begins to slowly, gently stroke her clitoris. Veronica shivers with each lick. As he continues to tongue-stroke, he picks up the pace and she begins to rock in unison. The rain outside seems to add a certain romantic edge to the action. Veronica's hands find the back of Marcus's head as he strokes her gently, now adding slight pressure, intensifying pleasure. He slips two fingers into her hot, wet pussy, searching the top inner wall until he finds the soft hump of the G-spot and then concentrates his finger pressure there.

"Oh God, Mark, baby. Don't stop! Oh, eat it! Mark, it feels so good!"

Marcus induces more speed and pressure. He thrusts her legs high into the air, forming a giant V shape, while supporting them with his palms at the backs of her thighs. More pressure, more speed. The thunder rolls and the lightning flashes as the rain pounds against the house. She gasps and pants with each lick; every finger-stroke over her spot induces another flutter through her groin. She feels heat, and cold; a wave is starting somewhere behind her groin and she grips his head in a vice lock of legs and hands as her vagina explodes in ecstasy. Veronica's gasp is instantly silenced as the wave continues to pulse through her whole body. She temporarily loses breath and goes light-headed, basking in the bliss of the orgasm. She's suffocating him, as she cums hard and slow.

Marcus grasps both legs and forces them to part away from his head as he takes in a deep breath of air. The excitement of the oral sex is stimulation enough to stiffen his dick again. As Veronica lies on the floor with her eyes shut tight, clutching her breasts while still convulsing in the orgasm, Marcus creeps over the top of her and gently but firmly shoves into her sopping wet pussy. She gasps hard, then screams in pleasure as he begins to jackhammer thrust in and out of her, stroking hard and fast while grunting between his clinched teeth.

She grabs hold of his back, edging him on with each deep stroke, and begins gibbering in intertwined English and Spanish. Outside, the lightning snaps sporadically in brilliant flash patterns; thunder rolls and crashes as if God is bowling the game of a lifetime; the rain relentlessly pounds against the brick house's windows. Veronica is screaming bloody murder as she wraps her legs around Marcus's lower back. She squeezes her pelvis with everything she has left. In between gasps, she looks Marcus in the eyes with a stare that he will never forget—the cold certainty of that stare brings home the reality of the current situation. He's seen that stare in the office on many occasions, when business was in order.

She speaks to him in a husky, raspy tone that almost scares him. "Marcus Jackson, fuck me harder, you son of a bitch! Fuck me like you've never fucked anyone in your life, dammit!"

Marcus digs deep and kicks into high gear. The tile flooring is beginning to scrape his knees, but still he pounds away like a madman set free of his shackles. Veronica continues to scream at him, her voice growing louder with each hard thrust. Marcus can see by the sweat forming on her forehead that the pelvic squeezing is beginning to take its toll on her, yet she persists to scream and clutch, gasp and pant. His heart is pounding inside his chest so hard that it's beginning to ache. His lower abdominal muscles are on fire; his triceps are screaming in burning pain, but he refuses to stop. He's going all the way with this one, until he either explodes or drops dead. He's determined to tear a hole through this pussy, even if his heart decides to burst through his chest. Sweat drips into his eyes, stinging—still, he thrusts away. His balls spank back and forth against her ass and his own, until they eventually go numb.

"Oh my God, Marcus! Oohh, shit . . . my God in heaven! Ohh, I'm gonna cum again . . . oh you fucking Marcus, you . . . oohh . . . ohhh . . . oh. God, I'm . . ."

Marcus, feeling his own joy juice about ready to flow, roars into a full-blown jungle holler.

"Oh, fuck me! I'm gonna—"

Veronica shudders and reflexively digs her nails into his back, drawing blood. At the same time, she pulls herself into a locked position and bites down on his right shoulder as she explodes in orgasm, sending a hot flush of wet juice flowing from her pussy. Marcus lets loose a violent spray that flickers back and forth between pain and pleasure. His body also locks up and simply shuts down, freezing them both in a weird sort of silent, petrified embrace.

Marcus feels warm, wet juice flow down his scrotum and between his legs as Veronica continues to let loose what she would later describe as the single most pleasurable pee she would ever experience. The wave between the forbidden lovers continues until they slowly relax and embrace each other, breathe together, holding on to each other as if life depends on the strength of the hug. Veronica's lips let go of Marcus's shoulder. She slowly collapses to the sweaty floor as she gasps for air. Marcus's arms give way and he simply falls on top of her, breathing heavily into her right ear. His stomach is performing topsy-turvy flips and his head aches.

"How'd we do, boss lady?" he whispers.

"We were wonderful, *Papi*," she whispers.

"Good. If you don't mind, I think I'm gonna go ahead and faint now."

"Sleep, hon. My God, you definitely earned a rest and a raise," she whispers.

As his breathing slows to a steady pace, Veronica gently kisses his right ear, then stares up at the patterned ceiling of her kitchen. A smile draws across her face as she strokes the back of her unconscious lover's neck with one hand and caresses his shoulder blade with the other.

"Sleep, love. Dream of a different time and place, where we wouldn't have to hide," she whispers.

Veronica Torres watches the patterned ceiling slowly begin to gray out as she drifts toward sleep. Just before passing out, she realizes that, outside, the rain has stopped.

# Sayulita Siesta

## BlissDulce

I had just rolled over to get deeper into Denzel's arms when the sound of a ringing phone snatched me right out of them.

"Shit," I mumbled as my heart galloped a thousand beats a minute. "A sista can't even get fucked in a dream."

I felt around for my saline container so I could rinse my contacts and *see.* There might have been a few streaks of light in the sky but I was squinting with dry eyes and wasn't sure. I squirted a few drops in each eye and everything in the room sprang to attention as my vision was restored. Just what I thought. It was barely light out. Who would be calling me before the crack of dawn? I sat up to look for the phone and it took a minute to remember that it was in the living room. Back when I'd first talked to the current owners about buying this house, it was cool that there were no phones in the bedrooms. I didn't plan to make any calls from here, and after the deal was done, I only expected to get calls from family, who I hoped would call only when I was awake and out of bed, unless it was an emergency. My secretary Karma had the number and instructions to call me only if she heard my momma and/or sister died and she wanted to make sure I had the news.

I scrambled barefoot into the living room, glad the tile floors were warm and worried that this *was* an emergency call.

"Hello?" I gurgled.

"Dee, what you doing, girl?" a voice chirped, too happy for this time of morning.

I cleared my throat. "Who is this?"

"It's me. Ticey."

"Ticey?" I echoed.

"Ticey, your sis-ter!" Ticey sucked her teeth.

"Ticey, you done lost your mind. Girl, it's still dark here," I lied.

"Dee, you a damned liar." Ticey laughed. "I checked the time on the Internet before I called you. What? You got some man in your bed and I got you up in the middle of something nasty? Tell the truth, Dee!" Ticey cackled. "What color is his dick, girl? Is it big? Is he circumcised?"

"Ticey, what do you want so early in the morning?" I asked, about to get an attitude. "I had too many damned margaritas last night, the *sun* is still sleeping, and no, I ain't got no man in my bed. I'm here to buy this house, remember? I ain't got time for nothing else."

I had to laugh at myself then because I knew how stupid I sounded. My sister and I were tighter than tight and she knew nothing stopped me from getting dick. I plopped down on the overstuffed couch and spilled my guts when I stopped laughing.

"Ticey, I ain't seen a man here yet who looks good enough to get this ass, girl. Can you believe that?"

"Whaaaaaaaaat?" Ticey drawled. "Dee, you lying! Here I am waiting for you to say our Latino brothers are swinging giant dicks. Sis, I swear I was gonna pack my ish and hop on the next thing smoking down that way." Ticey laughed loudly in my ear.

"Girl, don't waste your time. I've been here five days and ain't seen nothing worth taking my drawers off for." I laughed with her.

"Damn, girl. That must be hard for you. Where are you, anyway? I thought you were in Cancún but the operator didn't say Cancún."

"Operator? What operator? Ticey, I left y'all a direct number for the phone here at the house. Why you call the operator?"

"Dee, you know I don't know nothing about calling foreign countries. The operator was cool. It didn't take her no time to ring you."

"Chile, do you know operator-assisted calls are the most expensive? 'Bye, Ticey! We been on this phone too long. You gonna be mad when you get your bill and no, I ain't splitting it with you so don't ask!"

"Dee, you know you wrong. 'Bye, girl. Oh, wait! Where ya at?"

"I'm in a town called Sayulita. It's near Puerto Vallarta. 'Bye, Ticey." I hung up.

Since I was already up, I watched the colorful sunrise from the bedroom patio and did a fifteen-minute meditation. After a warm shower, I dressed for breakfast, ready to step out into another sparkling day. The bedroom mirror reflected my fine chocolate frame, looking voluptuous in my lime-green sundress. I put on matching thong sandals and pulled my waist-length locs up into a high ponytail, glossed my lips, then checked my side and rear views to make sure my dress repped my 36DDs and ass like it should. Perfection!

The restaurant that had become my favorite place to eat breakfast was a block away. It was one of the oldest restaurants in Sayulita and had a panoramic view of the surf. The señora and her husband who owned the restaurant were very nice people. Both spoke excellent Spanglish; I chose their company every morning because they reminded me of my momma and daddy.

The beach beckoned after my leisurely breakfast. There wasn't much else to do, and since my plan was to soak up as much sun as I could before heading back to dreary DC, I gave in. I would be sorry to leave the beauty and warmth of Sayulita but happy when the house was officially mine. The problem was that I had no clue how long it would take. Mexican laws on foreign property ownership are complicated so I had a *mexicano* attorney handling this for me. He called me the day I arrived but not since then, so I was basically killing time.

I lay out on my towel under my umbrella and opened one of the juicy novels I took out of my bag. I had to put it down after a few chapters into the book. It made me horny, and why should I be reading about some other woman getting her freak on if I had to walk around with hard nipples and a lonely coochie until I got back home? Uh-uh, I wasn't doing that. I closed my eyes, stretched out on my back, and let the soothing sounds and aromas of the beach make love to me while I thought about the benefits of having my own house near the beach. My purchase would enable me to take real vacations as often as I could get away and every time I came down, it would be like getting free accommodations because if I handled my business correctly, it would pay for itself with the extra cash I could make by renting it out to some folks I already had in mind.

When I opened my eyes, there was a man standing over me. He startled the shit outta me but I grew up in the hood. I wasn't scared. We stared at each other, neither speaking. Since he came to me, I waited. In the meantime, I assessed him with a practiced eye. I was squinting into the sun but the brotha was fine from what I could see. His jeans and white T-shirt were nothing fancy but they fit him well. He looked like he was taller than me, had broad shoulders, nice muscle tone in his arms, and a trim waist. He had smooth, deep bronze skin, an angular jawline, and thick, glossy hair that disappeared down his back. I could see that he wasn't as husky as my usual type but that was trivial. However, I did need to know if he could pass the T-bone test cuz I like my men the way I like my steaks: brown and meaty with a big bone in the middle. He was definitely brown and I was hoping the other two were part of the package as well.

Then my conscience kicked in: *You're on business in a foreign country, girl. Cool your hot ass down!* it hollered at me as I stared curiously at him. But unlike my conscience, I have no shame when it comes to sex. Am I a bad girl because I like my business to be as pleasurable as possible? And why should I make an exception just because I was out of the country?

*Shit, I've been here a week and he's the first man I've seen who ain't too light, too skinny, or too ugh for my tastes. It might take a little ingenuity to get the dick, but it's alright. If I can't do this, it can't be done. I can play this game in my sleep.* I giggled aloud as I visualized the kinky possibilities.

My laughter ended the staring contest and he spoke to me.

"Señora, you should cover up more when you are sleeping on the beach. Some in our town do not consider it proper for a lady to expose her . . . to expose herself in such a way in public." Then he left abruptly. I watched him disappear into a restaurant I'd eaten in a few days ago.

Well damn! Not even a polite hello. I didn't know what to think about that. I hope all this body didn't offend the dude. I know not every man can handle this much woman but I love every inch of me and I'm not ashamed to flaunt my assets. Maybe I dozed off and my legs were open or a titty fell out. I considered myself attired conservatively in my white two-piece. A sheer orange pareo covered my booty so what was the fuss about? It wasn't one of those itty-bitty, dental-floss-in-ya-crack bikinis either. I got tits and ass to spare and I fluctuate between a big size 14 and a smallish 18. I never could find an off-the-rack swimsuit that could keep all my goodies wrapped in the package. I have my bikinis custom-made to gently support my lusciousness while allowing my sexiness to play a peekaboo.

I thought about my visitor. I didn't see him when I ate in that restaurant earlier in the week. Did he work there? Hmmm . . . I had an idea about lunch. I stayed at the beach another hour before flouncing off to the house to get ready for the midday stunt I intended to pull.

. . .

Showering and putting on fresh clothes and makeup killed a half hour on my clock. It was too hot for too many clothes but a full-figured sista can't roll without the proper foundation. I wore black lace panties, a matching bra and a black half-slip under my turquoise crinkled-cotton dress. My makeup was minimal, just eye shadow and tinted gloss on my lips.

The restaurant was cool and dim in contrast to the midday heat and glare. I sat down at an empty table and waited for my waiter. He appeared at my elbow almost before I could put my legs under the table. Was it a coincidence that he was the guy from the beach? His name tag said RODRIGO and his eyes were sexy, what people used to call bedroom eyes. Mmm . . . my pussy threatened to heateth over.

"*Buenas tardes,* señora. I am Rodrigo, your waiter today. How are you today, señora?" he sang in a perfect blend of English and Spanish.

I looked up at him through my eyelashes and flashed what I hoped was a sweet smile. I was saving the drama for later. "I'm doing well today, Rodrigo. *¿Y tú?*"

"*Muy bien,* señora. *Gracias.* What can I get you to drink today?" He put napkins and a straw on the table in front of me.

"I'll have a lemon Perrier, *por favor.*"

"*Gracias,* señora. Would you like to order now or wait until you have your drink?"

"I'll order now, thank you. I will have the rice and beans with *plátanos maduros* and house salad, please."

"*Gracias,* señora. I will be right back with your Perrier. It will be a few minutes for your meal. In the meantime, please, if you prefer, you can sit on either of the outside patios. There is the one out front or the one upstairs, on the roof."

"*Gracias,* señor." I smiled demurely at him again. He smiled politely at me and walked away. I watched his ass as he headed toward the kitchen.

I had no intentions of sitting outside. It seemed to get hotter in exponential increments here, from 10 A.M. until the sun set, and although the restaurant was almost on the beach, the air was still today. I looked around at the other diners, noting that I was the only person there solo. I was also bored. I spotted the antiquated jukebox near the bar and recalled hearing it last time I ate here. I sashayed over and dropped a few pesos into the slot, closed my eyes, and picked random songs. I nodded my head and swayed to the upbeat tempo of my first choice as I returned to my seat to enjoy the music with my Perrier.

The waiter who brought my food from the kitchen was not Rodrigo. He was much younger, couldn't have been a day over sixteen. My disappointment must have shown.

"Is everything okay, señora?" he asked politely.

"*Sí,* señor. Everything is fine." I smiled nervously at him as he put my food in front of me. Everything tasted wonderful but I felt let down. My stunt required Rodrigo to serve my meal. I paid my bill at my table and hauled ass. I was halfway up the block when someone touched my shoulder. It was my young waiter, grinning at me.

"Señora, you forget this? It was under your plate." He held out a cream envelope addressed to *La Reina.*

I shook my head. "No, my name is not Lareina. I don't think this is mine," I said, pushing the envelope back into his hand.

He dropped his hands to his side, refusing to take the envelope. "*Sí*, señora, you are *La Reina*, the Queen." He nodded emphatically.

I guessed that was something I'd missed in high school Spanish. I smiled. "Okay . . . *Gracias,* señor." He gave me a salute and ran back into the restaurant.

"The Queen?" I said aloud. "Who would call me that?" I opened the envelope and read the enclosed note as I sauntered home.

> *Mi Reina,*
>     *You are lovely, a wonder for my eyes and heart*
> *to behold and embrace. Por favor, I would like to see*
> *you again. El restaurante will close very soon for*
> *siesta. If you permit, I would like to visit with you*
> *then. If you will hang a blue cloth from your*
> *window, I will know that you wish to see me, too,*
> *and my heart will sing with gratitude. Until then, I*
> *await with hope,*
>     *Rodrigo*

I could have been bought for a penny. Rodrigo was trying to mack me! I couldn't hate because I knew the game inside out. I *was* a teeny bit mad that he had made his move first but why should I care? Either way, I was all for getting my pussy done right so there was no need to resist. I fumbled with the key at the door, wondering if I had anything blue to hang out the window. I left the door open but locked the bars.

Snickering to myself, I tore through the closet in search of a scarf, a belt—anything blue. In light of Rodrigo's polite note, it seemed too tacky to hang out the turquoise dress I was wearing. *Shit, I hope this ain't some Mexican courtship ritual. I'm not trying to get married. I just want some decent fucking to hold me until I get back to DC.*

I hung a blue washcloth from a hanger on the patio and took a quick freshen-up that included inserting my contraceptive sponge and putting condoms in strategic locations. I heard the doorbell ring as I put my toothbrush in the charger. I checked my face for stray gobs of toothpaste, then answered the door. Rodrigo's lean frame filled the doorway as he entered. He took both my hands in his and greeted me with a two-cheek kiss and a hug.

"*Buenas tardes,* señora," he said as he released my hands.

"*Buenas tardes,* Rodrigo," I replied, stepping back to observe him. He had changed into black, loose-fitting linen trousers and a cream shirt that offered an enticing contrast to his bronze skin. I was caught off guard for a moment. I'd never fucked a man *this* fine. I was nervous. Not that I'd been laying up with the ooglies, but Rodrigo was from the "Hell yeah!" page in the Sophisticated Sista's Catalog of Fine Ass Men. I reminded myself that I'd been campus queen at my alma mater and though I was forty, I was mistaken for twenty-five quite often.

"Rodrigo, please make yourself comfortable." I smiled graciously as I regained my composure. "And please, my name is Deena. No need to call me señora."

"*Sí, mi reina,* I will call you Deena." He sat close, facing me, our knees touching slightly. "How are you enjoying Sayulita so far?"

"Sayulita is beautiful. So far, I like it here."

"Wonderful, Deena." He caressed my thigh as he watched me attentively.

*Aha! He's down with it. Good. Now I don't have to work so hard.* I could feel my pussy juices simmering.

"Do you think you like it well enough to buy this house?" Rodrigo asked.

"Yes." I smiled. "I like it well enough to buy the house. How did you know?"

"Deena, Sayulita is a small town. Remember that there are very few secrets here. That is why I admonished you at the beach. It would not do to have the name of our newest resident to be dishonored for something so petty." He smiled seductively at me, arousing me further when he traced my lips with his finger. An involuntary moan escaped my lips. I forgot to ask him what sin I'd committed at the beach.

"Deena."

"Yes?"

Rodrigo stood up. "*Mi reina,* my queen, I want to bathe you. Do you have any olive oil?"

"Olive oil?"

"Yes, it softens the skin. I use it in my own bath."

"Oh, yes. Sure. It's in the kitchen." Whew, for a minute I thought I'd mistaken *bathe* for *baste.*

Rodrigo held out his hands to me and my will became his. I led him to the Jacuzzi tub in the master-bedroom suite. He sat me on the vanity stool and I watched him run the water, then leave for the olive oil. When everything was ready, he undressed me and helped me into the tub. I watched as he stripped down to glistening skin. His dick wasn't hard so I couldn't tell how big it really was. I could wait. He got

behind me in the tub and I relaxed against his chest, luxuri-
ating in the dual embrace of Rodrigo's arms and the warm,
slippery water.

"Deena . . . I love the sound of your name. . . . Listen,
Deena. I have something to share with you."

He sang to me in Spanish as he buffed my body to a dark
cocoa sheen. His voice was as melodious as he was attractive, and even though I didn't speak enough Spanish to make
out a third of what he was saying, it put me in a trance that
had me believing all the good things I'd heard about Mexican men and sex. In between verses, we kissed passionately,
fucking with our tongues as our bodies would later, building
an explosive tension that threatened to singe my soul. Rodrigo's free hand alternated between teasing my clit and my
nipples, making it more difficult for me to delay what we
both wanted. I lost it when he began licking and sucking my
nipples.

He cupped both my titties in his huge hands, pushed
them together, and flicked his tongue from one nipple to the
other, rapidly sucking and nibbling until they looked like
shiny chocolate gumdrops and I was a woman on fire. I
pushed him against the tub and straddled him. His mouth
kept my nipples warm and hard while his hands dove under-
water. I felt his powerful fingers enter my pussy.

"Mmmm . . . Ahhh . . . Rodrigo . . ." was all I could say.
Our voices mingled as he joined me in a chorus of ecstatic
harmonies that rang to the ceiling. I realized the bathroom
shutters were wide open and, for a split second, I wondered
if we were too loud. Then, I was like, *To hell with it. Why get
fucked if I can't enjoy it to the fullest?*

I rode Rodrigo's fingers as he massaged my pussy walls

with precise timing. I wasn't surprised when I felt his finger working its way into my asshole. At that point, all holes were fair game and I welcomed it. My body climbed to incredible heights of ecstasy as Rodrigo rocked me into a state of bliss with his fingers, lips, and tongue. I saw the birth of a new galaxy as my body and mind were swept into an orgasm with the force of a tidal wave.

"Ohhhhh . . . Uhnnnnnnnnnnn . . . Wheeeeeeeeee!" I sang as I was taken under. My pussy burst into convulsive spasms of delight as I whirled in the ripples of release. When my ears stopped ringing, I realized Rodrigo was crooning to me in Spanish. Whatever he said, it sounded good to me. We locked eyes and kissed slowly, appreciating each other's tastes and textures. I was hypnotized.

We chilled in the tub until the water got cold, then headed out to the bedroom patio to play in the sun. Rodrigo had the towels and I had the condoms. He spread a towel on a comfortable chair for me.

"Deena, sit here, *mi reina*."

I shook my head. "No, Rodrigo, you sit there. It's your turn for pleasure." I knew I was grinning my Nasty Girl grin.

I saw that his dick was still limp but that was no problem. I am proud to be the Mistress of Making 'Em Hard in a Hurry, a title I've worked hard for and one I intend to have for a long time to come. Therefore, I welcomed opportunities to keep my skills current.

I lightly licked Rodrigo's lips and once again, he met my tongue with his own. Electricity raced through my body as we took turns sucking each other. I ran my fingers up and down his chest, playfully scratching his nipples with my nails until they hardened like raisins. Then I straddled his hips to kiss him again. His lips were beet red. I'm not sure why that turned me on but it did. Rodrigo's moans told me he was enjoying my efforts and that excited me, too.

Rodrigo's fingers tangled in my locs as I teased the flat button of his navel with my tongue and teeth, making sure not to bite him in my fever to taste his flesh. Finally it was time for the main course, my favorite part of every meal. I folded the other towel, put it on the floor, and kneeled on it. I pushed his legs apart and held his uncircumcised dick in my hand for the first time. I pulled the foreskin back and almost cried because it was so pretty. I battled with myself over sucking it right then or waiting. I wanted to be in control this time so waiting won the fight.

His dick was semihard, thick, and very heavy. I knew it would grow longer and fatter as I worked my magic on him. I cradled his large shaved balls in my hand to feel their weight. They were heavy as well, which probably meant he hadn't had any pussy in a while. I licked each of his balls, giving each one special attention before taking it into my mouth and rolling it gently around on my tongue. (I wanted to do both at the same time but they were just too big and I was scared I would bite him.) Rodrigo's moans came more often and louder, letting me know he was getting closer to full arousal. I took my time stroking his dick, aware that he was about to be overly stimulated. When his dick stretched out and grew heavier in my hand, any willpower I thought I had vanished. I draped my lips on that gorgeous mushroom and lowered my head until his dick touched my tonsils. I spit-shined his dick from head to base, making sure it touched the back of my throat with every downstroke. Rodrigo began thrusting so I slowed down because I didn't want him to come too soon. I put a condom in my mouth and rolled it on.

I removed my mouth from his dick and Rodrigo opened his eyes in time to see me backing my pussy onto his dick. He spread my cheeks to get deeper penetration, and I leaned forward to get my balance and good friction for us both. As the hypnotic rhythm of his thrusts seduced me into the clouds, Rodrigo began teasing my asshole with his finger.

This time I know the whole neighborhood heard us as we crashed, grunting and screaming, into an orgasm that was better that my first one.

"Ahhhhhhhhhhhhhhhhhhhhhhhh!" Rodrigo yelled as he almost bucked me off his dick.

"Oh shiiiiiiiiiiiit!" I cried as the waves came to drown me again.

"Mmmmmmmmmmmmmmmmmm . . ."

"Uhhhhnnnnnnnnnnnnnnnn . . ."

Rodrigo's dick burst into the condom as I felt my own orgasm vibrating through my core. I continued to move my pussy up and down on his dick, knowing the extra sensation would be something he would never forget.

Exhausted, we collapsed into a heap of heavy breathing and sweat. When we were able to breathe normally, we moved to the chaise and I sat between Rodrigo's legs and listened to his stories about life in Sayulita. Let him tell it, Sayulita was Paradise. As I listened, I wondered if it was true or if he had an ulterior motive, like the town's continued economic success (foreigners usually rented their properties part-time, which brought cash flow to the town), or if it was his way of making sure I would return to Sayulita as often as possible to be with him. We hadn't had time to discuss anything beyond the present but I found myself hoping it was the second option. My vacation in Sayulita wasn't over and the thought of fucking this man every night—or even every other night—for the next fourteen days was enough to harden my nipples.

A wicked smile curled my lips as I stroked Rodrigo's thigh.

"Rodrigo."

"*¿Sí, mi reina?*"

"Bathe me again, *por favor?*"

# Papi's Baby Girl

## Gwyneth Bolton

*The* bruja's *back*. His mother's caustic and cautioning words at Sunday dinner came back with resounding clarity as soon as Miguel Suárez walked into the offices of his multimillion-dollar company and saw *her* there.

Lissette Suárez had used a variety of racial epithets along with the Spanish word for *witch* because she'd never gotten along with the African-American woman her son married. She told everyone who would listen to her that the *bruja* must have put a spell on Miguel.

He hadn't believed that his mother had really seen his wife. He'd assured her that she must have been seeing things. Because there was no way Stacy Williams-Suárez would come back to town and not notify him. Estranged though they might be, his wife knew better than that.

But there she was walking down the hall, every sway of her delectable hips mocking him. The red suit she wore put the power in the phrase *power suit*. And as she walked down the hall toward him with a slight slant in her eye and her lips tilted in a soft, taunting little smirk, he recognized that was exactly the effect she was after. She wanted to give the semblance of power—control.

A genuine smile formed on his lips as he realized that his sweet, sexy wife was indeed standing in front of him. Judging from the way his dick jumped to life, he was more than a little happy to see her.

"Hello, Stacy. Glad to have you back."

Stopping directly in front of him, she put her hands on her hips. "You don't have me back. Your company does. There's a big difference, Miguel."

Allowing the grave misconception for the moment, he decided to take stock of the beauty standing before him rather than disabuse her of the misguided belief that he didn't have her back. From bottom to top, the woman was simply gorgeous. He'd always loved the color red on her. It worked nicely with her rich walnut complexion and brought out the soft red undertones in her skin. The silk stockings that graced her legs beckoned to be stroked. Her long shapely calves led to curvaceously firm thighs and hips that he could only imagine under the skirt but he remembered fondly. Remembering those legs wrapped around him while those hips met each of his thrusts almost made him want to take her against the wall in the hallway. The rest of the employees would no doubt be shocked if they walked in on such a thing, but Stacy should have calculated that risk when she decided that the workplace was the first place she wanted to be seen after her two-month disappearance.

Letting his eyes travel upward, he licked his lips at the slight, subtle lift each breath she took gave her breasts. The soft fabric of the suit and the silk blouse she wore underneath could not contain the bountiful bundle. He imagined the nipples underneath waiting for the caress of his tongue. Moving to her long, graceful neck, he paused and knew for certain that he needed to either make love to his tempting wife or move along to the confines of his office. The delicate ruby-and-diamond choker she wore around her neck made his dick painfully erect. That she still wore the choker meant *more* to him than the fact that she was also still wearing her engagement ring and wedding band. Those conventional trinkets may have held weight with the rest of the world, but the choker and the fact that she hadn't removed it spoke to him in ways that he could *never* fully express.

Deciding to move the discussion on, Miguel simply stated, "Mom said she saw you shopping on Saturday. I guess she was right?"

An expression of hesitation briefly traveled across her face before she put her game face back on. Shrugging and twisting her sweet thick lips to the side, she said, "Yes, I saw your mother. But I didn't really feel like speaking to anyone that day."

There had never been any love lost between the two women. But Stacy's attitude toward the Suárez matriarch still irritated him. His eyes narrowed slightly. "How long have you been back in town?"

Again her slight hesitation spoke volumes and clued him in on her nervousness. She took a deep breath and he noticed the gentle lift of her breast under the red jacket.

Tilting her head defiantly, she responded, "I've been back two weeks."

She'd been back a whole two fucking weeks and she hadn't come home!

She'd left their six-month-old marriage two months ago and took a leave of absence from her position at his company in order to "clear her head." Even though it had been the last thing he wanted to do, he'd given her space. Their relationship had been unconventional by typical standards and his decision to marry her had apparently freaked her out more than she let on because it had been the beginning of the end.

Emotions warred within him. And the biggest one of them—desire—had to be contained until he figured out exactly what Stacy was playing at. She wasn't a dumb woman. In fact she was the smartest woman he'd ever met. So, she had to know that coming back and still wearing the choker, his first gift to her, *his collar,* was as close to resuming their relationship as anything. Miguel knew that Stacy was well aware of the kind of man she'd married.

"So, you're back . . . only for your job?" He let the question hang as he trailed every curve and crevice of her body with his eyes. He then pinned his gaze on her and let her know with one look that all the red power suits in the world weren't going to stop him from getting her exactly where he wanted her. *Naked, splayed, and tied to their bed.*

Her eyes met his stare. Recognizing his meaning, she literally jumped and moved back a space. Her semblance of control faltered just barely.

A lesser man might not have noticed it at all.

She lifted her chin and smirked. "Yes, Miguel. I'm back for my job. We never should have breached those boundaries. I'm hoping that eventually we will be able to get to a place where we can put the unfortunate incidents of the past behind us."

*Unbelievable! No way, Baby Girl!* Miguel closed the space

between them in one giant step and pulled her into his arms. He took her lips quickly and roughly. The kiss was meant to show her that she was not calling the shots. She tried valiantly to refuse him, but he wasn't having it. Two long months without tasting her made him react like a starving man tasting a stolen morsel of food. Wrapping his arms around her and allowing his hands to rest on her ample behind, he pulled her tightly to him and allowed her to feel the press of his dick as his mouth ravished her. Mrs. Stacy Williams-Suárez had to know exactly what she was dealing with.

Stacy tried to catch her breath. The wind was being sucked out of her by Miguel's sweet lips. It was torture. Coming back to town had been a mistake and coming back to work had been a huge misstep. But Stacy knew that the old woman had seen her in the mall and it would only be a matter of time before she ran and told Miguel. She thought she was ready to face him but she must have been crazy to think so. She had stepped back into his grasp and he was seizing control again.

She couldn't let him have it. Could she? The last time she did, she swore she almost lost what she thought was her very self.

There was really no choice when it came to the kiss, however. If Miguel's penetrating gaze hadn't let her know, his probing tongue was making it damn certain. She was *his*. Her own tongue seemed to mock her as it rushed its way into his mouth and tasted him. The pleasure and pain of his rough, angry kiss had her lace thong sopping wet and it wasn't even nine in the morning. There was no way she would make it through the day without crawling to the man's office and begging him to fuck her.

But she had to. For her own sanity's sake, she would. Then she would send him her letter of resignation along with divorce papers and put this part of her past behind her once and for all. She tried to pull away but he held her tight. Groping her behind, he pressed his dick closer. His meaning couldn't have been clearer.

Just like that, he ended the kiss.

Stunned, she took a shaky step back and expelled air from her lungs that she was amazed she still had. She even found a voice from somewhere and it spoke. "That was un-called for, Miguel. And it is exactly the reason why things got out of hand between us in the first place. Please try and control yourself so that this doesn't happen again today. What if some of the employees—"

The raging desire in his eyes refused to be contained as he cut her off. He moved away from her as he spoke. "It's *my* company. I'm the boss, Baby Girl. I could care less if the employees come in and see me kissing *my* wife." Punctuating each *my* with a sharp slap on her behind, her husband walked away and entered his office.

The slaps on the ass, like the kiss, like the bulging swell of his dick, were all meant to let her know that no matter how much she tried to change the nature of their relationship, he wasn't having it.

Turning, she watched the retreating back of Miguel Suárez in awe. The man exuded sexiness and power. In the boardroom and in the bedroom, he exhibited dominance and control that most men would give their right arm to possess and most women would give anything to be possessed by.

*Most women except me, damn it!* She needed to retain her resolve and focus on something besides his tight ass and strong back. All that did was make her remember the way he used that back and behind like a well-oiled piston to bring her to mind-shocking climax after climax after climax.

No, coming back to work and confronting her sexy husband may not have been the brightest idea. It was too late now. She couldn't let his silky bronzed skin, the glossy black curls on his head, or the piercing onyx gaze of his eyes stop her from doing what needed to be done. So what if the man called to mind a sip of one of her favorite guilty pleasures, a caramel macchiato? Just like the specialty coffee drink, the sweetness of the caramel, vanilla, and milk lulled her into a temporary calmness right before the kick of the espresso and caffeine snapped her ass into overdrive. That was Miguel Suárez in a nutshell and thus her inner turmoil about their relationship. She just didn't know if she could handle everything that went with taking the entire package—the parts that made her feel safe and warm and loved along with the parts that pushed her to her limits and beyond. Letting out a sigh and taking a deep breath, she readied herself for what was clearly going to be the longest day of her life.

The pressure of a multimillion-dollar company, the motion and excitement that made her join the company a year ago, gave her a small reprieve in dealing with Miguel. But none of the hectic hustle and bustle could halt her heart's rapid beating or the shockwaves of awareness that trembled through her body when his fine Dominican ass walked into a room.

By the end of the day she wanted to hightail it out of there with the rest of the employees. But she knew that she hadn't *really* faced him yet. She had to go into his office and firmly let him know that although their little explorations had been interesting, she was ending their relationship, severing all connections.

Once she was pretty sure that even his secretary had gone for the day, Stacy walked into Miguel's office for the facedown and hoped to God her visit wouldn't end with her facedown, ass up and spread across his rich mahogany desk.

Miguel glanced up from the papers on his desk when the door to his office opened. He thanked God that he was at least spared the scene of having to barge into Stacy's office and demand that she tell him why she left. The truth was he knew why she left. He didn't condone it and he wasn't about to let it happen again. But he understood that sometimes the intensity of their relationship scared her more than she let on.

Standing in front of his desk, her red suit jacket open to reveal the soft silky cream blouse she wore underneath, she presented a less formidable picture than she had earlier that morning. But her eyes still held her stubborn, willful challenge. She was going to make this hard.

"I just wanted you to know that I came back today to see if at least the business part of our relationship could be salvaged. And after careful consideration, after the way you behaved this morning, I have come to the conclusion that it would be best for all involved if I resign my position. Effective immediately." Her hand went to her neck, softly fingering her choker, and then moved behind as if she was about to remove it.

He couldn't let that happen. That wouldn't do at all. "And who gave *you* the authority?"

She faltered slightly. He got up from his desk, blocking any and every move she made. He was behind her in a matter of seconds, boxing her neatly between himself and his desk. He removed her hand from the choker and caressed the hand as he placed both her arms firmly at her sides. He could feel her soft shudders of breath and he smiled.

Pressing his lips to the back of her long, graceful neck, he inhaled and for a minute he envisioned what a drug addict or an alcoholic must feel like after taking that first fall off the wagon and sabotaging their sobriety. The scent of her traveled through his nose and made him want more. He let his tongue trail her neck slowly and seductively, trailing a pattern along the edge of the choker and making her aware of his collar before repeating his question. The way she trembled at his touch let him know she had forgotten that he'd asked her anything at all.

"I said, who gave you the authority, Baby Girl?"

"I—I . . . what? What do you mean? I gave myself the authority. I don't need anyone giving me any authority to make a decision about *my* life, *Miguel*." She said his name with force and spun around to face him.

Her alert nipples pushed through the silk blouse as her chest firmly pressed against his own. The defiance in her eyes was breathtaking. All fire and passion, she asserted her control firmly and decisively.

Impressed, but not waylaid, he lifted her blouse from its

neat, tucked position in her red skirt and let his hands caress her belly before moving up and squeezing the full taut mounds of flesh encased in lace.

"Well. We both know that's not true. Don't we? You have absolutely no authority whatsoever about what is best for all involved. And you certainly have no authority to say how it will play out, much less how, when, or if it will end. We both know that is my domain. Don't we, Baby Girl?"

She closed her eyes. He could see she was trying to hold back her reaction. Squeezing her breasts tighter, he pressed his lips to hers and enclosed them in a kiss. Her mouth opened to him immediately and for that he allowed a calmer exploration than he had that morning. He took his time probing the depths of her mouth and reclaiming his space. As he let his finger scrape the protruding nipples in her lacy bra, the moans that escaped her lips urged him on even further. He moved down to her skirt and lifted it enough to give himself access to her stockings, garter belt, and lace thong.

The thong was drenched. *Yet another thing to add to her growing list of infractions. Cumming without permission is a no-no.*

First two, then three of his fingers slid their way into her slick folds and penetrated her in ways the dick straining against his zipper longed to. With her silk shirt bunched up to her neck and her skirt scrunched up around her hips, she looked exactly as he had imagined her many times for the past two months. Burying his head in the lace of her bra, he grasped a nipple in between his teeth and bit down as he finger-fucked her. Nibbling on the nipple as he probed her

G-spot, he then pressed his thumb tightly to her clit and felt her burst. Her pussy spasm squeezed his fingers and she rocked rhythmically against him.

He let go of her nipple but kept his fingers in her soft, wet hold. "Did you just cum without permission, Baby Girl?" He tsked in mock annoyance. "Someone has allowed her little hiatus to make her forget all her training. We'll have to deal with your infractions later. Right now, I have to fuck you, Baby Girl."

Her eyes widened as he lifted her onto his desk, swiftly pushing everything onto the floor in one sweep. Pulling her hips to the edge of the desk, he wasted no time entering her. He pushed into her hot, slick, wet pussy all the way to the hilt. He was home.

"Ahhhhh!" She threw her head back and cried out as she wrapped her legs around him and pulled him closer to her with her arms. "You see," she accused. "This is exactly what I was talking about. We shouldn't have . . . ahhhhh . . . Oh God!"

"Don't." He smiled when she fought back the orgasm that threatened to rip through her. Even though he knew she was nowhere near ready to submit fully—to assume her role and ask for permission—the brief exchange of power was not missed.

She took deep, panting breaths and expelled a sharp hiss. "This is wrong, Miguel. We shouldn't be doing this. We should have had better control over our desires and we never should have given into them. This has to end, now."

He lifted her off the desk and walked with her still firmly impaled on his dick to the large brown leather sofa in his office. Laying her down, grabbing her arms, lifting them above her head, and holding them in the grasp of his hand, he continued to fuck her as he spoke. Enough was enough. He had given her the time away because he realized that their last scene together had taken them to such an incredible place of pleasure and pain that even he had been caught off guard by the intensity.

He loved her more than words could ever express, but maybe his mother was right and he had married a witch. For only a spell-casting temptress could have caused him to go against every dominant bone in his body and let her leave. It wouldn't work this time. As far as he was concerned, if she wanted to remain free, she should have stayed gone. Coming back to town and work firmly placed her back where he wanted her all along.

"This is not wrong. What's wrong is you thinking for a moment that I'm out of control. Or that you can come in here and dictate anything at all. The mere fact that I let you walk away for two long months, come back here, and went a whole day without fucking *my* pussy right there in the hall for every single one of my employees to see is a testament to the amount of control and restraint I have." He measured each of his words with sharp penetrating stabs of his dick.

"Ohhhhh . . . Oh. Shit. Oh shit!"

"And don't you dare cum, Baby Girl!"

Her eyes glazed over and she swallowed.

"Don't you think you have cum enough for one day?" He lifted her leg and buried his dick deeper inside of her. She felt so unbelievably inviting. So tight. So warm. The sticky sweetness of her was about to send him over the edge. He bent his head and bit down on her nipple to take the edge off himself. He couldn't cum yet. Not until they were clear.

He pinched the other nipple between his thumb and forefinger, pulling and tugging it as he sucked and nibbled on the other. He felt her pussy tightening around him and knew it was only a matter of time until his Baby Girl exploded. But first she had to acknowledge that was exactly who she was—*his.*

Stacy couldn't believe she was right there writhing under her husband, both of them partially clothed and fucking on the sofa in his office like they didn't have a lick of home training. That was the biggest problem of all, wasn't it? From the first time she laid eyes on him, Miguel always made her forget all her inhibitions.

The man unleashed things in her, desires and wants that she never knew she had. She was a successful, strong black woman, for goodness sake! There was no way in hell she could possibly want the things he offered her. She didn't want to be sexually dominated. Did she? She was the independent woman that Beyoncé and the girls sang about before they started giving lap dances on awards shows, singing about catering to a man. She couldn't be both. Could she?

Everything that had happened to her since she'd taken the position in his company had been under his control, at his command, by his desire. You would have thought that she would have hightailed it out of there when she found herself having the kinkiest, wildest sexual encounters she had ever experienced anywhere, let alone in the workplace. But their affair had been so sudden and so breathtaking that she had gotten swept up in it. And before she knew it, they were in Vegas, closing a business deal and then sealing her own fate with a quick marriage. By the time she had a second to process it all, she was Mrs. Miguel-fucking-Suárez. That she hadn't hauled ass then was a testament to how caught up she was.

The day-to-day aspects of their life, the way they conducted themselves as intelligent colleagues, all went out the window when they came together sexually. The night before she left, he'd both stripped her of any remaining semblance of control she thought she held and given her more intense pleasure than she'd ever known.

And she'd loved every moment of it! Just like she loved him. The pain. The pleasure. The power. The pull of his love. The push of her own. It all just became too much for her and she had to leave before she could no longer recognize herself.

But lying there with her husband's dick stretching her and filling her and feeling the sweet torture of her nipples as she all the while fought even her own reason and held back the screaming orgasm that threatened to escape any minute—all so that she wouldn't displease him—she recognized more about herself than she had been willing to face. She could be both the independent woman and cater to her man, at least in their intimate lives. She *was* both—independent *and* submissive.

A low, keening moan escaped her lips and she bit down to gather the strength to fight off cumming, so that she could find the strength within her to say what needed to be said.

He removed his mouth from her nipple. He continued to work the other nipple as well as his hips. "I can't let you go, Baby Girl. I tried. I can't. I won't. I know what you need and you know I do. So tell me, Baby Girl, tell me." The last of his words rushed out in a mumbled groan and she could tell that he was as close to bursting as she was. "Tell me what you need, Baby Girl."

"I need . . . I need to cum, *Papi,*" she managed to pant out. "Please. I need to cum and I need you, *Papi.* I need you so very much." It didn't surprised her how easily she fell back into the groove of their D/s relationship, how quickly she became Baby Girl to his *Papi.*

His mouth covered hers and he slowly moved his tongue in and out of her mouth in tandem with his dick. He fucked her mouth as he fucked her. And he hadn't said she could cum! As he pulled away from her lips, he nipped the bottom one in his teeth in a piercing grasp and demanded, "Cum, Baby Girl. Cum for me."

The orgasm was instant and ripped through her the moment he uttered the words. If she had any doubts about where she belonged and who she belonged to, she didn't have them anymore.

Her pussy cleaved to his dick, latching on and trying to pull it further in, as if that were at all possible. He let out a bellow and held her tightly as he released his hot burst of sperm inside of her. "I love you, Baby Girl. I love you so much. But if you ever leave me again, I'm going to spank that ass of yours until it feels like it's on fire and then I'm going to make you beg me to fuck you, knowing that the next time you see an orgasm would be so far away you might even forget what it felt like." His tone held no hint of play and she knew he was letting her off easy.

She took a deep breath. She embraced herself and his love for her. "Permission to speak, *Papi.*"

"You may speak, Baby Girl."

"Since we both know there is no way I'd ever forget what

a climax brought on by your wonderful lovemaking feels like, can we move this party to our home so that I can show the man I love and adore just how much I've missed him and . . . begin my penance for being a *very* bad girl? Can we go home now, *Papi?*"

Miguel smiled before kissing her slowly and seductively. "Yes, my love. Let's go home."

# Peaches 'n' Cream

## Amie Stuart

I had a plan.

I bit down on a fat, juicy strawberry and chewed slowly as the tart sweetness filled my mouth.

My name is Fiona Menard and in my opinion, the highlight of Carthage, Texas's Peach Festival is seeing Chris Whittier, never mind that he usually comes with a different woman every year (pun definitely intended).

I never took my eyes off him as I stuck my tongue out and caught the bit of juice that had escaped. "The strawberries are very good this year."

"I see that." He'd been staring at me *and* the strawberries for ten agonizing minutes, as if debating his next move.

Though he wasn't exceptionally tall, Chris was the epitome of tall, dark, and handsome, with short chestnut hair and delicious green eyes. A bit of chest hair peeked out from the top of his T-shirt and I found myself distracted, wondering just how hairy he was. If he had a soft pelt that covered his chest and tapered into a yummy happy trail that led into his denim shorts, and would I have to hunt for his nipples to nibble at them.

"Nice to see you again, Fiona."

Every year we seemed to play the same game of cat and mouse. Though it was also my job to flirt with the customers, to sweet-talk them into buying more than they came for, Chris always got more than his fair share of flirting.

Rumor had it he was from Tennessee, where he did something in the music business. He usually spent the festival weekend eating himself silly on peach cobbler (usually mine) or peach ice cream and the remainder of his vacation fishing and drinking beer with the friends he brings with him.

This year was different, however. Not only had he come sans an entourage, he'd come sans a woman. I'm not much of one for poaching, so beyond the usual chitchat about his vacation, I'd never managed to learn much about him. No one had. The man liked his privacy and I could respect that, but I had every intention of getting in his bed this weekend. Or getting him into mine.

I threw the last of my strawberry in a nearby trash can and slowly licked my fingers clean. "Did you decide?"

"How about just a bowl of fruit?"

With a smile, I filled a bowl with chilled peaches, cantaloupes, and strawberries and handed it over to him. He accepted it and returned my smile with one that crinkled the corners of his brilliant green eyes. Even dressed in nothing fancier than denim cutoffs that showed his thickly muscled thighs to perfection and a faded T-shirt stretched across broad shoulders, he was yummier than any damn peach. My nipples puckered under the covering of my own baby-blue shirt as I accepted the bills he handed me.

Thankful for a lull in the crowd, I leaned over and rested my arms on the pitted wooden countertop, giving him a peek at my cleavage.

"Where are your friends?"

"I came alone this year. Wanted some privacy." He popped a slice of cantaloupe between his lips and chewed thoughtfully.

"Good?"

"Worth waiting all year for." He gave me that grin again, the one that turned my insides into a puddle.

"My cousin brought them up from The Valley. Just picked this week." Texas's Rio Grande Valley was nearly as famous for its fruit as were Florida and California.

"No wonder they're so good," he muttered, slipping another piece into his mouth. "Let's talk . . . cobbler." His voice dipped dramatically on the last word.

In Carthage my peach cobbler was nearly as famous as my cleavage. The women stopped by my booth to chitchat and try to wrangle my secret cobbler recipe out of me—the men, well, they came for my cleavage. I flicked a long dark curl behind one ear and gave him a smile I knew bordered on a smirk. "I made *six* this year. I hear three are gone and the bidding is fierce over the last three."

"I know . . . those assholes outbid me!" He leaned in so close I could nearly count his eyelashes, his freckles, and every shade of green that made up the brilliant hue of his eyes. "I dream about your cobbler. All. Year. Long."

"Poor baby." I laughed, then pursed my lips thoughtfully. "Is that all you dream about?"

"I'll never tell." His eyes lingered on my cleavage before meeting mine again. The husky tease of his voice made my skin tingle. The late-afternoon breeze ruffled his hair and plastered his T-shirt to his chest. "I think you should come home with me and make one for me every day."

"Come home?" I quirked one eyebrow and chuckled. "To your little fishing cabin?"

"No, Nashville. Since you won't give me the recipe for my cook."

"You don't need me, *querido,* if you got a cook," I purred, leaning closer.

*"Querido?"* he repeated with a frown.

*"Darling,"* I translated with a smile and added, "or *dear,* if you prefer."

"Ah, I see. So, my little peach, what would it take?" He fished a slice of strawberry from the bowl and slid it into his mouth, then licked his fingers just as slowly and provocatively as I'd done earlier.

"I like a man who knows how to use his tongue."

Even as Chris howled with laughter, a deep sound that drew more than one censorious stare, I heard a gasp from behind him. It was my seventeen-year-old assistant, who I'd surely corrupt if she spent any more time in my company. Poor Fankie took naive to a whole new level. I should've behaved myself, but I wasn't a woman to let something like that stop me, and I wasn't afraid to go after what I wanted.

"You want my recipe? What's it worth to you?" I murmured while quickly assessing the crowd. We only had an hour or so before we closed down for the day, and all of downtown became a dance floor. Surely Fankie could handle the last hour by herself.

"The sun, the moon, the stars—all my earthly riches for just a taste—"

I licked my lips, aware of those eyes focused on my mouth. "Maybe we can come to some sort of arrangement."

His eyes warmed noticeably. "What did you have in mind?"

"You'll see," was all I'd say.

Instructing Fankie to finish cleaning up, I untied my apron and tossed it on the hook by the door. Stepping outside the almost claustrophobic confines of the booth, I took a deep, cleansing breath and crooked a finger at Chris, assuming curiosity would propel him to follow.

I managed to wade through the sea of peach-happy humanity while occasionally checking over my shoulder to be sure Chris was behind me. He was. Finally, I reached the corner of Main and Vine and slowed down enough to allow him to catch up. With an extra swing to my hips that made my skirt swish against my knees, I kept moving, but at a slower pace. The heat of the late-afternoon sun quickly soaked into my scalp as the heat of anticipation built between my thighs. I was already walking a fine line with the townspeople. If I got caught . . . I'd just have to make sure I didn't.

"Where the hell are you taking me, Fiona?" he demanded, grabbing my hand.

"You'll see." With a sly smile, I nudged him into an alley. A few more steps brought us to the drugstore's recessed delivery area. We had a shaded concrete pad covered from the heat of the sun and safety from the prying eyes of anyone who might wander past the alley's entrance. Prying ears, however, could be a whole other matter, if I wasn't careful.

"Do you like me as much as you like my cobbler, Chris?"

I spun around and gave him my most seductive smile. My panties were already damp and my insides quaked the tiniest bit at having him within my reach. My nipples were so hard they hurt but I refused to give into the urge and pinch them like I wanted to. Not yet anyway.

He chuckled and stepped closer as if he was finally aware of what I had in mind—of what I wanted.

I took the bowl of fruit he still carried and set it on a chair someone had left outside, then hooked a finger in the collar of his shirt and pulled him closer. "Do you?" I whispered.

"Do I what?"

"Like me as much as my cobbler." The backs of my fingers traveled lightly up his neck and across his stubble-kissed jaw.

"Definitely."

I sighed in pleasure as he leaned down and caught one finger in his mouth. His teeth exerted just enough pressure to not be ignored while his tongue gently laved at the pad of my finger. He moved closer, close enough so that his denim-clad thighs were pressed against mine and the brick wall bit into the tender flesh of my bottom through the thin material of my skirt. He was hot and hard and the slightest bit rough as he ground against my mound and continued making love to my finger.

Aching to relieve the ever-increasing pressure, I pushed my hips toward him, then shivered and gasped in pleasure as rough denim made contact with my pussy lips.

Finally, he released my finger and pressed his lips to my neck. "Now what exactly do I have to do to get some of that peach cobbler of yours?"

His callused hands were under my skirt, traveling up my

thighs, squeezing the cheeks of my ass, probing, spreading them wide and delving lower to tender lips filled with nerves, flushed and swollen and already hungry, and I realized I'd just lost control of him and this.

I pushed him away with a flirty "behave," and forced air into my lungs. I'd never given my recipe out. Ever. To anyone. I couldn't believe I'd consider it now, but Chris was worth it and by the time I was through with him, I doubt if he'd remember how to make it anyway. "You have to be a good boy and do what I say, and in exchange, I will give you some . . . cobbler."

"I'm not very good at taking orders. I'm more used to giving them."

"But this is a vacation—no need for giving orders when you're on vacation, right, *querido?*"

With a smile, I hooked my thumb in the waistband of my skirt, pushing it and my skimpy bikini panties off my hips to reveal his prize—if he was good. His eyes immediately dropped to my neatly trimmed snatch, and a hungry smile spread across his face.

I had a feeling he was going to be very, *very* good.

I leaned against the brick wall, briefly covering my swollen pussy, shielding it from those liquid green eyes, despite the provocative outward thrust of my hips. Then I gave him a playful smile as my hands ever so slowly skimmed across my belly and under my shirt, pushing it over my breasts so I could unhook my bra. "Well?"

He nodded, never taking his eyes off the set of C-cups I held in my hand.

"You like to watch?"

He nodded again and swallowed hard three times as I

pinched the cinnamon-colored tips, then rolled them between my fingers.

"That's good, 'cause I like it when you watch. Do you like peaches and cream?" My words caught his attention, and his tanned brows puckered in a frown. "Get a piece of peach, lover." I nodded toward the bowl he'd bought and released my nipples.

With an indulgent smile, he followed my instructions, finally aware of what I wanted. I reached down and pulled the lips of my sex apart, then gasped as the cool juicy treat made contact, sliding between the hot, slippery folds. I couldn't help myself. I spread my lips wider and arched my hips upward.

"Like that?" Chris asked, moving closer.

I felt the fruit slide inside me the tiniest bit and forced myself to stand still, but that didn't stop a moan from slipping out as peach juice trickled down my legs. "That's good . . . very good, *querido.*"

"I've got something better," he whispered against my skin, then pressed a kiss to one painfully taut nipple, pulling it into his mouth.

"Not yet. Do that some more."

From far away I could hear the low-level hum of the crowd, and the sultry scent of peaches and sex tickled my nose. Chris's wet tongue slid out and circled my nipple while he never took his eyes off my face.

He continued to tease me with the fruit and his fingers, sliding them in and out of me, fucking me until my legs shook and I couldn't hold off my orgasm any longer. Between his fingers and the peach, I was a goner.

"Don't stop. Don't you dare stop, dammit." I locked my

arms around his neck and latched onto his earlobe as I rolled my hips against the slick fruit tickling my clit. The soft material of his T-shirt chafed at my nipples, pushing me to a fever pitch. I stiffened against him and my hips took on a mind of their own as I climaxed with enough force to steal my breath away and leave me weak-kneed. Thankful for the wall at my back, I pushed myself upright, despite my pounding heart, and gave him a sleepy-eyed smile. "Eat it."

He never even hesitated. Just slid the peach, coated with my juices, between his lips like a good boy and sucked it clean before cutting it in half with those sharp white teeth. He fed me the rest on my order and watched as I licked the last of my juices from his fingers.

With another deep breath to clear my head, I rehooked my bra and pulled my shirt down. "If you want . . . some"—I gave him a long hard look, taking in the prominent erection straining against his shorts—"you have to help make it."

It, of course, being peach cobbler.

Slipping from his arms, I retrieved my skirt and shimmied into it before turning and tucking my panties in the pocket of his shorts.

"You're gonna kill me, Fiona," he mumbled with a shake of his head.

"But you'll die a happy man." Smiling, I grabbed his hand and led him out of the alley. We turned down the sidewalk, heading away from the commotion of downtown Carthage.

"How far are we going?" he finally asked. We'd only gone a block.

"Not too far, why?" I turned and smiled at him over my shoulder but didn't stop.

"Baby, I'm hurting," he groaned softly.

"Just a little bit further," I coaxed, turning onto my street. Two houses later we were turning into my driveway. I gave a last glance over my shoulder at the neighborhood. All was quiet. The tidy old houses with their tidy little lawns, pristine and sparkling in the early summer sunshine. Not one curtain moved. Good.

"How bad do you ache, *querido?*" I slowed my pace as we neared my Mustang. "You want it now, or should I make you wait a little longer?"

"Now, inside." Pushing me against the car, he lifted my skirt and ground against my bare ass. A move that made my belly tighten with need.

"How about now? *Right here?*" I challenged, smiling to myself. Chris had no idea what he'd gotten himself into.

"What if someone sees us?" he growled against the crook of my neck. He sank his teeth into my skin and the memory of those same teeth cutting the peach in half flashed behind my eyes.

"Right here, or you wait. You have to be good to get what you want—"

"I'm always good," he softly insisted.

"I know, but this time you have to be good *my way*. Remember?" I forced myself to breathe through the feel of his erection against my naked bottom and the heat of the car searing into my thighs as I bent over the hood of the car.

"Dammit, Fiona, I can't!"

"Then you don't want it bad enough." My pussy clenched as I pushed my hips against him in challenge. "Did you like how I taste?"

"Oh God, yeah."

"Do you want to taste me again?" I bit back a moan and

waited to see if I'd break him. Then sighed as a warm breeze caressed my bottom. I fixed my skirt and turned to find him leaning against the side of the house, his chest heaving with every breath.

"No. I do, but not like this."

"Fine." I was disappointed, but far from bested. I had all afternoon to reel him in. I led him up the porch steps, aware of the slippery slide of my pussy and the ache between my thighs. Inside, the cool air washed away the day's heat but not the heat of my need.

"Damn, it smells good in here."

My kitchen still smelled like peaches and cinnamon.

"Is food all you think about?"

"Absolutely not." He spun me around and pulled me toward him. His lips were on mine and then his tongue was pushing into my mouth, hot and heavy and demanding. I responded in kind, but this wasn't *his* game. It was *mine*. I let him have his way, gave the tiniest fractional bit of control over to him until he broke the kiss. Kicking off my sandals as if nothing had happened, I circled around the kitchen island to the oversized refrigerator and reached inside, pulling out two beers and a large bowl of sliced peaches.

"Do you know how to cook?" I turned and set the bowl on the island's black granite countertop and opened both beers, handing him one.

"No way, baby," he said with a laugh. "I don't have to cook."

"You do today," I said, quirking an eyebrow in challenge. "So come wash your hands." I took a long pull of my beer and set the bottle down, wincing as the beer burned a path to my stomach. At the sink I flipped the lever upward, while listening for the sound of Chris's approach over the rushing water. I filled my hands with liquid soap, then smiled at the feel of him pressed against the length of me. His arms circled my waist and his hands joined mine. Warm water sluiced the dark hairs on his arm smooth and carried soap bubbles down the drain.

*Who knew handwashing could be foreplay?*

The last thing I wanted to do was make another damned cobbler, but Chris had a lesson to learn. I was all business as I snatched two towels from the rack above the sink and handed him one, then fished a clean pot out of the dishwasher.

"Pour the peaches in while I get everything ready."

He propped his hands on his hips and gave me a skeptical look, before he threw the dish towel on top of mine and did as I asked. While he poured, I gathered up sugar, cinnamon, flour, and everything else we'd need, piling them on the island next to him.

"Now what, Miss Bossy?" Despite the doubts lingering in his eyes, he'd obviously decided to play along.

I handed him the measuring spoons and a large glass measuring cup. "Measure out a cup of sugar and a tablespoon of cornstarch."

While the oven was preheating, I moved up behind him and deliberately cupped one cheek of his ass as I wrapped my other hand around his wrist and helped him pour the sugar over the peaches. "Now the cornstarch."

"Done," he said, tapping the measuring spoon on the side of the sauce pot.

"And lemon juice."

His hand shook as he spun the lid off the juice, slowly,

unconsciously learning to follow my orders. Something that could come in handy later. I held his wrist again and slowly added the juice. "Put it on the burner."

He arched one eyebrow at me in challenge, but silently followed my instructions.

As he set the pan on the cooktop beside us, I dug a spatula from the drawer on our other side and held it out to him. "Now stir."

While he stirred the fruit, *I* stirred *him*. Taking advantage of his captive position, I ran my hands as far down his thighs as I could and then back up to squeeze the rounded cheeks of his bottom again. I yanked his T-shirt free and slipped my hands underneath. The skin of his back was smooth, muscles rippled under my fingers.

"How am I supposed to stir this with you distracting me?"

My hands traveled across his stomach and upward to palm a set of heavily muscled pecs covered with just enough hair to tickle my fingertips. "Looks good. Just a little more," I said, peeking around his shoulder.

I forced myself to stop teasing him long enough to pull a casserole dish out from under the island and set it next to the cooktop. Once I was back behind Chris, I let one hand trail down the warm plane of his stomach to the waistband of his shorts. Chris leaned into the counter's edge, pinning my fingers in place so I couldn't explore any . . . lower.

"Pour it in the dish," I softly instructed. I shut the burner off with my free hand and wiggled my fingers where he'd trapped them against the countertop.

"Not till I finish, Miss Bossy."

Once he was done, Chris clamped a firm hand down on

my wrist, turned, and pulled me against him. Our eyes locked and we smiled at each other as he casually draped his other arm over my shoulder. "We could finish this later," he whispered against my cheek.

The feel of his hand delving under my skirt, the warm firm pressure of his fingers on my damp curls tempted me.

"Put the peaches in the oven," I murmured, pressing my face into his chest to smother my groan of frustration. I was ready to put the entire cobbler in the oven so we could move on to bigger and better things. "They need to stay warm."

His movement freed my hands to quickly measure out the ingredients for the crust and dump them in a bowl. From another drawer I pulled out a pastry blender and handed it to him with my most serious expression on my face. "Now the crust."

"I thought we were done?"

"Not quite, *querido.*"

While Chris cut in the crust with almost determined precision, I went for the pantry and the brandy.

He glanced at me, one dark eyebrow arched. "Beer's not enough? Or do you just need that so you can handle me?"

"Please!" I giggled. *As if I couldn't handle him.* "Don't ask questions. Just take notes. You have to remember all this so you can tell your cook in Tennessee how to make it for you . . . or maybe you could make it for her?"

"Or maybe you could come back home with me and make it every day."

"You want me to move to Tennessee just so I can make cobbler for you every day?" I took the pie cutter away from him and added milk, handing him another spatula. "Stir."

"I told you, I dream about your cobbler."

"You have a one-track mind *and* you're crazy," I said with a laugh. "Now mix that up real good."

"I might be crazy, but they've never been able to prove I'm insane."

His words gave me pause as I turned toward the oven and pulled the warm peaches out.

"I'm kidding . . . it's the job that makes me crazy," he said. "Now you gonna drink that brandy or what?"

With a grin and a shake of my head, I measured out a liberal amount and slowly poured it over the peaches. "How's the crust?"

"Take a look for yourself." He held the bowl up so I could see.

"Perfect." I nudged the brandy-covered peaches toward him with a nod. "We'll make a cook out of you yet. Now, drop spoonfuls of dough on top and then we can bake it."

I sounded like Julia Fucking Child. While Chris finished the cobbler, I sipped my beer, contemplating my next move. The countertop was too high for sex. But the old pine table that ran the width of the kitchen was perfect.

"So it's the brandy?"

"Shhhh." I grinned and held a finger to my lips. "Put it in the oven and set the timer for thirty minutes."

"So what do we do for the next thirty minutes?" he asked once he was done.

"I'm sure we can think of something." I took my beer and sashayed across to the table, turned, and leaned against it with my legs crossed. Now that the business of baking had been taken care of, it was time to get to more important matters. "Still got my panties?"

Chris followed my path across the kitchen, pulling the panties out of his pocket as he got closer. Smiling, he held them to his nose for a heartbeat or two before tossing them on the table beside my beer. My granny would have had a fit . . . if she were still alive.

"Lose the shirt." He nodded his head with a determined gleam in his eye.

"Ha! You lose yours."

He gave me a hard once-over, then peeled off his shirt, revealing the heavy pecs I'd fondled earlier. They were covered with a light dusting of dark brown hair that tapered down to a thin line and disappeared into his shorts.

"Now the shorts." My mouth was practically watering. He was tanned a light golden brown and while he didn't exactly have a six-pack, he *definitely* had nothing to be ashamed of.

Chuckling softly, he unsnapped the button fly on his shorts but left them on.

"Tighty whities," I teased, peeling off my own shirt and dropping it to the floor beside me.

"Those are nice," he said, indicating my breasts.

"I like 'em," I said, winking.

"I noticed." He reached up and unhooked my white cotton bra, pushing it off my shoulders. "You just don't seem like a girl who'd wear cotton."

"It's not about the boring cotton, *querido,* but what's in it." With a grin, I delved inside his shorts and cupped the firm cheeks of his ass, pulling him against me.

"I promise there ain't nothing boring in my cotton, sugar," he whispered against my neck. His stubble tickled, but I didn't move as he pressed a soft wet kiss under my ear. "You have the softest hair . . . the softest skin. Come back to Tennessee with me and make us both happy."

I leaned back, reclining the length of the table, my skin so hyperaware of everything that I swear I could feel every scar and pit in that old table. "Take off my skirt."

"You didn't answer me." He obliged, working the skirt over my hips and letting it fall somewhere below me.

I continued to ignore his insistence about Tennessee, because frankly, I didn't take him seriously. Instead, I focused on what I wanted. I watched him through half-closed eyes as my hands skimmed across my rib cage and the flat plains of my stomach to between my thighs. "Touch me, lover."

In response, he pushed his shorts off his hips and slowly ground his cotton-clad crotch against my naked pussy.

"You want me to fuck you?" he growled, my legs held firmly in his grasp.

I shook my head and smiled. "Not yet. I'd much rather you touch me . . . with your mouth. That sweet mouth. Yes?"

"You are enjoying watching me suffer way too much." He frowned in obvious frustration and splayed his hands across my ribs.

"Be a good boy and I'll give you hot cobbler with ice cream later."

His frown turned into a grin and he chuckled as he propped my legs open wide. He nodded and planted a soft kiss in my belly button before trailing lower. On a happy sigh, I closed my eyes and bit my lip in anticipation and he didn't disappoint. Chris's tongue was good for more than eating fruit. My hips arched upward as he deftly teased my clit and licked every inch of me. I refused to wiggle or give in to the ever-increasing need to pull him in deeper, by his hair even, and come all over his face. Instead, I forced myself to breathe though the tension coiled tighter and tighter low in my belly until I almost couldn't stand it.

"Stop . . . stop it, Chris!" I pushed at his shoulders and wiggled away.

He finally came up for air, planting another soft kiss on my belly. "What's the matter?" he asked, frowning.

"There's more of me that needs attention." I lifted one leg and traced the length of his chest with my big toe, being sure to pay special attention to the one nipple I could reach.

Smiling, he grabbed my foot and nipped the fleshy part near my toe. "You are a demanding mistress."

"I can be." I sighed as he pressed a soft kiss to the arch, then my ankle.

"Maybe I won't take you back to Tennessee with me." He sank his teeth into the tender flesh behind my knee.

"Then you wouldn't get any more peaches and cream." I tugged my leg from his grasp and sat up, pulling his head down to mine. "And then what would you do?"

"Guess I'd just have to come back to Texas for a regular fix." He sealed my mouth with his own cool, firm lips and delved inside. He tasted like peaches and brandy and me. I pushed his jockeys down, pausing long enough to assess the size and girth of his cock, before I released it and landed a smack on his bottom.

"Mmm!" He scowled down at me, one of my wrists firmly clamped in his hand. "What the hell was that for?"

"You got in the peaches!"

"So!" His scowl morphed into an outrageously shameless grin.

"I should spank you. Or maybe something worse?" I reached down and cupped his sac, smiling as it twitched ever so slightly in my hand.

"How many licks do I get?" he asked, snickering.

"How many peaches did you sneak?" I gave his balls another squeeze, firm enough so that he knew I meant business, but not painful. Then I leaned over and gave the head of his cock a light lick. When I looked back up at him, he had his lower lip caught between his teeth, and I couldn't resist giving him another swat on the ass.

"I ate three," he said with a grunt, "and they were *so* good. Now do that some more."

"What's the magic word?" I could taste him and I wanted more.

"Please," he whispered, nodding and tangling a hand in my hair.

I propped one foot in a chair for support and leaned over, drawing his cock into my mouth. My hands trailed down the length of his back and across his ass, landing another smack that echoed through the cozy kitchen. His breath hitched and he grunted, bucking in my mouth.

"You make me wanna come so bad," Chris ground out in a shaky voice.

"Then no more of that for you. It's not time." I slipped off the edge of the table but left one leg propped on the chair and tugged him toward me by his cock. "First, I punish you, *then* you get to come."

"Fine, whatever you say." His eyes at half-mast, the tiniest smile on his face, Chris wrapped his arms around my neck, as if he'd given himself over completely to whatever pain/ pleasure I might dole out. The sight of his surrender left me weak-kneed and achy.

"Move a little closer," I whispered, giving another gentle tug.

He did as I instructed and I started a slow rhythmic pumping with one hand. We ended up forehead to forehead, whispering soft lover-talk to each other: *Do you like that . . . Harder . . . Can I touch you . . . Spank me.* A request I was happy to fulfill, smacking one plump muscular cheek while I continued to jack him off. I forced my eyes to stay open, forced myself to breathe, to stay in control despite my own growing need.

We stood there, our breaths mingled, the musky perfume of sex mixed with peaches and cinnamon and brandy. Chris's long dark eyelashes fanned out under his eyes, his breath came in short huffs as he demanded I go faster, demanded I spank him again. Of course, that's when I didn't. Never mind that my pussy had grown slicker and wetter every time my hand connected with his bottom, so wet in fact, the tops of my thighs were damp.

I didn't change a thing, not the speed of my hand on his cock, nothing, until he reached the point where he was begging. Begging for faster, begging to be spanked. All his earlier playfulness was now long gone.

"Relax," I instructed as I fought the urge to give him what he wanted. Me.

"I can't . . . I wanna come so bad." His face was tight, his teeth gritted together and his body hummed with tension.

"Not yet, okay. Now relax or it'll hurt more when I spank you. I don't want to hurt you, *querido*."

"I know you don't, but if I relax, I'll come," he insisted.

The hand wrapped around his cock sped up. "Relax," I hissed. "Breathe, Chris . . . breathe." Under my other hand his right cheek muscle softened the tiniest bit and I smacked him again just as I released my grip on him, and he found himself thrusting into air.

"God!" He reared back, every muscle in his body tense as he sucked in a deep breath and fought for control. "Dammit, Fiona!"

"Touch me, lover." I lightly fondled every inch of his erection with my fingertips. The head of his cock was nearly purple and the shaft swollen to delicious proportions.

His large, gentle hands wandered from my hair to skim the length of my back and caress the soft underside of my breasts, my shoulders, my arms, and my legs spread wide between us. Goose bumps popped up on my skin, and I hummed in pleasure as my nipples puckered even harder.

We kissed, wet, sloppy, breathless kisses until Chris came up for air, nipping at my earlobe and begging to fuck me.

I lay back on the table, closed my eyes, and handed him the reins, smiling as he jerked my bottom to the edge and thrust inside me with a rude grunt of satisfaction. I caught my breath at the sudden sharp invasion, then locked my legs around his waist and met every hard, hungry thrust. He'd definitely been more than worth the wait.

"You're a . . . damned . . . tease . . . Fiona . . ." he insisted with each lunge.

"And you love it. Now c'mere." I held out my arms and reveled in the hot, heavy length of him in me. Then slipped one hand between us. There was no way I could catch up with Chris, who was already beginning to climax, but I followed quickly, squealing and bucking against him and milking us both for all we were worth.

We lay there the longest time. Until the air-conditioned air cooled the sweat on his back and our heavy breathing had returned to normal.

Chris's legs shook as he slowly pushed himself up on one elbow. "So what about Tennessee. Did you decide?"

I smiled but before I could answer, the oven timer went off.

# The Salsa Connection

## Anna Black

*She moans beneath him as the rhythm of his hips
matches the tempo of the music. Each thrust of his cock into her cunt
goes deeper and deeper, like the steady beat of the timbales. Sweat
coats his skin and hers, the bed creaks beneath them, a breeze, redo-
lent with the smell of the ocean and of mariposa lily and the intoxicating sounds of the salsa band playing beneath their open window
sweeps across their frenzied bodies. His hands grip her wrists, holding
her firmly against the mattress, his lips sear her throat, his teeth nip
at her skin. She feverishly rubs her breasts against his chest, the black,
curly hairs strafing her throbbing nipples.*

*His moans echo hers and he punctuates them with fiercely whis-
pered words in Spanish that she does not understand but the meaning is as clear as his pelvis grinding against her, his cock pulsating
within her, his body possessing hers.*

"Pay attention, Gloria."

Startled out of her daydream by Eduardo's words, Gloria
twisted her ankle as she tried to turn where he was guiding

her. She stumbled and was slipping toward the hardwood floor of the dance studio.

Eduardo quickly grabbed her, his arm snaking around her waist. She looked up at him. His dark eyes glittered with annoyance, his firm, sensual lips twisted with irritation.

"I'm wondering whether you and I are wasting our time."

She squirmed away from him. "Wasting our time? Haven't I been coming here every week for the past month?"

He crossed his arms over his chest, his black cotton shirt stretching over his broad shoulders and lean, muscular arms. "You do not feel, Gloria. And because you do not feel, I cannot teach you."

"What do you mean?"

"You take the lessons but you do not *experience* what you are doing. Tell me, why do you want to learn to dance the salsa?"

"What does it matter, why I want to learn?"

"I want to know what is in your heart."

"My heart? What the hell does my heart have to do with it?"

Eduardo shook his head, as if confronted with a misbehaving child. "There's no need to curse, Gloria."

"You call that cursing? Trust me, when I get to cursing, you'll know."

"When you asked me to teach you to dance the salsa, I made it quite clear that if you were not serious about it, I would not waste my time teaching you."

Gloria clenched her hands. "I am serious. Why do you keep saying I'm not?"

He tapped her on her forehead. "You are not here when we dance. Your thoughts are elsewhere."

*No shit,* Gloria thought. Her thoughts were definitely elsewhere. For example, in bed with Eduardo as he thrust with what she imagined was a most delicious cock inside her, at the beach with Eduardo, waves washing over them as they fucked, on a—"

"There you go again. Daydreaming."

Gloria focused back on Eduardo's face. The smoldering dark eyes framed by thick black lashes, the classically sculpted face, the sensual lips. Why did he have to be so goddamn gorgeous? And how in hell was she supposed to concentrate on dancing when all she could think about was being naked with him, his long brown limbs wrapped around her, his thick, long cock (and, yes, she had no doubt it was thick and it was long) pumping steadily inside her hot, juicy cunt.

"I'm not daydreaming."

"This is not going to work," he said.

"What?"

"I am not going to waste my time teaching you, Gloria."

"But . . . I've paid you—"

"I will return your money."

"Why?"

He touched her forehead and then moved his hand, lightly touching her chest. Her nipples tingled. "In your head and in your heart, you are not here. I cannot teach you."

"You are such a pompous ass," Gloria blurted out, her sexual frustration finally lashing out as anger.

His eyes widened. "Pompous?"

"Yes, pompous. Why do you have to make such a big deal

out of everything?" She waved her hand at the other instruc-
tors who, along with their students, were staring at her and
Eduardo. She didn't care. "They don't make such a big deal
out of it. They're just having fun."

"Fun?" Eduardo nodded as if something had been confirmed for him. "If that is what you want, only to have fun,
perhaps you'd be better off with one of them."

"Fine. Maybe I would."

"I'll see that your money is returned."

He walked away and Gloria, despite her disappointment
and anger, couldn't help noticing what a nice ass he had.

Damn him. Well, if that's the way he wanted it, she would
find another instructor. Maria's wedding was five months
away. She still had time to learn to dance the salsa.


"Why didn't you just tell him you wanted to learn to dance
so you don't make a fool of yourself at your friend's wedding?"

Gloria, her feet tucked under her as she sat on the couch,
shifted her cell phone to her other ear.

"Because it isn't any of his business," she told her friend,
LaShonda. "I paid him to teach me, not to find out what is in
my head or in my heart. What does that have to do with
teaching me how to dance?"

"Girl, you are such a fool. The man asked you a simple
question and you had to turn it into World War III."

"And I didn't like the way he was teaching me," Gloria
went on. "He was too hard."

She bit her lip at the irony of her statement. That was the
problem. He hadn't been hard enough.

"But he was fine, right?"

"He was all right."

LaShonda laughed. "Ain't what I heard. I heard he's more than all right. I heard he's one fine piece of Latin love. Sexy, dark eyes. Nice, tight butt. And he dances like he could make a woman come until her throat is raw from screaming."

Gloria's cunt tingled at LaShonda's words. It was true. All of it. But it didn't matter. She was never going to see him again. But, damn it, she also couldn't stop thinking about him.

"You should apologize." LaShonda's voice cut into her thoughts.

"Why?"

"Because the person at fault is usually the one who apologizes," LaShonda said dryly.

"I'm not at fault."

"Yes, girlfriend, you are. You're at fault because it's obvious you've wanted to screw that man since day one. But you're too scared or prudish or stupid to tell him."

"LaShonda," Gloria said, her voice rising.

"So, either you apologize, finish your lessons so you don't look stupid at your friend's wedding, and then ask him out, or you sit there and masturbate. 'Cause, girl, you got it bad. Real bad."

LaShonda said good night and hung up. Gloria put the cell phone down. It was uncanny how LaShonda knew her so well. But this time it didn't matter what her friend said. There was no way Gloria was going to apologize to Eduardo. He'd made it quite clear how he felt about her. She wasn't going to make a fool of herself by apologizing to him. Because if there was anything Gloria hated, it was making a fool of herself.

But, Lord, he was so fine. Even now she found herself fantasizing about him.

*His mouth moving slowly across her cunt, his lips rubbing against the wet lips of her labia, his tongue seeking her searing core, licking slowly at the wetness seeping out of her, the tip rasping against her clit.*

Gloria shivered. She shoved her hand down her sweat-pants and underneath her panties. Her finger slipped across her cunt the way she imagined Eduardo's mouth would. She moved her finger inside her and imagined it was his long, agile tongue, invading her, tasting her, ravishing her.

She threw her head back against the couch, her thighs slackening, her legs opening wider as she stroked faster. She imagined Eduardo's dark head moving between her thighs, his mouth engulfing her sex, his tongue lapping hungrily at her.

She bucked her hips, her finger moving wetly in and out, twisting and rubbing against the sensitive inner walls. She massaged her juices over her clit, slowly circling.

"Yes, lick my pussy, lick it," she whispered.

She moaned as she fell deeper into her fantasy. She spread her legs wider, her finger moving quickly as she imagined Eduardo's long, wet tongue licking and probing her cunt. She tossed her head back and forth, her pelvis humping as she stroked and rubbed her swollen clit.

"Oh, yes, yes, yes," she moaned. "Oh, God." Her fingers flew over her clit, her body shuddering, her hips quivering.

The phone rang. Gloria gasped, her orgasm just on the edge of peaking. Then she realized it wasn't her cell phone. It was the house phone. The only person who typically called her on the house phone was her mother. She jumped up and ran for it, picking it up on the fourth ring.

"Hello?"

"Gloria?"

She nearly dropped the phone. Eduardo's sexy voice flowed into her ear like honey.

"Yes?"

There was silence for a moment on his end. "It is Wednesday night," he finally said.

"So?"

"You are not here for your lesson."

"Excuse me? Didn't you tell me not to come back?"

"No, you said you were going to find another instructor. But you have not. I checked and you have not contracted with any of them."

It was true, Gloria had not found another instructor but only because she hadn't had the time to look for one. "Maybe I'm taking lessons at another studio."

"You are not."

"And just how the hell would you know that?"

"Why do you curse so much, Gloria?"

"This is not cursing. When I really start cursing—"

"Are you coming or not?"

Gloria's lips twisted. I was coming, she thought, until you interrupted me. "No, I'm not. You're right, Eduardo. It wasn't working. We're obviously not compatible."

And she definitely wasn't going to risk getting hurt by him. Just stay away from him. That was the best course of action.

"Gloria—"

"Good-bye, Eduardo."

She hung up the phone and released a deep breath. She thought about resuming her masturbating but realized she was no longer interested. Damn him. She wanted him, not her fingers.

The phone on her desk at work rang. Gloria contemplated not answering it. She was already days behind on her report. But, as she glanced at the display, she recognized the phone number. A smile broke across her face.

She picked up the phone. "Hey, girl!"

"Gloria!" María's voice blared from the receiver. "How you doing, *chica?*"

"Okay."

"Bad day?"

Gloria's lips quirked. "What else is new?"

"How many times have I told you to get out of that white man's rat race and come help me with my catering business?"

"You know I don't like humid weather."

"That's the only way weather should be, *chica*. And it's what you need. Lots of sun, warm beaches, and hot men."

Gloria shook her head. The sun and beaches sounded great but the last thing she needed was another hot man upsetting her equilibrium.

"So, how are the dance lessons coming?"

Gloria blinked. She had forgotten she had told María about the lessons.

"Umm, okay."

"Just okay?"

Gloria made a sound she hoped sounded encouraging.

"I can't wait," María said. "My brothers are already drawing straws as to who is going to dance with you first."

María cheerfully went on giving Gloria the latest details about the wedding but she barely heard her friend. She'd tried to find another dance instructor, but either they were all booked up or they'd clearly been unqualified or they wouldn't stop staring at her breasts.

"Gloria, did you hear me?"

"What?" She quickly brought her attention back to María. "Umm, yeah, I heard."

"No, you didn't. I'm sorry. I shouldn't have called you at work."

"That's okay. But I should get back to work. I'm so glad you called and I can't wait until August."

"Me neither, *chica*."

They exchanged good-byes and Gloria hung up the phone. She stared at the walls of her office. What was she going to do? The wedding was in three months. She wanted to at least learn enough Latin dancing so she wouldn't look like a complete idiot at the wedding. Eduardo had been an excellent teacher. If anyone could get her ready for the wedding in time, it was him.

She chewed her bottom lip as she stared at the phone. For all she knew he was completely booked up. Or he would resent her for having quit and refuse to take her back as his student. Or a meteor could smash into the earth and solve all her problems.

She sighed, picked up the phone, and dialed the number for the dance studio Eduardo taught at.

"In Motion Dance Studio."

Gloria frowned. The receptionist sounded like her mouth was full of food.

"May I speak to Eduardo Reyes?"

"Who?"

*Oh, good Lord,* Gloria thought, *where did they find these people?*

"Eduardo. He's an instructor there."

"Hold on."

Gloria drummed her manicured nails on the desk. Then she noted that one of her nails was chipped. Before she could make a mental note to have it fixed, the receptionist was back on the line.

"He's not here."

"Do you know where he is?"

"No."

Gloria gritted her teeth. "Do you know how I can contact him?"

"No."

"Will he be in later?"

"I don't know." The woman's voice grew flatter with each response.

*Yeah, screw you, too,* Gloria thought. "Well, if he does come in, could you please tell him that Gloria Berner called?"

The woman hung up without replying. Gloria stared at the phone. The nerve of some people.

She glanced at a postcard she'd thumbtacked to the wall. María had sent it to her as part of her campaign to convince Gloria to move to Florida. White sands and an ocean as blue as the sky. She cupped her chin in her hand and sighed.

*Eduardo is wearing swimming trunks and she a bikini. He walks next to her, his hand holding hers. He pulls her across the sand until the two of them are running. Up ahead is a grove of palm trees. They run in among them. He presses her against a tree trunk and puts his hand on her breasts, his fingers squeezing her nipples. She gasps, her sex moistening. He pulls the bikini top down, exposing her breasts. He lowers his head and wraps his mouth around one of them, licking steadily at her nipple.*

*Gloria grips his shoulders. He wraps his hand around her other breast, pinching and tweaking the nipple. He sucks hard on her breast, while his other hand slowly works its way down her stomach, then in between her bikini bottom, his long agile fingers exploring her cunt lips, teasing her, stroking her, flicking her hard little clit.*

*He moves his mouth over to her other breast, rubbing it with the flat of his tongue while his fingers part the lips of her moist cunt, and he slowly, maddeningly, slides his finger in and out.*

"Earth to Gloria."

She started and whirled around.

Her coworker, Jared, grinned down at her, his pale green eyes, as always, flicking down to her breasts. "Didn't mean to scare you. What were you doing? Daydreaming?"

She frowned. Jared was management's latest golden boy and resident stooge. "What do you want, Jared?"

He smirked. "Mr. Paterson wanted me to check and see if you're done with that spreadsheet he needs for his meeting."

Gloria turned back to her computer. "Yes, I'm almost done." *Now, go away.*

She felt him standing behind her, then he finally walked away. Her lips twisted. What a prick. Then she sighed. What was she going to do about her dance lessons?


Gloria got out of her car and stopped. Eduardo was pacing in front of the entrance to her condo. He looked amazing. She supposed not having seen him for two weeks made him look even sexier, but she didn't think so. That man always looked good.

"Eduardo."

He stopped pacing and looked over at her.

"What are you doing here?" she asked as she walked toward him.

"You left a message for me at the dance studio."

Gloria laughed. "She actually gave it to you?"

Eduardo smiled as if sharing a secret joke. "Darla knows better than to play her little games with my messages."

Lord, but when he smiled he was nothing short of make-you-want-to-shout-glory-hallelujah gorgeous. He hadn't smiled much during their lessons. But he was smiling now and as Gloria looked up into his dark-chocolate eyes, she saw something she hadn't seen before.

Appreciation. Warmth. Lust.

He moved closer until she was not only surrounded by the lush masculine scent of him but she could feel the warmth of his body radiating against hers.

"Do you wish to continue your lessons? Is that why you called?"

Gloria nodded mutely, as she was too preoccupied in looking at his finely sculpted lips to speak. She imagined his lips on her mouth, on her breasts, on her sex, nibbling, licking, sucking.

He wrapped an arm about her waist and pulled her gently but firmly against him.

"Good. Then we shall start from the beginning."

He lowered his head and kissed her.

When he pulled away, Gloria looked up at him, almost too shocked to speak. "What . . . why . . . when?"

"I've wanted you from the first time I saw you, Gloria. But you were my student and I never mix business with pleasure. I was going to wait until we stopped our lessons to ask you out but then you quit."

"But I quit because—"

"Because you wanted me also?"

She nodded.

"So we are both fools, agreed?"

She nodded again, still too surprised to speak.

Eduardo glanced around. "Now, are we going to stand out here and give your neighbors something to gossip about or are you going to invite me in?"

She opened the door and stepped inside, Eduardo behind her. As soon as the door was closed, she turned to him. They looked at each for the space of five heartbeats, then, without a word they began pulling at each other's clothes—buttons were unbuttoned, zippers unzipped, and his shirt and his pants, and her blouse and her skirt drifted to the floor.

Gloria gazed admiringly at his naked body, the lean, solid look of him. There wasn't an ounce of fat on him. It was a dancer's body. He pulled her tight against him, his naked skin smooth and hot.

"Dance with me," he murmured. And, as he guided her, naked and barefoot, to the bedroom she fell into the steps he had taught her.

Once they were in the bedroom, Eduardo laid her gently on the bed. He gazed down at her.

"You are so beautiful, Gloria. I've wanted you from the first moment you walked into the studio."

"But you were waiting until our lessons were finished," she said.

He nodded. "I do not date my students."

Gloria tilted her head and smiled up at him. "I'm no longer your student?"

Eduardo got onto the bed and lay next to her. "Not tonight. Tonight you are my lover. When you are ready, we will resume the lessons. And once we are done, then we will be lovers again." His eyes grew worried. "If that's what you want, of course."

"If that's what I want?" Gloria shook her head and laughed. "Of course it's what I want. Since the first moment I saw you, too."

"Then it seems we were in sync even before we started dancing."

Gloria put her arms around him. "Yes, it seems."

Eduardo's eyes moved slowly over her breasts. Gloria's nipples were hard and erect. He reached over and lightly ran his hands over them. She shivered and a soft moan slipped from between her lips.

He leaned over and lightly kissed one of the nipples. He flicked it with the tip of his tongue. Gloria moaned and pulled him closer. He drew her nipple deeper into his mouth, running his tongue over it as he sucked. She moaned louder, the blood rushing madly through her veins.

Eduardo sucked and tongued both her breasts until Gloria was squirming wildly on the bed, the juices of her cunt flowing. He released her saliva-glistening breasts and kissed his way slowly down her body until he reached her navel. Lazily, he swirled the tip of his tongue around the tiny depression. Gloria bit her lip and arched her back as a current of heat burrowed from her navel deep into her womb.

"*Tú eres muy hermosa,*" she heard him murmur.

"What?"

Eduardo looked up from where he lay between her legs. "You are very beautiful."

He continued downward. Gloria lifted her hips. Her cunt juices were flowing, dampening her inner things. Eduardo moved his head lower, his kisses soft and wet, his breath moving across her clit.

She whimpered, longing for him to lick her there, but he moved past her quivering nub and down to her cunt. He softly kissed her, his tongue sliding slowly along her cleft.

Gloria gasped. It was so much better than her fantasies. Eduardo ran his tongue up and down her pussy, and she felt her body rising inexorably toward its climax.

No, not yet. She had fantasized about this for so long; she wanted it to last. She tried to move away from Eduardo's mouth but he held her tightly by the hips. He licked and sucked at her sex, causing wave after wave of pleasure to gush through her.

"Oh, it feels so good." She pushed her fingers through his dark, curly hair. "Make me come, please, make me come."

Eduardo moved his tongue up to her clit and flicked it across the nub. Gloria shuddered and jerked against the bed. He slid two fingers inside her, thrusting them in and out as he tongued her clit. Gloria's hips bucked hard as she came, and the orgasm was so good, so sweet—thick and rich like the tastiest cream.

Her hips slowly ceased their frantic pulsing as she came down from her orgasm. Eduardo moved next to her. She turned and looked at him. He leaned over and kissed her. She tasted herself on his mouth.

"Oh, Eduardo," she whispered. "That was wonderful."

"*La pequeña muerte,*" he said softly.

Gloria smiled. "What's that?"

"You probably know it better as *la petite mort,* or so the French call it."

"*The little death.* An orgasm. It sounds much more beautiful in French. And in Spanish."

"Just as you are when you come, Gloria."

She turned on her side and stroked his chest, her fingers trailing over the crisp black hairs. "I want to see you come, Eduardo. I want to see your *pequeña muerte.*"

He took her hand and put it around his erection. "Then touch me, *mi mujer caliente.* Touch me.

Gloria put both her hands around Eduardo's cock. It hardened and lengthened as she stroked it. She slowly moved her palms up and down.

"*Sí,* Gloria, *sí.* Hmmm, *sí,* like that. Just like that."

"I want to do more than this," Gloria whispered.

She rose from the bed and knelt at the end of it. Eduardo looked at her and a smile spread across his face. He scooted down and sat on the edge so that Gloria's head was between his thighs. She ran her hands up and down his legs. Then she lowered her head to his groin and kissed the tip of his cock. She licked softly at the salty sweetness of his pre-cum. She slid her tongue along the shaft and down to his balls, lightly kissing them both. Eduardo's hips shivered and she heard him draw in a sharp breath.

Gloria smiled and drew each of the heavy balls into her mouth, swirling her tongue around them. Eduardo hissed between his teeth. Gloria released his balls and kissed her way back up the shaft, swiping her tongue across the hard heat. Reaching the bulbous head, she drew it into her mouth.

She looked up at Eduardo and smiled at him with her eyes. He caressed her shoulders and returned her smile.

Continuing to gaze up at him, Gloria licked around the head of his cock. She reveled in the taste and feel and scent of his sex. As she watched the passion flood his face, her heart swelled with the knowledge she was giving him such pleasure. She slid her tongue around the head and drew it into her mouth.

Eduardo adjusted his hips, his hands on her head as the two of them worked together until all of his cock was deep in her mouth. She slowly pumped her mouth up and down, her tongue swirling around the thick heat of him.

His hands tightened around her head. "*¡Dios! ¡Lo siente bien!* Yes, faster, baby, faster!"

Gloria moved her mouth faster.

"*¡Dios!* I'm going to come! *¡Dios!*"

She felt him try to pull away. She kept her mouth tight around his cock. A hot stream of liquid gushed down her throat. She moaned and moved her head faster.

Eduardo groaned. "*¡Por favor, no pare! ¡No pare!*"

She wasn't sure what *no pare* meant, but she assumed he was telling her not to stop. She didn't. Eduardo's hips bucked hard around her head as he jetted his cum down her throat.

"*¡Dios mío!*" he shouted, then fell back on the bed.

Gloria crawled onto the bed and slid next to him. She kissed him, aware he was now tasting himself as she had tasted herself on his mouth. They kissed for a long time and nothing had ever felt more right to her. When they finally broke their kiss, she looked deep into his dark-chocolate eyes.

"I've been a fool," she said.

Eduardo held up his hand and almost pinched the thumb and forefinger together. "Maybe just a little."

"No, not just a little. If I hadn't been so—"

"Stubborn," he offered.

She smiled. "Yes, that, too. And afraid. If I hadn't been so afraid—"

"I was afraid to get close to you, too, Gloria. And it made me strict and proud. I know that. So do not be so hard on yourself."

She looked up at him, batting her lashes in what she hoped was a coquettish manner. "How do you say *fuck me* in Spanish?"

"There are a number of ways. But I would rather you say *quiero que me coges,* as I believe you curse enough already."

"Don't start," she said, laughing. "Because when I finally do get to cursing—"

"I know." Eduardo chuckled. "I will know it."

"You're damn straight. Now, what was it you said?"

He repeated the phrase until she could say it perfectly. Then she arched a brow. "Well?"

"Well, what?"

"Are you going to fuck me or not?"

Eduardo looked at her, then down at his groin. "I think I am once again ready." He grinned. "Listening to you practice has adequately prepared me, I think."

"You think?" Gloria put her hand around his long, thick cock.

Eduardo pulled her close and slid inside her. But, Gloria, feeling mischievous, rolled over until she was on top of him.

"This time you will follow and I will lead," she said grinning down at him.

Eduardo gave her a slow, lazy smile. "*Sí,* you can lead. This time."

Gloria rocked against him, letting her swollen cunt swallow him completely. Eduardo's throat worked as he matched her movements. Gloria gripped his shoulders, while he grabbed her breasts and squeezed them, his fingers pulling and twisting her nipples.

She slammed her body onto his, fiercely twisting her juicy cunt around his thick, stiff cock. His hands clenched her gyrating hips as she rode him hard and fast. It was like the dancing, Gloria suddenly realized, the two of them hot and synchronized, the two of them moving as one.

She cried out, her back arching sharply as she climaxed and, as Eduardo was still hard and thick inside her, his mouth now sucking hungrily at her dangling breasts, she looked forward to a long night of their salsa connection.

# The Birthday Present

## (El Regalo)

Penelope Flynn

The only party anyone would bother attending at the beginning of August had to be near a pool. The Florida sun had beat down all day heating the sand, brick, concrete, and tar, raising the temperature well into the high nineties. Miguel stood at the balcony, overlooking the barrel-tiled roof of his Miami Beach home, and watched the sun slowly sink into the west. His dark brown eyes took in the splash of colors across the horizon as he backed into the relative cool of his bedroom and closed the French doors against the heat and humidity.

The bedroom was generally what one would expect to see in a well-dressed man's room. His clothes and shoes were neatly arranged in his closet and in the dark wood wardrobe and chest of drawers, which held the remainder of his personal items. The large king-sized bed sat close to the French doors, giving him a view to the pool area beyond. He shut his eyes tightly, then inhaled a deep breath and blew it out slowly, dreading the next few hours. He turned up the music on his sound system and began preparing for the evening. He slipped his arms, sunkissed to a warm café au lait, into a short-sleeved white silk shirt and heard the doorbell ring as the guests started arriving. He was an attractive man with a slim, angular face and an engaging manner that had been absent the past few weeks. He pulled his thick, black, wavy hair into a ponytail and was looking for his shoes when he heard the frantic rapping on the doorsill.

"Happy birthday, Miguel!" Kelly giggled as she flung open the bedroom door, skipped into the room, and kissed him noisily on the lips. Kelly was a tallish, attractive girl with a slim build and high, perky breasts. Her light brown eyes sparkled with anticipation. Still in her early twenties, she was a little younger than what Miguel was used to. They'd been together for three months . . . the first of those was while he was still living with Ebony.

"Come on." She laughed. "People are starting to show up."

Kelly hurried him along, chiding him for waiting so long to get dressed as he stepped into his loafers. He was really in no mood to entertain. He simply wasn't feeling himself lately. Kelly thought a party might pull him out of his funk, and even though he didn't think so, he didn't argue too much when she began planning and inviting everyone they knew. When he was finally ready, Kelly dragged him downstairs to greet the early arrivals.

Miguel could hear the music floating down the hallway as he was ushered toward the patio on Kelly's arm. He had met Kelly when he was photographing a spread for a department store. She was a pretty, modelesque girl, and wore her blond hair in a classic flip. She said it was her trademark. Kelly was a little too short for the runway but just fine for the print

work she was often called for. She confided that she wanted
to be an actress. Miguel wasn't certain she had the talent but
didn't discourage her from taking her classes and rushing off
to auditions whenever she found a role to her liking.

"The Big three-O!" Charlie yelled as he waded through
the arriving guests. He gave Miguel a big bear hug and patted his back while simultaneously leering at Kelly. Miguel's
uncle Carlos, or the Americanized Charlie, which he preferred to be called, was the quintessential dirty old man.
Now in his late sixties with no wife and children, he was
spending a lifetime of earnings on pampering "sweet young
things" and getting as much as he could out of them before
they grew tired of him.

"Kelly, *bonita,* you're more beautiful every day." He
smiled. "You should let me introduce you to some producer
friends that I know. They'll be shooting a film here in Miami
in about three months and I know you'll be perfect for one
of the parts."

"Really?" Her eyes glittered.

"Yes, really."

Then Charlie smiled that smile Miguel recognized as the
one he used when he thought another sweet young thing
was about to take the bait.

"Can I steal Kelly away for a moment?" he asked, flashing
his mouthful of bonded and capped teeth.

"Sure," Miguel said, giving Kelly's arm a squeeze.

Miguel didn't see the point of holding Kelly there. She
was pretty good at handling herself. Besides, his attention
was focused elsewhere. He had heard the distinctive laugh as
soon as he stepped into the hallway. Ebony had come to his
party, even though she hadn't been invited. He prepared

himself mentally before he approached her. Their breakup hadn't been a pretty one.

They had been together, in one form or another, for a little over three years. It had taken almost two years for them both to become serious about the relationship at the same time but, after that, it was actually all he could ever have hoped for. Of course his mother didn't like Ebony at all. She often complained that Ebony couldn't really cook . . . and she complained that Ebony was Amercan . . . and nagged that Miguel should date a nice Cuban girl . . . and that Ebony was too old for him.

It was true that Ebony was three years older than he was. She was already thirty when they met, but it was impossible to tell. She looked no older than Kelly, who was nearly ten years younger, and Ebony had one of those Coke-bottle figures . . . all hips, ass, and thighs with not a whole lot up top. He remembered making love with Ebony, her riding him high and hard, his hands sliding up her arms, to her shoulders, then down over her breasts, almost completely covering them as he massaged her nipples in time with her rocking motion. The thought made him smile. She had talked about a breast enlargement a few times but they had both laughed it off.

"*¡Feliz cumpleaños, hermano!*" Miguel felt Alex's big hand slap him congenially on the back.

"*Feliz cumpleaños* my ass, man!" Miguel smiled, returning the slap and following up with a hug. "I see you came to my place empty-handed. Where's my present, you cheap son of a bitch!"

"It's been a rough quarter."

"Not so rough you didn't get new rims for your Corvette."

"Hey, you know I have to keep up my image. Keep it lookin' good."

"God knows you need all the help you can get with that!"

"You're cold, man." Alex pantomimed a shiver, then laughed with Miguel as they made their way down the corridor.

Miguel had known Alex for as long as he had known anyone. They had grown up together and had lived down the street from each other most of their youth. They went to the same grade schools, even played ball together, but while Miguel was about six feet tall, sinewy and lean, Alex was a big, heavily muscled man. Miguel's ball-playing career ended in high school but Alex played college ball and even had a stint in the pros. Alex was nearly six foot five and still maintained his body as if he was training to play professional ball. He deftly rode the cusp between handsome and pretty. He had sparkling hazel-green eyes and "lashes like a girl," they all used to kid him, but the women loved him. They loved his big hands, sensuous lips, and easy manner. Even Kelly blushed in his presence. The only woman who never fell at his feet was Ebony.

Miguel used to notice the way Alex looked at Ebony. He wanted her, but Miguel also knew that Alex would never approach her. He and Alex had been friends for too long, and for that he considered himself fortunate. He knew that Alex generally didn't care if a woman had a man or not. If he wanted her, that was all that mattered. But Miguel really didn't worry too much. Ebony was always pleasant around Alex, but never tripped over herself like the others. Bonni was in love with him and was always his alone.

"Sooo." Alex grinned. "I see you took my advice."

"What advice?"

"The girl—Kelly. I told you, you should go younger. They're easier to handle . . . lower maintenance."

"What are you talking about?" Miguel laughed. "You've never dated a woman under thirty in your life!"

"Exactly." Alex smiled. "I like women . . . not girls. I like high maintenance."

"You're crazy!" Miguel laughed as the two strolled into the large sunroom together.

"Hey," Miguel said, becoming serious. "Bonni's here."

"Yeah, I know," Alex replied.

"You know we didn't end on the best of terms."

"I'm aware," Alex answered as they slowly moved toward where Ebony was standing, talking and laughing with a group of women.

"You don't think she's gonna make trouble, do you?"

"No." Alex smiled as he stepped up behind Ebony and wrapped his arms around her. "She's with me."

Miguel was speechless as Alex leaned forward, nuzzling and kissing Ebony's neck. Ebony turned, still in his arms, and gave him a soft peck on the lips, asking, "What took you so long?" When she saw Miguel, the momentary flash of hurt was replaced by a pleasant smile. She extended her hand affably and gave his hand a light squeeze, saying, "Happy birthday, Mickey."

"Thank you," Miguel muttered, still trying to overcome the shock.

Miguel could see that Ebony had changed—a lot. Her haircut was conservative, cut shoulder-length into a bob, but it brought out her dark, luminous eyes and full, pouty, vermilion-painted lips. She was wearing a red halter dress that exposed large expanses of her smooth brown skin, leaving nothing to the imagination. She had put on a few pounds . . . not much, but enough to make her look even more curvy and luscious, but the biggest change—her breasts. It seemed Alex had been able to convince her to get that breast augmentation, transforming her body from a Coke bottle to an hourglass.

"You look good, Bonni," Miguel choked out as he watched Alex's hand travel up and down Ebony's bare back.

"You, too," she replied, then looked around the room cautiously. "Where's Kathy?"

"Kelly," Miguel corrected. "She's talking to Charlie about some part in a movie."

"Oh?" Ebony batted her lashes mischievously. "He's associated with that *porn* outfit, isn't he?"

"Bonni . . ." Alex warned.

Ebony smiled, then continued, "I sincerely hope she is very successful in her career endeavors."

"I'll certainly convey your sentiments." Miguel smiled sarcastically. "Well, I better check on the other guests."

Miguel left Ebony in Alex's arms and made his way through the house, out onto the patio and to the pool, hugging and kissing the women, and shaking hands with the men. He downed three drinks in the first hour and danced several dances, but he couldn't keep his eyes from wander-

ing over to the table where Alex and Bonni were sitting with
another couple. Ebony was snuggled close under Alex's outstretched arm, laughing and talking with the other woman
and her date. Alex sat quietly, leaning back with his eyes
closed, intermittently stroking Ebony's hair, taking sips from
his margarita, then laughing as he kissed her lips, letting the
sweet and salty alcoholic beverage run from his mouth into
hers. Even from across the room, Miguel could see the drops
of perspiration on Alex's forearms as he shifted in his seat,
then kissed Ebony's face, surreptitiously brushing his fingertips against those round heaving breasts and whispering in
her ear before moaning softly and again leaning back, closing his eyes.

Miguel was furious. He knew all too well this scenario.
Hadn't he been the man, sitting there with Ebony too many
times before, feeling her hands stroking his inner thighs,
then squeezing and teasing his cock through the weave of his
pants, working him into a frenzy? It wouldn't be long before
she left the table, a signal for him to follow her to a bathroom or an empty bedroom where she would peel down his
trousers and let her mouth finish the job her hands had
started. His cock began to stiffen at the thought of her hands
and tongue and lips on him.

"*¡Putana!*" He hissed through his teeth as he watched her
slide out of her seat, straighten her dress, and head presum-
ably for the bathroom.

Miguel made a beeline behind Ebony and entered the
house just in time to see her quickly climbing the stairs. He
slowly walked up after her and stood outside the bathroom
door, trying to decide if he should confront her. After all, he
was the one that had cheated on *her*. He remembered stand-

ing outside that very door, listening to Ebony sobbing and vomiting.

She could hardly speak. She just kept asking, "What did I do, Mickey? What did I do wrong?"

He couldn't answer her. He didn't know the answer, not until later when he guessed that it was just that she loved him too much. Or maybe he loved *her* too much. Either way, the relationship had suddenly seemed permanent and heavy. He was still young and it was all happening too fast. When he met Kelly and she began to flirt with him, it seemed like someone had opened a window and let cool fresh air into a stifling hot room, that someone had opened a route of escape.

He and Kelly had been seeing each other for nearly a month openly, daring Ebony to say something. Finally, when she did, he reminded Ebony that they weren't married, that he felt affection for her but he hadn't signed on for a lifetime commitment. He was sorry as soon as he said it and followed her when she grabbed her purse and hurried to the bathroom. After half an hour of tears, she emerged calm and resolute. She told him that she was moving to her sister's house and that someone would pick up her things later. Then she walked downstairs and left the house without looking back. That was just over three months ago.

When he told his mother that he and Ebony had ended it, his mother cried for days. Despite her complaints, she knew that Ebony was one of the few people who even bothered to deal with her. Ebony came to see her every week, even in the face of her constant abuses. His mother even suggested couples counseling, anything to get them back together, but he assured her that it was over, for good.

As he stood outside the bathroom door, Miguel knew he had had a little too much to drink and was probably being irrational by watching Ebony so closely. He shook his head and sighed. He was about to leave when he saw Alex making his way up the stairs. He knew Alex was past the point of mere arousal and was looking to Ebony for release. He and Alex were friends but he knew how Alex was with women. He wined and dined them, used them up, threw them away, then moved on to the next. The thought that he was going to do that to Ebony pissed Miguel off. So, he gave up his position next to the bathroom door, descended the stairs, and cut Alex off at the landing.

"*¿Qué pasa, Miguelito?*" Alex smiled a little tipsily, with sweat still beading on his forehead. "*Tengo que ir al baño.*"

"Yeah, well this one is out of order—you'll need to use the one downstairs," Miguel said, maintaining his sentry.

"Oh," Alex replied, not moving. "So is there another bathroom?"

"Sure, you know, the one downstairs by the coat closet."

"Yeah, right." Alex smiled, trying to keep the edge out of his voice as his eyes drifted up toward the room where Ebony had disappeared. He took a step forward, but again was cut off by Miguel taking a side step. Alex's brow furrowed, but instead of arguing, he stepped back, throwing one last glance at the bathroom door, then turned and headed back downstairs. Miguel watched as he left, then exhaled deeply. He climbed the stairs toward the bathroom. Knowing the door would be open, he turned the knob and slipped inside.

•  •  •

Ebony was sitting on the closed toilet lid. The halter top of her red dress was bunched around her waist as she sat waiting for Alex. When Miguel stepped inside and closed the door, she tried to hide her large grapefruit-sized breasts, embarrassed.

"What the hell's wrong with you, Bonni?" Miguel asked sharply, "Why are you doing this shit in my house? And on my birthday?!"

"I—I'm sorry, Mickey," she stammered, gathering her purse while trying to hold the dress over her breasts. "I wasn't thinking, okay? I'm sorry."

"So you finally did it." Miguel smirked, moving to block her path to the door.

"What?" she asked warily.

"You got your breasts done. Did Alex convince you to do it?"

Ebony looked even more uncomfortable. Her short bangs began to stick to her forehead, more from nervousness than from the heat.

"Alex has nothing to do with my breasts. It's my body. I do what I like," she jeered as she tried to push past him to the door.

"Why did you go so big?" he asked, already hard from the moment he saw her sitting there, breasts exposed, waiting for the attentions of her new lover.

"That's none of your business, Mickey."

"Maybe you're the one doing the porn flicks, huh?" He laughed.

"Why do you even care? You've got your new girl; she's right downstairs. Bother *her*. Leave *me* alone," she said as she squeezed by him and grabbed for the doorknob.

"Wait," Miguel protested, grabbing her around the waist. "You get the shits done for Alex and won't even let me take a look, huh? Is that how it is now?"

Miguel pressed his hardened love stick against Ebony's derriere and felt her body quiver. It seemed natural and right as he rubbed against her, his hands on her stomach, his tongue tickling her neck and earlobes. He shifted her body to face the mirror and she let the halter top drop.

"Damn!" Miguel whispered in her ear as he viewed the reflection of her large milk-chocolate breasts in the mirror. "They're beautiful," he murmured as he traced her dark areolas with his fingertips, then fondled and caressed her dark nipples into hard peaks. She moaned out loud, despite her obvious attempt to remain silent as he slipped his hand between her open thighs and tickled the creamy wet spot in her panties. She pressed back against him, opening her legs wider, giving him the access he wanted. He moved the warm, slick material to the side and began to slowly strum her clit.

"Please, don't. Don't Mickey . . ." She pleaded as she instinctively began to grind her ass against his hardened cock while he paid homage to her pussy.

He groaned in her ear between kisses to her neck and shoulders. "Yesss, yes, *ay, Mami,* that's it. You know what I like."

Ebony's back stiffened as she pulled away, hissing, "You didn't think I knew three months ago. Then, Kelly knew what you liked. I was just in the way."

But Miguel was quick and grabbed her by the waist again, not allowing even an inch of space to open up between them.

"C'mon, don't be mad, baby," he crooned in her ear, as his hands slid downward to grip her hips. "I made a mistake. You know I love you, don't you, Bonni?" he asked as he held her body close to him, moving gently from side to side. "It's fucking torture to see you with Alex. I can't stand to see another man touch you. You know that." He murmured in her ear as his hands slid forward, caressing her stomach.

"You know this is how it's supposed to be," he said as he raised the hem of her dress and slid his hand into her panties before slipping a finger inside her.

Miguel stood swaying in time with his "ex," dancing a slow rhythm with her pussy. His finger entered her, retreating then circling her clit, repeating the cycle again and again until her legs became weak, all the while whispering and moaning, *"Te quiero, Mami. Sabes que te quiero."*

She relinquished control to Miguel, letting her body rest against him. In the mirror, their eyes locked, but only for a moment before her brown eyes fluttered closed. *There.* He had seen it . . . only a fleeting glance, but it was there . . . Ebony seeing him as the man he used to be . . . a thoughtful and tender lover, not the man who told her that he wasn't in love with her, or the man who let her walk away without so much as a good-bye. That cruel, insensitive man was Kelly's lover. Remorse for what he had done to Ebony began to surface, but he suppressed it and held her tighter.

"You believe me, don't you, Bonni? It's just you and me . . . like it used to be, *solamente nosotros, mi corazón,"* he said as he massaged her mound until his fingers were coated with her honey.

"Don't do this to me, Mickey. You know you don't mean it," she pleaded.

"You know I could never love anyone the way I love you, Bonni. *Te juro que sí. Dime que sí sabes que es la verdad,*" he whispered, softly kissing her face and neck.

Ebony turned and threw her arms around him and held him tight, almost as if her life depended on never letting go. She slipped her hands inside the smooth silk of his shirt and ran her fingers down his well-defined abdominals toward the waistband of his pants. She dropped to her knees as his shirt fell from his shoulders and rested her forehead against the thick rod jutting from his groin, then her fingers quickly unbuckled and unzipped him. Miguel slowly licked her cream from his fingers, taking his time, anticipating the moment when she would caress and pleasure him.

Clear, thick fluid dripped over her fingers as she gripped the base of his cock and began to squeeze and stroke him. "Ahhh, *sí, Mami,*" he moaned, moving his hips in time with her hand's up and down motion.

"Mmmm, you're gonna make me cum, Bonni," he groaned.

"That's the idea," she cooed seductively.

"Yeah, but not here," he said, abruptly grasping her hand.

Miguel opened the door, pulled Ebony to her feet and led her into the adjoining bedroom.

When they reached the center of the room, Miguel stepped out of his pants and briefs, then reclined on the bed, his stiff cock stretching skyward like a glistening, caramel missile. He turned onto his side and watched hungrily as Ebony walked around to the middle of the floor in front of him. Her hips gyrated an intimate seduction in time with the music that wafted in from outside. Ebony had never been in the business but she danced like a stripper. He had always taken her little private shows for granted until he realized that most men's women weren't quite that talented. With Kelly as his new woman, he had joined the ranks of most men.

"Slow," Mickey panted, squeezing his erection anxiously. Ebony slowed her routine, exaggerating every movement. She rolled her hips and displayed the chocolate brown orbs of her ass bending forward in a motion so sinuous and deliberate that it drove him wild. When she leaned toward him, hugging her smooth breasts, her nipples just barely brushing his lips, he was certain he would pop. Every lick of her lips, the sultry look in her eyes, brought him closer to the edge and easily suppressed any guilt he originally felt for making off with the woman his best friend brought to the party. He was justified in his mind. He rationalized that Alex would only use her, while he really loved Ebony and needed to be with her.

"*Venga,* come here, baby," he said, stretching his hand toward her. "Let *Papi* look at you."

Ebony hesitantly moved onto the edge of the bed.

"Come on." He grinned and gently pulled at her arm, coaxing her to lie beside him on her back. He didn't touch her right away. He looked at her. It really did seem so natural to have her there. His eyes were again drawn to her breasts, which were even lovelier as she lay there. He carefully straddled her hips and she giggled as he leaned over and slowly suckled on her nipples, licking the smooth skin of her breasts and the medallions of her areolas. He watched the amusement on her face as he touched, fondled, marveled, ooohed, and ahhhed over her breasts.

"You really are such a big titty-baby, aren't you, Mickey?" She grinned.

"I dunno," he answered, laughing. "They're just so perfect."

"You're silly." She laughed along with him.

"And you're beautiful." He smiled, then lowered himself downward until their lips met in a deep, soft, wet kiss. He slipped his fingers inside the waistband of her panties and tugged them down past her knees as he continued to make love to her mouth.

"I've missed you." She sighed as she kicked off her panties and spread her thighs wide to greet him. She was swollen and open, her pink treasure glistening in the dim light.

"*Dame una prueba.* I'm gonna have a taste of this." He smiled as he softly tweaked her clit, making her whimper the way he knew she would. He moved down her body, kissing every inch of her chocolate skin until he slipped his tongue inside her molten cream pot. She gasped and moaned, moving her hips up to his hungry mouth as he spent what seemed like a sweet eternity lapping at her clit and tasting her, expertly plunging two fingers inside her warm, slick canal and stroking her sensitive spot.

"Please, Mickey, I need to feel you."

"*No entiendo lo que estás diciendo, Mami.*" He smiled mischievously.

"Oh please," she whined. "I mean . . . *Por favor, Papi, dame su pene lindo.*"

He laughed and raised her thighs and ass high off the bed and placed the thick head of his cock at the opening that he had for so long felt he owned. They gasped in unison when he made the first deep stroke.

"Awww shit, *Mami*, that's so damn good!" he groaned.

"Don't stop," she urged while her fingers trailed upward against the sensitive skin of his rib cage. Then he started that hard driving rhythm he knew she loved. "That's it, *Papi*." She sighed. "Do me like you used to. Take your pussy."

Miguel was beyond ready to explode as Ebony rolled her hips, squeezing and massaging his dick until he could hold out no longer.

"Oh, God damn!" He bellowed as he slammed into her erratically, his back arched and rigid as he pumped his seed into her while she cried out, "Oh, make me cum, baby! That's it, baby, make me cum! Make your pussy cum!"

Five more strokes and they were both spent. Miguel flopped down beside her, with sweat still beading on his body. He rolled in next to her, pulling her body into his, saying, "I want you to move back home, Bonni. You'll do that, right?"

Ebony hesitated a moment before she answered, "I don't know if it's such a good idea right now."

"That's all right. I know it's going to take some time. All I'm asking is that you consider it. Give me a chance."

"It's your birthday, Mickey. You've been drinking. You feel this way tonight, but what about tomorrow?"

"I know how I feel. I'm only asking you to have faith in me."

Miguel tenderly squeezed her thighs and stroked her breasts, then after a moment, asked matter-of-factly, "If you don't mind telling me, you know, as a little something for my birthday?"

"Depends on what it is." Ebony yawned as she nestled into his arms.

"Well, not that it matters," Miguel asked, "but is the baby you're having mine or Alex's?"

Ebony was quiet, her body rising up and down with slow, measured breaths.

"I know you're not asleep, Bonni." Ebony flinched as Miguel admonished her with a pinch.

"What makes you so sure I'm pregnant?" she responded defensively after a moment.

"Come on, Bonni. Those breasts? Too perfect. I'm a photographer, remember. I've seen and felt more fake breasts than most plastic surgeons and those are not fake. Besides . . . you're keloidal. If you'd had surgery, you'd have scars . . . and like I said," he remarked imperiously while stroking her breasts, "These are perfect."

"You're a little too smart for your own good, Mickey," she grumbled, exasperated.

"Yeah, I know," he said with a self-congratulatory smirk as he gave her body another squeeze.

"Yep, you're a regular Cuban Sherlock Holmes," she groused as he nibbled playfully at her ear.

"Bonni!" Alex's voice cracked through the room like the sound of a broken timber.

Both Miguel and Ebony flinched as Alex made his presence known, standing in the doorway of the adjoining bathroom. He held Ebony's discarded dress in his hand and without looking at Miguel, crossed over to the side of the bed where Ebony lay. He handed her the garment and said quietly, "Get dressed."

"You don't have to go anywhere, Bonni," Miguel said sharply. "She doesn't need to leave. She has a home right here."

"Right, until you find the next younger, sweeter thing to turn your head. Then what? You'll put her out again?"

"Check your own glass house, Alex. You're with a different woman almost every week."

"So that gives you license to fuck my woman?" Alex asked incredulous.

"*My* woman, you mean," Miguel countered as he hastily rose from the bed, grabbing his robe. "Ebony is mine, Alex. You know that."

"No, Mick, she *was* yours, but not anymore."

"Maybe I should get dressed," Bonni said, scrambling out of the bed and hurriedly recovering her panties before rushing into the bathroom.

The two men were silent at first, fiercely glaring at each other, until Miguel sneered. "You think you've got a shot with Bonni?"

"More than a shot. Bonni's mine, man. You need to get used to that."

"Yours? Well, it didn't look like that tonight." Miguel smirked as he pulled on his robe.

In that split second, Alex advanced on Miguel so quickly that he didn't even have time to raise his hands in defense. Alex's big hands collared the robe around Miguel's throat and Alex snatched him up close and hissed, "I expect you to respect what Bonni and I have."

"You don't have anything," Miguel said.

"When you were with Bonni, I never touched her. But she comes here as my date and I turn my back for two minutes, Mick, and you're all over her. What the fuck is that all about? You're supposed to be *mi compadre, mi hermano*."

Miguel knew Alex was right but he was too angry to

think straight. He slammed his fists against Alex's chest, and pushed away from him, then began pacing back and forth like a caged tiger, gesticulating wildly.

"Bonni was the only thing that was ever mine, and you couldn't wait to get your hands on her! You could have any other woman, but you just *had* to have Bonni. Why do you think that is?!"

"You need to get your shit together, Mick." Alex laughed cruelly as he shook his head and walked toward the door. "Bonni is mine, and you put your hands on her. You know the only reason you're still standing here drawing breath now is because I thought you were my friend. Consider *that* your birthday present."

Without waiting for Miguel's reply, Alex left the room and walked downstairs, leaving Miguel alone listening to the sounds of celebration and considering life in the coming year without the love of his woman or the companionship of his best friend.

# Tomorrow's Saints

## Kathleen Bradean

*Mamá* wasn't dying of anything, except embarrassment. She broke her hip. Instead of calling an ambulance, she phoned me.

*"Me resbalé cuando estaba fregando, mi hija,"* she explained, apologetic. *I slipped while mopping, little girl.*

The emergency medical technician told me that older women could easily break their fragile bones. I stared at him, wondering what old woman he was talking about. Then they wheeled *Mamá* past us on the gurney and, for the first time in years, I didn't use my memory to filter the truth. She looked so frail, and her beautiful brown face was lined with wrinkles.

She looked even worse in the intensive care unit. Spindly metal IV poles hovered over the head of her bed like praying mantises. Machines beeped quietly as green lines trailed across their screens. Tubes were taped to her arms and under her nose.

*"¿Cuando me puedo salir?"* she asked. *When can I get out of here?*

It worried me that she'd lapsed into Spanish since having her accident. We rarely spoke it anymore. That was my fault. I wasn't interested in anything that made me different. When she had called about her accident, I was shocked how long it took me to understand what she said.

"I want to go home, Esme."

I grasped her hand, careful not to disturb the taped IV tube. *"Sí, Mamá, pero . . ."* I wasn't up to it. I was *sin lenguaje,* without language. "Please let them watch you for a few days. After that, I promise you'll go home."

"Are your sisters here yet?" *Mamá* snapped.

Her flash of temper was comforting. She sounded more like her usual self.

"They're driving down from Paso Robles, *Mamá.* They'll be here tomorrow."

An orderly came into the room, followed by one of the nurses I'd seen by the metal doors of the ICU. She didn't tell me to leave, but I got the hint that I was in her way as she bustled around me.

"I'm stepping out, *Mamá,* but I'll be back."

There was no privacy in the ICU. As I stood in the wide, white hallway outside the room, I could watch through the floor-to-ceiling glass wall and see everything the nurse did.

In the room next door, a *muy papi* man gently brushed the silver hair of an ancient grandmother. He set aside the brush and stroked his brown fingers across her cheek in a caress.

I heard *Mamá* fuss at the nurse and hid a smile.

The nurse came out of *Mamá's* room. "She's doing well. As soon as the doctor approves the move, your mother will go to the regular ward."

"Tomorrow?"

"I can't say." She gave me a curt nod and went back to the nurses' station.

I followed her. "Can you give me some idea?"

"It's up to the doctor." The nurse picked up a chart.

"I'm only asking—"

"And I told you that it's up to the doctor."

She moved away before I could say anything else.

Taking deep breaths, I forced my temper down. I turned around and leaned against the counter, my arms crossed.

The man caring for his *abuela* wore a dark-blue wool suit that hugged his broad shoulders. I loved the crisp line of barbered hair above the stiff collar of his white shirt.

He put a dab of lotion on his hands and spread it over her transparent skin with small, soothing circles.

I bet that felt nice.

He took his time, his touch lingering.

I could use a little of that myself.

When he bent over the woman to kiss her forehead, his pants tightened over his muscular butt.

Frowning at my wicked thoughts, I wondered why I couldn't simply concentrate on *Mamá*.

I glimpsed at him again.

A man built like that would look so good walking toward my bed in a tight pair of boxer briefs that hugged his package. He'd look even better with the underwear off.

*Dios.*

Seven months without a lover was taking its toll. Lately, my blood was in a permanent simmer. It didn't take much desire to make it boil over.

He leaned over her again.

I sucked air between my clenched teeth.

*In a hospital,* I scolded myself. *Really, you'd think you'd have some restraint.*

Worried that I might get caught ogling, I hurried to the visitors' lounge.

A large family filled the room. While the adults paced, the kids fought over the channel on the television. A talk-show host chatted with her guest. The picture flicked to a reporter clutching a microphone, and finally, a cartoon. The kids plopped to the floor, content.

That would be us tomorrow—sisters, nieces, and nephews everywhere. Noise and family, the way it was meant to be. It didn't feel right to be alone in a hospital.

I took the chair in the far corner. It wasn't clear if *Mamá* would need in-home care when the hospital released her, and I had no idea what her insurance would cover. I stared down at my hands. Cupped together in my lap, they held no answers.

Several minutes later, the man came into the lounge. The only open seat was next to me. He sank into it with a groan and put his hand over his eyes.

His spiced aftershave was a pleasant change from the astringent odor of the hospital. The scent touched the back of my tongue as I inhaled. His long, lean thigh rested against mine. I could feel the heat of his body through my skirt.

He leaned forward and clasped his hands together. I glanced sideways at him, catching a glimpse of his thick eyelashes. He was praying. As soon as I realized that, I felt guilty for the tingles between my legs. Following his example, I thought of *Mamá* and thanked God that her stay in the ICU would be short.

"Just a precaution," the nurse assured me. I repeated her words, like prayers, and believed.

My thoughts returned to the man beside me. Where was his family? Quick glances down at his hands spied no ring.

"Twenty more minutes."

His voice startled me. I glanced up at him. He nodded toward the door. "The nurses will let us back in soon."

"Oh. Yes."

The coffee in the pot next to the television looked as thick as syrup, but I needed something to do with my hands, so I poured a cup and brought it back to my seat.

He must have seen me wince. "Bad?"

I scraped my tongue with my teeth to get rid of the burned flavor as I dropped the full cup into the trash can. "There isn't enough cream and sugar in the entire world to make that motor oil taste like coffee."

I wasn't that funny, but lines crinkled around his smoky topaz eyes as he chuckled. The dimple in his cheek was a test of my waning self-control.

He towered over me when he stood. "I'm going down to the cafeteria. Hopefully the coffee is better there. Can I bring you back something?"

How incredibly sweet he was.

"No. I'll go, too. Maybe I'll find something I like if I go down." I didn't mean it as suggestive as it sounded, and I most certainly didn't plan to get caught eyeing his bulge. When I glanced up at him, his eyebrow raised a bit.

"Go down. To the cafeteria," I blurted. *Madre de Dios,* the words that came out of my mouth.

He followed me to the elevator. I tried to walk like a nun.

His name was Luis. He worked in a bank, played soccer in a weekend league, and he showed me pictures of his sons.

"They live with their mother in San Diego. I have them at

Christmas and for a month in the summer. It isn't enough, but what can I do?"

I agreed that it was sad, but wasn't sorry to find out he was a free man.

Even though he didn't have to, he paid for my coffee. We sat on opposite sides of a wobbly table in the cafeteria and talked about *Mamá* and his *abuela,* because the hospital was what we had in common.

Luis's voice was a nice, rumbly baritone. When he talked of his *abuela,* his eyes were so sad and soft that I reached over the table to touch his hands. His squeezed back and didn't let go.

"I don't think she's ever coming home," he admitted.

"Are your parents here in LA?"

"*Abuela* raised me. She's all I have."

I couldn't imagine growing up without sisters, brothers, or cousins. How horrible to be alone.

When it was my turn to talk about *Mamá,* his thumbs stroked the back of my hands. I imagined him stroking my hair as it fanned across the pillow on my bed. I bet he took his time with a lover, caressing her until she begged him to move his hands lower. Under my clothes, my skin ached for warm, feathery touches.

Our knees knocked together. Jolts jumped between my thighs. The thought of our legs tangled together in crisp white sheets sent a rush of heat to my belly.

He sighed. "My only regret . . . Well, not my only one. I wish my marriage had lasted until after my *abuela* passed. Sometimes I think she took the divorce harder than I did."

"At least you were married."

My hands escaped his and fluttered like hummingbirds as

I talked. I tried to make them land in my lap, but they took flight again as I imitated *Mamá*. "Esme, you're not getting any younger. Esme, when are you going to give me grandchildren?" I brushed back a trailing lock of my hair. "*Ai* . . . It never stops, you know?"

"Oh, yes." He did understand. We were from the same place, the same people, the same culture. No explanation needed.

"Every time I get a wedding invitation, I grit my teeth. *Mamá* gives me that look."

Luis laughed. Tension seemed to release from his muscles. The dimple showed again.

After getting nasty looks from the morose visitors in the cafeteria, we leaned across the table, conspiring to confine our wicked chuckles to the small space between our bodies. I looked only into his eyes, even when someone across the cafeteria dropped a tray.

He said his job wasn't as exciting as mine, but he modestly shared his victories as a goalie for his soccer team. My fantasies of him took a raw turn. I pictured him in the shower, rinsing the mud and sweat of a game from his skin, and had to close my eyes for a moment.

Thick, white soapy lather sliding down his broad back to the curve of his butt, and then him turning to me, smiling but a little shy, showing me a muscled abdomen and below that, his—

Luis touched my arm.

I squeezed my legs together. My engorged sex pulsed. I squeezed my thighs again because it felt so good.

"Did you play in college, too?" I asked.

"Yes. And two seasons of professional before I ruined my

knee. But tell me, how did you get to be a line producer? Do you ever go on location when you're working on a movie?"

I shrugged. "Sure. It isn't as fun as it sounds. Just stressful, especially if the production is running behind schedule."

He took my hand again. His touch sent a good shiver pinging through my nerves. My muscles clenched, aching for his long fingers to work miracles inside my body.

"I bet you handle it well." He gazed directly into my eyes.

Dios, *what a flirt!* And I was just as bad.

"Well, one time . . ."

The cleaning crew came in to wax the cafeteria floors. I glanced around. We were the only people sitting at tables. A look at my watch told me that two and a half hours had passed.

"Shit!" I jumped up and knocked the table, sending my empty paper cup rolling under my chair. Luis kneeled down to pick it up for me. I saw his nostrils flare, so I tugged at the hem of my skirt, but that freed another, stronger whiff of my scent. Heat spread across my cheeks. He set the cup on the table. Our eyes met, and a private smile pulled at his lips, but he said nothing.

The ride up to the ICU was agony. I ran my tongue over my lips, which were flushed with blood and hot. Tendrils of hair trailed into my eyes when I bowed my head. I brushed them away only to have the black waves cascade around my face. Inside my bra, my nipples were tight.

A doctor stepped into the elevator on the second floor. He inhaled deeply and smirked. Luis stepped closer to me. The smirk faded.

The hallway outside the ICU was quiet. The television in the visitors' lounge played to an empty room.

I pressed the flat, silver square that opened the doors to the ward. Nothing happened.

Luis peered in through the small window. "Someone is coming."

We waited, standing close, until a nurse opened the huge door only enough to poke out her head.

"Visiting hours are over. You can come back tomorrow."

It was that same nurse. She gave me a hard look. I stepped forward. "Listen——"

"I'm sorry." She shut the door, not sorry at all.

I shoved at the door but it wouldn't budge, so I tapped the call button until Luis lifted my hand from it.

"It isn't your fault, Esme," he told me. As he walked back toward the elevator, his shoulders slumped.

There was nothing to do but give up for the night. I cursed myself for being so selfish. *Mamá* probably asked the nurse a dozen times where I was. No wonder I had gotten such a nasty glance.

I'll make up for everything tomorrow. I'll be a good daughter and think of nothing but her. Tomorrow. There was nothing else I could do until then, I bargained with my conscience, but I didn't feel absolved.

I stared down the hallway at the white walls and harsh fluorescent light fixtures; he rested his head against the wall. Luis had his hands in his pockets so that his jacket strained to cover his muscular back. My gaze swept slowly over the white collar showing above the dark-blue wool, down to the narrow cut of his waist, and stopped at his belt.

My tongue flicked over my lips as I pictured a dimple on either side of his spine, just above the curve of his butt.

I rolled my eyes up to the ceiling tiles, and beyond that,

God. What had I done to deserve so much temptation? And why did I give into it so easily?

"I could have looked at my watch." He touched my arm again. "But I wanted to listen to you laugh. I needed a break from death."

He bent down and pressed his warm lips to mine, at first as if the kiss were a question, and then like a hungry man.

It was my chance to prove that I'd learned my lesson. I could have walked away but as his tongue parted my lips, I realized I'd already conceded the day. Tomorrow was my fresh start. And then I wasn't thinking, but melding into his arms.

We breathed deeply, as if winded by sudden urgency. Heat exploded from the friction between our bodies. His hand slid to the back of my head as his other arm brought me closer. He was hard.

"Not in the hallway," I whispered.

He nodded, understanding that I wasn't saying no.

He led me into the visitors' lounge. I leaned against the wall as Luis pushed the door closed. I knew we could get caught, but that only spurred me on.

He unbuttoned my blouse while we kissed. His hands felt good against my skin. I wrapped my arms around his neck and pressed my lips below his ear.

When he pushed my bra over my breasts and flicked his thumb over my hard nipple, I gasped.

"Too harsh?"

"No, but they get very sensitive."

"Poor baby," he crooned as he ducked his head down to kiss it better.

He kneaded my breast while his tongue flicked over the brown nub. Every little twinge traveled straight to my sex.

When he suckled, it was as if he put his mouth right on my pussy. I squirmed.

His hand was still on my breast as he kissed me. I closed my eyes to the bright overhead lights as he tasted my mouth.

My hands groped for his zipper. Inside, his pants felt hot and humid from the drops of pre-cum wetting his briefs.

I teased his cock as he'd teased my nipple. First, I lightly pinched the head.

Luis moaned.

"Too rough?"

He smiled down at me. "It's sensitive."

My devilish grin should have warned him. I ran my fingernails lightly across his glands, and then with more pressure, until his cock twitched inside his briefs. When I felt his hips pull back from me, I grasped him and stroked. With a firm hold on him, I brought him closer.

"Careful, Esme. I'll follow a woman like you to the ends of the earth—especially if she has my dick in her hands."

I chuckled as I stroked the full length of his shaft. His eyes softened and his lips parted. I released his cock and loosened his tie. He watched while I unbuckled his black leather belt, as if he'd never seen anything as fascinating as my hands. I pushed his pants down past his knees.

His thighs were sparsely covered by dark hair that only emphasized the sculpted muscles. My imagination hadn't done his body justice. I saw surgical scars on his knee and longed to run my fingers over them, but teased his nipples through his white shirt instead.

Luis's hard-on pushed against his white briefs. I admired the outline, and then worked my hand around the tip until another drop of pre-cum soaked into the cotton.

Luis pushed my skirt over my hips. His insistent hand urged my thighs apart. He smiled when he felt the soaked lace.

"I thought so," he teased. But as his fingers parted my lower lips and tested my swollen pussy, his kisses grew harder.

My muscles gathered tight and I loved the way it felt. They pulsed in the rhythm of sex until the throbbing waves no longer ebbed.

He got to his knees. "Put your foot up on the chair." Then his mouth pressed to the lace and I felt the heat of his breath as he exhaled. "You smell so good." He pulled the material tight and rubbed it from side to side until my legs shook. Then he lapped against my aching sex.

I melted. My hand grasped at the back of the chair as I fought to stay on my feet. The fast, hard clench of pleasure robbed me of breath.

Fingers pinched my sex, holding back the wave that threatened to break over me. I thrust forward, riding his tongue, and wanting more.

"Fuck me," I gasped.

His tongue hesitated between suckles.

"In my purse. Here." I tore the foil packet open with my teeth and threw it empty to the floor.

His face was slick with my juices. He released his hard-on from his briefs when he stood. Thick and rosy-brown, his cock pointed toward his flat stomach. I grasped him and rolled the condom down his long shaft, teasing him by taking my time reaching the dark nest of hair at the base. With him still in hand, I wrapped a leg around his waist and guided him to me.

His hard cock pushing into me felt sinfully good. Every pulse through my groin bounced off that solid cock and magnified. I moved my hips against him, holding him inside, not letting him thrust.

He put his hands on my hips and took control. Each hard slam knocked me into the wall.

Luis bit at my lips until they were as swollen as my sex. His cock rubbing against my underwear sent another gush through my pussy.

I pulled back from him. Kneeling on a chair with my back to him, I shoved my lacy underwear down to my knees and pulled my skirt up.

"Like this," I told him. "From behind."

He entered me with a harsh thrust, pulled all the way out, and slammed back in again. His balls slapped my sex each time. I tried to stifle my moans.

"You're so wet. Your juices are drenching my balls."

A tight clench shuddered through me.

"That's right; milk me," he said.

I pushed my hand between my legs and stroked his balls when they swung close enough. Then I tugged at my sex. My fingertips pressed hard and made tight circles right where my nerves clustered. My pussy grabbed him tighter and tighter with each of his long thrusts.

Perfect pleasure hung over us for delicious seconds.

I arched for him. His cock rubbed all the right spots. Heat flushed across my face and lips. I could hear him groaning. His fingers dug into my hips.

My pussy clamped tight around him, grasping as his cock amplified the release inside me. I hit the peak and rode the waves down.

I groaned.

Luis thrust once more, and then held still inside me. I could feel the throb as he came.

There was nothing I could do about our scent in the air, but I straightened the chairs and smoothed my skirt. He stared at his shoes while he dressed.

In the elevator, he slumped against the handrail.

God, what had I done?

Tomorrow, I'll be good, I vowed. Tomorrow, it will all be about *Mamá*. She'll sit up in her bed and scold me for neglecting her. I'll bow my head, knowing that I deserve it, and be grateful that she's feeling like herself again.

Maybe I'll brush her hair.


We walked through the deserted lobby. The gift shop was closed. Tomorrow, I'd bring *Mamá* irises, tulips, and daffodils—spring flowers of renewal. She'd scold me for spending the money, but she'd be pleased.

"I'll walk you to your car," Luis offered.

The door to the hospital chapel stood ajar. It offered sanctuary from an awkward moment.

"I think, maybe, I'll go in there for a while." It wasn't the best way to say good-bye, but at least he could escape cleanly.

Luis followed me inside.

There were three rows of smooth, dark, wood pews, separated by an aisle. A small pulpit stood on a raised dais. The dark-brown carpet showed vacuum tracks.

I knelt and crossed myself before taking a seat. The pew was hard and cool on the backs of my thighs. Luis sat close, but didn't touch me. I stared at the brass cross on the wall behind the pulpit and wondered why I couldn't be the girl *Mamá* had raised me to be. Was it right to face God with fresh sin still damp between my legs?

My head tipped forward. Hair cascaded, hiding my face, but not my shame. I prayed for *Mamá,* for her nurses, the doctors, and Luis's *abuela,* with my hands clutched tight.

Tomorrow, I promised God, I'll be a saint.

Luis put his warm hand on the nape of my neck. I glanced up at him, hoping the tear stinging the corner of my eye didn't sparkle. Guilt weighed at the corners of his mouth.

"Do you think we'll be forgiven?" he asked.

I nodded toward the cross. "If we ask for it sincerely, we're forgiven. Unless you mean *Mamá.* She's a little tougher on me than God is."

# South South Bronx

## Hugh Smith

Enormous rats scurried among the shadows, pausing here and there to pick up scraps of garbage that spilled from Dumpsters lining the South Bronx alleyway.

Every so often a face appeared at the alley's entrance. Addicts, probably, or homeless, wondering what a brand-new Mercedes (with Connecticut plates, no less) was doing parked in a filthy South Bronx alley at this hour of the night. They would have to keep wondering since the streetlight couldn't penetrate far enough into the murk for them to see what was going on. But I'm sure they wish it did, since my moans and screams made it clear what was taking place.

The night had been much more stressful than usual. My restaurant, Cabaña, was a zoo. Over the past year I had worked my ass off and Cabaña had blossomed into a genuine Manhattan hot spot; a place to see and be seen. In addition to the usual Friday night crowd of rich Manhattanites and wealthy tourists who waited months for a reservation, to-night there was an Oscar-winning actor, a former New York

City mayor, a rapper and his entourage, and a private party for an up-and-coming European tennis star.

Everything had to go perfectly, so I personally greeted every table, made sure the food was perfect, soothed the ego of the rapper, who thought the waiter was coming on to him, arranged a private table for the Oscar winner so no one would notice that the young lady he was with wasn't really young or a lady, and later escorted the young tennis star out through the service entrance so the paparazzi wouldn't see that she was so high she didn't even know her own name. By the time the bulk of the patrons were gone, I was exhausted and decided to leave my managers to close up. After a night like I'd had, I needed some relief, the kind my husband, Miguel, couldn't provide and that I could only find in one place.

I've had lovers in the past, but after too much wasted time and effort, I found I had no use for the young personal trainers who only wanted to brag about fucking the rich, older woman. I couldn't stomach the models either, or the athletes, actors, and assorted trust-fund babies who spent their money at my restaurant and their time flirting with me, trying to seduce me with their looks and Daddy's money. Even more pathetic were the executives, Fortune 500 types with manicured nails, soft hands, and hair plugs. Those pampered punks didn't know a thing about what I wanted. Plus, they weren't used to a woman like me, a sexy, full-figured Latina who overpowered them with more breasts, hips, ass, and thighs than they had any clue what to do with. I needed someone from the streets, a man who knew what it was to come up hard and have nothing except a dick and the ability to use it. I needed someone rough around the edges. I needed someone rough, period, and the best place to find men like that is the South Bronx.

I must be *loca*; even the cops don't venture into the South Bronx without a damn good reason. Hell, I could get robbed, raped, or worse. To tell you the truth, the thought of rape turned me on. There was something exciting about the thought of being brutally used to within an inch of your life by desperate men who don't give a damn about you.

Still, sometimes I wondered whether or not what I did and who I did it with was more to hurt Miguel than to plea-sure myself. Miguel would be mortified if he knew his *prin-cesa* was associating with the kind of people he called "the dregs of society." He's forgotten that those "dregs of society" are the same people we grew up with, laughed with, cried with, and dreamed with. The only difference between us and them is our dreams came true.

Miguel and I both grew up in poverty in the South Bronx but we both worked hard. He landed college and law-school scholarships and eventually became an associate, then later the first Hispanic partner at one of the city's most presti-gious law firms. I went to culinary school, then honed my skills working for some of the best restaurants in the city before opening my own restaurant. They were tough, those early years, but those were great times. We didn't have much, but we had each other and our dreams. We couldn't have been happier. Now we're living our dreams and we have everything but each other.

I put those thoughts out of my head and twenty minutes after leaving the restaurant, I exited the Major Deegan Ex-pressway at 161st Street in the shadow of Yankee Stadium. The night was rain-forest humid, typical for August in New

York. Ghetto folks, most too poor to afford air-conditioning or even a decent fan, were still outside at this late hour, lounging on stoops or just standing around, leaning against the rough concrete, holding ice-cold bottles in their hands of whatever would help them make it through the sweltering night.

Music from my favorite bump-and-grind CD played from the Mercedes's Blapunkt speakers as I cruised for my choice for the evening. It didn't take long to find him. He was a thug, twenty years old at the most, and not too tall, around five nine or ten, dressed in the standard drug dealer uniform—bandanna, white wifebeater, much too baggy jeans, and $150 sneakers. A thick gold chain with a Puerto Rican–flag pendant dangled between his thick, chiseled pecs. He walked with his head slightly down, but always vigilant, not missing a thing.

He and his boys crowded into a cuchifrito spot just off Willis Avenue. I double-parked in front, shot a nasty glare at the crackhead eyeing the Mercedes, kissed *mi abuelita*'s crucifix, and followed them inside.

The restaurant, if you could call it that, was filthy. The ghosts of fried things lingered in the air. A fan leaned in one corner, wearily oscillating and doing nothing but rearranging the humidity. A strip of dirt dislodged from its metal grillwork and soared on an invisible current before coming to rest on a plate of empanadas in the grimy display case. The stools lining the counter were occupied with the type of men I would expect to see in a place like this at a time like this eating food like this.

My target was seated on a stool at the far end of the counter, surrounded by his boys. Conversation ceased as I strode the entire length of the restaurant to get to him, the only sounds the clack of my heels on the dirty floor and staticky salsa squeezed from an ancient radio. A dozen pairs of eyes followed my every step, but I didn't give a damn— I'm used to the stares. At forty years old, I still look good. I might be thick, but I work out for two hours every day, my double-d breasts are still firm and impressive, and thousands of hours of step classes ensure that you can bounce a quarter off my ass. My tanned skin sets off my dark hair and eyes, those unmistakable Puerto Rican features inherited from *mi mamá*. It didn't hurt that the dress I was wearing almost fit me like a second skin or that I hadn't bothered to wear either panties or a bra.

I approached him and in two minutes, we were in my car. I didn't get his name. I only wanted one thing, so name, rank, and serial number were unnecessary. Ten minutes after that we were parked in the alley, and I was naked and riding his long, hard dick and getting it exactly the way I liked it— hard and rough! I would be bruised all over my body tomorrow, for sure. Miguel almost never noticed my "souvenirs" even though I made sure to flaunt them in front of him. On the rare occasion he did notice, I told him they were from my kickboxing classes, and he actually believed that lame excuse. *¡Idioto!* I've never taken a kickboxing class in my life.

The thug squeezed my left nipple hard. My eyes watered from the pain, but I loved it. That sensation, combined with the feeling of the head of his monster dick grinding against my cervix, was powerful. Suddenly, the unmistakable sound of gunshots rang out. They were close, a block or two away, from the sound of it. The thug heard them, too, and lifted his head up, instantly alert. I wasn't about to put up with any distractions, not even gunshots, so I grabbed his hair and forced his face between my sweat-slicked breasts. He refocused his attention, regained his rhythm, and stroked me violently, biting my nipples so hard it felt as if he were trying to make me pay for daring to be forceful with him. I ground down on him harder, grabbing a fistful of his dark hair, and forced his head back and bit his neck, leaving a livid red bruise. If he had a girlfriend, he was going to have some explaining to do tomorrow. In return he grasped my long hair with one hand and now it was my turn for my head to be painfully wrenched back. He took a firm hold of my neck and squeezed. My air was restricted and it was harder and harder to breathe, but I didn't stop riding his dick. As spots danced before my eyes, I screamed in ecstasy.

"Ohhhh, *Papi*! I'm cumming! I'm cumming! I'm cumming! I'm cumming! I'm cumming! I'm cumming!"

Even as the orgasm took over and made my body shake and buck like a marionette on a string, he didn't stop, and continued pounding away as surge after surge of pleasure flowed throughout my entire body, finally ending with a flood of cum gushing like a waterfall from my pussy, saturating his dick and balls and the leather upholstery.

I collapsed, spent, on the thug's chest, trying to catch my breath, but he wasn't having it.

"Yo, wake the fuck up, bitch," the thug said. "Come suck my dick."

I don't take shit from anybody in this world, but his words turned me on more than I would have thought possible. Instantly, my pussy became soaking wet again.

"*Sí, Papi,*" I said, and rose up off the thug's dick, unlocked the car door, and led him outside. After the relative comfort of expensive German air-conditioning, the humidity was like a physical force bearing down on us.

I pushed the thug down onto the hood of the car. He lay there, his *pene* standing up and at attention. Thick veins ran up and down its length, still slick from my juices. I removed the condom, threw it to the rats, and stroked him slowly, feeling his dick become even harder by my attention. A single tiny droplet of pre-cum oozed from the tip and I bent over to taste it, then put the head in my mouth, savoring the flavor of our combined essences. His balls also got attention from my skilled tongue, swirling around them before I put his entire huge sac in my mouth and sucked gently.

His moans became louder and lights flickered on in the windows of the apartments that overlooked the alley. If the residents were watching, they were getting an eyeful of me, naked except for heels, bent over with a mouthful of dick.

I put his hardness in my mouth again, sucking furiously. He responded, his hips rising to force more of his length down my throat. I let him, knowing he was close and I wanted it all, every last drop of him. His body twisted and levitated off the hood of the car and he grabbed two fistfuls of hair as he came, ramming his dick into my mouth and down my throat, gagging me. Waves of hot cum exploded down my throat and I swallowed as fast as I could, but still some of his cum escaped out of the sides of my mouth.

"You better swallow all of it, bitch. Don't waste it!" he said, and I obeyed his order, licking his dick and balls to collect every drop of cum that had escaped my eager mouth.

After draining him dry, I removed a tube of lubrication and a condom from the Hermès purse Miguel bought me for my last birthday. I squeezed a healthy dab of the gel in my palm, put the condom on his dick, and lubed his erection well, spreading the gel over the shaft and the head before assuming the position on the hood of the car.

Naked and defenseless, lying ass up, facedown on the hood of an $85,000 luxury automobile in one of the worst neighborhoods in the city, I was at my most vulnerable but I felt the most alive. All my senses were in high gear. My skin tingled; I felt the heat from the still-warm hood and my asshole quivered in anticipation of what was to come. I felt the thug's hands on my hips as he braced himself to ravage me. I heard the fearless Bronx rats still feeding in the dark and more windows from the apartments above opening, voyeurs preparing to witness my violation at the hands of the young thug.

"Damn, you a sexy bitch, you fuckin' nasty *puta!*" the thug said, in awe of my shapely ass.

I felt the substantial weight of his dick as he used it to slap my ass. He positioned the head at my tender opening and gave an uncertain push, probably skeptical that my tight hole would accommodate his massive manhood.

Another push, harder this time, and the head slid in slowly. Aided by the lubrication, I felt myself opening to accommodate his width. His dick was well lubricated, but the pain was still unbelievable.

"You like that shit, bitch?" he asked.

"*Sí, Papi, sí, sí, dame más, dame más!*"

He rammed a few more inches into my ass and the world exploded in pure agony. I heard a scream, then realized it was coming from me.

I closed my eyes, but the tears managed to find a way past

my eyelids and down my face. I cried, not only because of the thug's huge tool was inside me, but because I wondered why it was that *mi amor,* would not, could not, make me feel a fraction of what this common street criminal could. I cried because I have everything a person could want, yet I was dead inside, only alive when I risked my life for cheap thrills.

The thug continued to stroke my ass; his entire dick was inside me now, stretching me wider open than I'd ever been before. My moans came louder, harder; I couldn't help myself. His rhythm was perfect, pistonlike, steady, and not too slow or too fast, the perfect speed to allow me to feel and savor every last inch of his huge tool in my asshole.

I felt my body responding, the pain was now gone and the pleasure almost equally unbearable. I had thought that his whole length was inside me, but I was wrong. There was more, and my moans got louder still, almost screams, as more and more of him was forced inside me. I had never been penetrated this deeply before; my ass was on fire. I couldn't move, paralyzed by my violation. Just when I felt as if it was impossible to endure any more of him inside me, I felt his heavy balls slapping against my pussy as he stroked me and realized that he had finally managed to fit his entire cock inside me.

The sensation was indescribable, an almost out-of-body experience that caused a mammoth orgasm to rip through my entire body. My mouth opened wide, but no sound came out, and the tears flowed down my face to join the pool of sweat evaporating on the hood of the Mercedes. I blacked out for a few seconds, but came to my senses just in time to feel the thug's cock throbbing inside of me, then a wet heat as he withdrew from my asshole, ripped the condom off and blasted a huge load of cum on my ass and back.

Depleted, I lay almost senseless on the car, my body shaking as the tears rolled softly down my face.

Minutes later I recovered enough to stand. I was sore and knew it was going to be much worse tomorrow, a painful reminder of my latest outing to *el barrio*. I got into the driver's seat and started the car. The thug said something, but I tuned him out. He had served his purpose and I had no more use for him.

As I backed out of the alley, I pulled some bills from my purse and threw them out the window. I didn't look back.

I was still naked but I didn't care. My ass was sore but I didn't care. My scalp tingled and ached where the thug had savagely pulled my hair. I didn't care. I was numb. I drove like a robot, the smells of sex and new car mingled and the tears rolled down my face all the way home.

# *Are You Available*

Mitch

"Are you available?" Chas asked a Linda Darnel look-alike. She was the spitting image of one of the movie star's Latina characters. Beautiful, bronzed, busty, and draped in a burgundy dress designed to emphasize her figure and draw attention to her cleavage.

Smiling, she took his hand, said, "*Sí*," and then led him toward a counter where an older lady was sitting. With only a hint of an accent, the older lady said, "Linda doesn't speak English well so you need to talk with me. She's one of our best and costs ten dollars. Is that okay with you?"

"Yes, that's fine," he said, reaching for his wallet.

Chas was in a Juárez bordello, San Miguel's, with three of his army buddies. It was the middle of February 1953; they had spent the past four weeks training on the M55 mount and the 90-millimeter cannon at Fort Bliss and were enjoying a weekend pass in Mexico. After entering, they had a drink and decided to go their separate ways, find a lady, and meet again about eleven o'clock.

He handed her a ten.

"Follow Linda down the hall. There's a room where you'll be checked for VD and given a condom. Kissing is against the rules and Linda's tatas are off limits. If every Juan who sees her used them, she'd be too sore to work. Is that clear?" she asked sternly, but with an understanding gaze.

With a nod, he returned her look.

"Have a nice time," she said as he turned.

He was directed to a room where a woman in her sixties or seventies had him drop his khakis. She grabbed his penis with a gloved hand and gave him two quick jerks. He didn't emit any fluid, indicating he was free of clap. Handing him a condom, she shooed him away.

Linda stood in front of a door and stepped inside as he waddled down the hall, struggling with his pants. Entering the room, Chas saw a flash of red falling to a chair and Linda crawling into a single, metal bed sitting low to the floor. She had a beautiful face, long black hair, light brown skin, dangling mammary glands, pubic hair glistening from recently applied lubricant, and long shapely legs.

She lay with her head on several pillows, her legs bent and spread wide. Chas undressed and rolled the condom the length of his erection. Watching emotionlessly, she gestured and said in heavily accented English, "Come on."

*She wants me to hurry,* he thought. For her this was

business—for him, however, it was an event he had been looking forward to ever since he had screwed Marti on Christmas in New York.

Crouching between her legs, he advanced toward her slick pussy while devouring her breasts with his eyes—even in the back and down position, they were marvelous. Penetration went smoothly, but before he was fully seated she exploded, moving her body in all directions at the same time. Shocked, Chas had never experienced such motion; he guessed her frenetic actions were an attempt to cause him to cum quickly. The faster he finished, the sooner she could entertain another customer. This method probably worked most of the time because her customers were usually horny, drunk, or both.

Chas hadn't had a piece of ass in over a month, and he maintained control because there had been no foreplay. Up and down, side to side, back and forth Linda's cunt gyrated swiftly around his shaft. His full weight settling on her body forced her to slow. Chas rested on his haunches and enjoyed the ride. His long, thick cock was being bombarded beyond belief, but he retained his load, a gift he couldn't explain.

Linda opened her eyes, astonished because this handsome, muscular, young gringo had her impaled and nearly powerless. His striking features and powerful body gave him an authority that countered her plan.

"Come on!" she commanded.

His body mass caused her to slow further. Looking at him defiantly, she gathered her strength, placed her legs around his waist, and energetically propelled her *puka* against him. Chas rode her like a bronco buster and beamed at her stunned glare. Finally tired and breathing heavily, she stopped, grabbed him by the ass, and repeated, "Come on."

As an alpha male, he thwarted her attempt to control him. He dropped to his forearms and rested above her heaving, perspiration-covered breasts. It was his turn. Rocking back and forth inside her slippery channel, he increased his movements until he was firing on all cylinders, like a 50-caliber machine gun. Concentrating and massaging her with long powerful strokes, he stared into her now-accepting eyes and said sarcastically, "Come on."

She enthusiastically lifted her hips to meet his thrusts. He continued plunging into her. With one last shove that looked and felt like the recoil of a 90-millimeter canon, she climaxed and screamed, "¡Si! ¡Si! ¡Si!"

Chas enjoyed the delicious flow of fluids from his throbbing cock. She sighed and tightened her grip under his continuing spasms. He held her securely and didn't let go until his secondary eruptions ceased.

"Come on," she whispered quietly. "Come on. Please?"

His sexual energy spent, he rolled onto his side and she scurried away, leaving behind the odor of sex and a vision of bouncing buns. Who said you could lead a horse to water, but you couldn't make a hormone? Apparently he had done just that.


The lady at the desk stopped him as he left. "Linda said you were *El Toro* in there," she said with a wise smile and a hint of admiration in her voice. "She suggests you return on a Wednesday or Thursday when she's less busy. You'll get a reduced rate and be able to spend more time with her."

"Please tell her I've never had a female so active. Her body and movements gave me great pleasure. She was worth the price."

"Come again soon," the madam cooed. "We appreciate your business."

Chas went to the bar, ordered a Seven and Seven, paid scant attention to the sound of the mariachi band, but he liked the floor show, especially the scantly clad ladies wandering in, around, and between tables.

"Chas!" a loud voice called to him. "Come over here and sit down. We've been wondering what happened to you. Did you get laid?" Mark asked.

"I've been standing at the bar, sipping my drink and watching the floor show."

"Chas, this is María and Silvia. They are Mark and my dates," Paul said, indicating the two of them.

"They were good and only cost three bucks. It's hard to beat a fucking deal like that, if you'll pardon the pun."

Chas smiled, nodded, and said hello to the ladies.

"Who did you spend your time with?" Ben asked.

"Linda."

Both María and Silvia looked startled, smiled broadly, pointed at Chas, and said together, "*¡El Toro!*"

The guys looked at each other and then at the girls. Mark asked, "*El Toro?* What the hell does that mean?"

Maria responded with excitement, "*El Toro,* the bull. Linda has called your friend the bull. To be called *El Toro* is a great compliment because he pleasures all the heifers, and he certainly pleased Linda. She told us that he nearly tore her a new pussy with his prolonged pumping."

"Chas, you have a new nickname, *El Toro,*" Ben said. "I didn't know the three of us were friends with a stallion."

Then all of them were talking and laughing at the same time. Chas planned on taking a lot of razzing from now until the end of their training.

"I know that's real funny, guys, but I'm ready to leave. I got what I came for. I'd like to look around before going back to the hotel."

"Chas, you're a party pooper," Paul said with a meaningful grin. "We just got here. If we stay long enough, I'll be able to take María back to the room again."

Chas chuckled and said jokingly, "Paul, all you're going to do is get drunk and waste your money buying these ladies expensive, watered-down drinks. You'll be lucky if you can get it up again in a week."

Ben and Mark snickered.

"What do you mean? I'm a friend of *El Toro,* the bull, and I'll be ready to get fucked again in minutes."

They all laughed. It seemed as though they had already had enough to drink, but it was hard for some guys to stop once they get started, especially since they hadn't been near booze or women since they arrived at Fort Bliss.

"You guys can stay if you want, but I'm going to go down the street, take a look around, and go back to the hotel. *El Toro* is just about petered out."

They all laughed with him.

"Did you hear that, guys?" Paul asked. "*El Toro,* the bull, is all *petered out.*" He grinned at his own joke.

After a short discussion, it was decided that the three of them were going to stay and meet him back at the hotel.

Chas left San Miguel's about midnight. He wandered down Avenida Juárez, peering into the shops but finding little of interest. As he passed an alleyway, he thought he heard a cry, and instinctively, he ran into the darkness.

He woke with excruciating pain at the back of his head and his left arm and shoulder were sore. Opening his eyes, the vision he saw was the opposite of his agony. The image was a beautiful, oval-shaped, cinnamon face with brown eyes framed in a trellis of flowing black hair. He was either in heaven or hell.

A flashing smile crossed the face as it rose and a low, husky, lightly accented voice said, "Señor Marshall, I'm so glad you're awake."

He noticed as she approached his bed that she was short, petite, and voluptuous. A loose-fitting peasant blouse with a scooped neck covered her considerable assets. Leaning over him, she felt his forehead as for a fever. Her action gave him a glimpse of her plump pendulums. He decided he was in heaven.

"I've been so worried. You've been unconscious for hours."

He tried to speak but only emitted a groan.

"You're hurting and probably dehydrated. I'll get you something for pain and a drink."

As she walked out of the room, he observed her narrow

shoulders and rounded hips. He wondered about her legs. His thoughts were short-lived because of the pain.

His eyes were closed when she returned. She lifted his head with an arm, pressing a breast against his cheek, and offered him a pill and a glass. He slipped the pill between his lips and the fluid flooded his mouth and throat. It was welcome relief but his thoughts were focused on the feel of her flesh against his.

Finally he spoke. "What . . . ?" his voice trailed off.

Hovering over him, she said, "You were mugged in an alley late Friday night, or early Saturday morning. My sister and some friends found you and brought you here. Please drink some more."

He drank and fell asleep, in spite of himself.

When he woke, he was cold, hungry, and his head ached. She was sitting at the foot of the bed, knitting.

"I'm cold," he said.

She was instantly by his side. "I'll get you some broth and tea."

Before leaving, she covered him with another blanket. Hearing conversations from the kitchen, he wondered what had really happened to him, how she knew his name—and why was she alone with him?

To his surprise, Linda returned with a bowl and a coffee mug on a tray.

She placed a second pillow under his head, then spoon-fed him some chicken broth and warm, sweet tea. He gladly accepted the food and beverage and observed her captivating movements as she tended him. Flashes of breasts and the warm food raised his physical and emotional temperature. He was no longer cold and his headache subsided.

"I crushed some aspirin into the soup. I hope it helps with your pain," she said with concern on her face.

Speaking with a weak voice, he said, "It's working. I feel better and I'm no longer cold. May I ask where I am and what I'm doing here?"

"You're in my home. I live here with my sister, Gabriela. Some friends and I found you in an alley on the way home early this morning and brought you here."

"The lady at San Miguel's said you couldn't speak English, but that obviously isn't true."

"That story's a ruse, used to speed up the process. How are you feeling? I'd like to find out if you're as good the second time as the first," she said, allowing her robe to fall to the floor.

Her hair was still damp from a bath or shower and her bodacious body was slick with oil. Gabriela returned to the room and stood beside her; she, too, was nude. Chas was stunned. He was looking at two of the most beautiful and well-built women he had ever seen.

"Last night was for business but today is for my pleasure, our pleasure," she said, nodding to Gabriela.

She tore the blankets from his body. "*El Toro* is limp," she said, joking.

Taking his penis into her hand, she stroked it erect. From behind and above him, Gabriela lowered her breasts to his face and dragged them back and forth sensuously. His body stiffened at the unexpected pleasure and he groaned when Linda kissed the head of his cock and her tongue encircled it. She took his dick deep into her throat and massaged it with her tongue. At the same time Gabriela forced his mouth open with a long, hard nipple.

Linda stroked the length of his erection, while Gabriela continuously filled his mouth with one succulent nipple, then the other. His body was on fire. Linda sucked faster. He licked harder until he was about to explode.

As if by intuition, she stopped and Gabriela stood. He was released momentarily from pleasure and wondered what to expect.

He felt their bodies crawl onto the bed, one from either end. Gabriela's flat stomach passed over his face and chest until she settled her snatch over his face. At the same time, Linda straddled his body. He felt soft hair at the tip of his cock, and the warm walls of her vagina surrounded his penis.

Chas caught his breath as his nose and mouth were stimulated by the smell and taste of a ripe cunt, while muscular coils were wrapped around his cock. He grabbed Gabriela's hips, pulled her closer, raised his head searching for her core, and lifted his hips to increase the stimulation of Linda's pulsating pussy.

He was in heaven. His penis was inflamed by vibrating spirals, while his tongue was feasting on a similar but smaller genital. Linda pumped faster and faster and Chas increased the speed of his tongue. Gabriela's body stiffened and she sighed in pleasure, climaxing. She fell, leaving his face and mouth covered with warm, wet fluids. With Gabriela gone, Linda fell to his chest, placed a luscious treat in his mouth, and, as he sucked, she went wild, caressing his cock with pistonlike regularity. Chas tried to maintain control, but multiple stimulations overtook him. Spitting her nipple from his mouth, he exploded in a volcanolike release. Wave after wave of pleasure shook his body as he erupted again and again into Linda's depths, her loud orgasm followed his.

"*El Toro* . . . *El Toro* . . . *El Toro* . . ." she droned in his ear.

It was dark outside when he awoke. Linda was gone but Gabriela sat at the end of the bed. He observed her through half-closed eyes. She was more beautiful than her sister. They were both well-endowed but Gabriela's appearance was more pleasing.

"What time is it?" he asked.

Startled, she looked up from her knitting and gave him a smile. "It's time for you to eat," she said. "There's a basin of water in the washroom. You can clean up and come to the kitchen."

As she stood and turned, Chas observed a flash of curves and watched her step erotically from the room. He cleaned himself in the rudimentary facilities and hurried to the kitchen. He wanted to be in her company, as soon and as long as possible.

They sat across the table from each other. She had prepared lentil soup with bread and hot tea. He asked her how they knew his name.

"The muggers left your military ID card at the scene," she said. "So we discovered your name, but that's all we know. Tell me about yourself."

Chas told her he was from New York. He talked about his family, his schooling, the fact he had been in the army since October, and at Fort Bliss since early January.

She told him she was nineteen. She and Linda had lost

their parents in a bus accident four years earlier, and Linda had gone into "the business" to support them. Linda made more in one night than Gabriela made in a week working for an import/export company that specialized in trade with U.S. companies. Her work explained the quality of her language abilities.

Finishing their meal, Gabriela cleared and cleaned the kitchen while he watched, fascinated by her elegance and practiced skills.

"I'm feeling better now," he said as she finished. "My head still hurts and I'm sore, but I should be getting to my hotel, My buddies will be wondering where I am."

Gabriela looked disappointed and said, "We were expecting you to stay tonight and go back tomorrow. Linda said she wanted to see you again before you left. Besides, I want you to stay."

She walked to him, took his hands, looked into his eyes, and said in a low, husky voice, "I'd like to know you better. I told Linda, when you were brought here, that you were the most beautiful man I'd ever seen. Ever since we pleasured you this morning, I've been hoping for more."

They kissed. His desire surprised him and he was aware of her warm, firm, but soft body. Her scent was a mixture of food, soap, shampoo, and body odors. Her lips were soft and pliable and tasted of lentil soup. Their embrace lasted a long time and their hands roamed freely over each other's backs. She responded to his gentle, rubbing touch with shivers of delight and he discovered her bra strap.

Excited, he pulled her into his protruding erection and massaged her buns vigorously. She responded by grinding her pelvis into him. They kissed passionately. He forced his tongue into her mouth, savoring the sweetness of her breath and the texture of her tongue. Expertly, he unfastened her bra, picked her up, and carried her toward the bedroom. She redirected him to her room, not Linda's.

Entering the room, his heart was pounding, his breathing was labored, his hands were sweating, and his penis was leaking. Standing her on the floor in the dimly lit room, he slipped her out of her clothes, then stood back and reveled in her beauty and her bounty. She smiled as he stared, and stood holding her hands folded in front of her pubis while he removed his clothes.

"I've dreamed about you since I was a little girl. I've always seen a tall, dark, handsome stranger making love to me. Since I've been a teenager, I've been waiting for that man and it's you. I want to please you because I know you'll please me."

He sat her on the bed and knelt between her legs. Tilting his face toward hers, they kissed, their lips and tongues aflame. He massaged her shoulders and the rounded edges of her breasts. Leaning back, he rubbed his hands lightly over her neck, chest, and the top of her breasts. She sighed and pulled her shoulders back to push her trophies toward him. They were the color of milk chocolate with dark, upright nipples surrounded by lighter-colored areolas. His mouth watered. He used his tongue to wash over and around her breasts and nipples. He took one gently into his mouth. Sucking and licking, he savored her sweetness. With one hand, he rolled the other breast in all directions. His pulse quickened as she quietly groaned. He changed sides and treated her teat like royalty with increasing ardor.

Running his tongue down the valley between her peaks,

he stopped when he reached her pubic hair. Spreading her
legs wider with his head, he nuzzled her wiry, soft fuzz and
the lips of her vulva until they were soaked. His tongue circled her opening, then moved inside probing for her clit.
Like a snake meticulously looking for prey, he rooted until
finding her miniature penis. She gasped.

No longer a random search but now a focused longing,
his broad tongue captured her essence with a frenzied embrace. She grabbed his hair, arched her back, and almost
stood as she reacted to the rapierlike dashing and darting of
his clapper around her organ. Her vaginal fluids increased
and her body shuddered as she succumbed to his ceaseless
stimulations with a deep moan.

"Stop, stop, please stop," she cried, pulling his face from
her. "That was wonderful."

Standing, he moved her body until her head hung over
the edge of the bed. He rubbed his dribbling penis over her
sensuous lips, and pushed forward until her mouth opened
and engulfed him. He groaned at the pleasure and gazed
at her hooters as they hung downward in an unusual but inviting position. Using his hands, he manipulated, rolled,
pushed, and pulled them, attempting to calm the itching of
his palms. Bending to one side, he took one breast into his
mouth, sucking, licking, and running his tongue over and
around her nipple. At the same time, he gently moved his
penis within her fervent mouth and enjoyed the sensations
shooting through his body.

He moved to her other breast and treated it adoringly,
lovingly, reverently, and with increasing passion. The multiple stimulations were incredible and he focused on the strain
in his legs and back to forestall his pending ejaculation.

Standing and pulling himself from her, he marveled at the beauty of her body and the growing fire in his loins.

Returning to her breasts, his hands manipulated and marveled at their softness and smoothness. His desire to become one with her was overwhelming, and her positive, audible, visible responses to his caresses drove him on. Dropping to his elbows and forearms to protect her body from his weight, he nudged her legs apart and his mouth eagerly sought her sexual interior. His tongue went straight to her clit and she moaned unceasingly as he ravaged her. She grabbed him by the ass and pulled him toward her, but stopped short of taking him into her mouth because her body experienced a series of convulsions, and she screamed in pleasure.

"I'm ready! I'm ready! Give it to me! Give it to me!" she begged.

Chas spun her like a top and pulled her to the edge of the bed. She appeared shocked, with tight lips and a stunned look in her eyes. He spread her legs, lifted them to his shoulders, and then inch-by-inch penetrated her until he could go no deeper. She swooned when his penis contacted her core.

"Stroke me! Stroke me!" she said, urging him on.

The walls of her canal enclosed his probe and squeezed tight. Stooping and holding her by the hips, he thrust slowly and incrementally increased his speed. Gabriela groaned with each shove and her moaning never stopped. He pumped faster and harder. Her constant cry, the grimace on her face, and the swaying of her breasts in rhythm with their movements energized him. Physically and emotionally, he was approaching his limit.

In a crescendo of pleasure, she raised her pelvis to meet his thrust and sobbed, "Now! Now! Now! I want it now!"

He continued until, with one last shove, he released his pent-up passion in a series of spasms. He flooded her fissure with fluid and emitted a howl from deep within his being. The flow was indescribable ecstasy. He pulled her closer because he wasn't ready to leave the comfort of her body.

After a long time being entombed, he fell to the bed and they cuddled, indulging in the afterglow of mutual satisfaction. They fell asleep, entwined in each other's arms.


It was six A.M. Linda had had a long, busy night, more tricks and pricks than she could remember. She was sore and tired but anxious to see Chas again. Strange that neither he nor Gabriela were in the living room. She looked in her bedroom but they weren't there. *Maybe he left to return to the States,* she thought. Looking down the hall, she saw a light in Gabriella's room. Quietly opening the door, she looked in. Startled, she stepped back, then silently, in her bare feet, strode to the side of the bed. Gabriela, with a smile on her face, lay naked, her head pillowed on Chas's arm. Her shapely derriere was tucked into his crotch like part of a jigsaw puzzle and his left hand cupped her breast as a basket holds a melon. Chas's handsome face was buried in Gabriela's mane of black hair and the lean muscles of his body were articulated by the shadows cast by the muted light.

Looking at them, she was disappointed and angry. Disappointed because she craved his gorgeous body and penile skills. Angry because he had despoiled her sister. Disappointed because she remembered his large dick impaling her on the cot at San Miguel's, holding her in place and bringing her to an unwanted, unwelcome, unexpected but incredible orgasm. Angry because she could understand why a guy the caliber of Chas wouldn't want a *puta* when he could have a young girl like Gabriela. Disappointed because she remembered the unexpected, exhilarating thrill of the desired orgasm he had brought her with his throbbing cock and succulent mouth. Angry because her sister, who she loved more than anyone in the world, had stolen him from her. Disappointed because she had plotted to have him waylaid and taken to her home. Angry because her plan had not worked as she wanted.

With tears in her eyes, she backed from the room, silently and solemnly. Through a mist she gazed at the serenity of the lovers and the beauty of their entangled bodies. Thinking sadly, she would always remember his looks, his talent, and his first words: "Are you available?"

# *Borderline*

## Kim Rose

Lorna Landry has never been fucked like this before. In all of her thirty-one years, she has never been lifted from her feet and placed down gently on her back to await the next levels of stimulation. Never been thrown down forcefully in anticipation of a good, rough screw, for that matter. Strong hands have never massaged and cultivated a channel from her scalp to the spaces between her toes. Never has an eager tongue followed the same path. It's a shame that wet, hungry lips have never met the backs of her kneecaps, meandering north like a balloon in the wind. There has never been much activity on Lorna's lean thighs, much less a raging hard-on pressing urgently into her soft flesh.

Can you believe that a confident scholar like Lorna, who has penned and been published amongst the highest-profile academics, could not before this moment translate into words the feeling of her generous breasts feeling small and secure within the palms of a man's insistent hands? Had never even considered that her nipples could fit so neatly in the webs between his fingers? That there might be a flavor to the underside of them, and that he might hunger for it? Might beg to taste her inside and out? But this is exactly what she imagines.

"Lorna."

This feels so primal, so jungle, that the rumbling down deep in Lorna's gut warns of a devastating storm. Sure enough, that hurricane tongue sends her ducking for cover, desperately awaiting the heavy downpour like the barren Mojave. Calling her name like the howling category-5 wind.

"Lorna! Damn it, Lorna!"

And just like that, it is gone. Lorna is used to falling short of a climax, but this time feels especially real. Unforgiving.

"Jesus Christ, Lorna! Focus! If you are not up to the job, then please step aside and let a competent photog relieve you of your duties."

Today, Lorna is among over fifty zealous do-gooders who show up on Arizona Avenue before the rays of dawn. They are self-appointed and self-righteous, and stopping the employment of illegal immigrants is their cause. Tucked away in high-end haciendas beyond the city limits of San Diego, they are mostly white-collar with white skin, and that's how they'd like to keep their neighborhoods, and this country for that matter. Among them are Lorna and her husband, who, like the rest, are committed to the cause and obsessed with the pursuit of national recognition.

Across the street an unsuspecting white cargo van pulls into a liquor store parking lot promptly at eight A.M. Within seconds, the vehicle is surrounded on all sides by a swarm of brown men looking for work, eyes as intense as their heavy accents and sun-baked skin.

The crowd looms even larger through the lens of the MiniDV camcorder Lorna has trained on the scene. In the past year she has seen hundreds of these men: harmless, indigent congregations of carpenters, landscapers, and cleaners paid to do the work that not even the poorest Yankees will accept. Truth be told, Lorna can't tell one from the next. To her, they are little more than objects to be captured and studied. So every day she stands video vigil like an obsessed voyeur, and records the every move of the "undesirable foreigners," the monotonous mass of paper-bag complexions.

But this one is a god among men. He stands a full foot above the heads of the others. He is fresh from the border, Lorna figures, on the scene now less than two weeks.

His plaid cutoff shirt is merely a distracting prop for sturdy shoulders and rippling arms that look capable of sup porting two men on each. His tan pants, the only pair he seems to own, are tattered at the knee and frayed at the hem, bulging in the middle. Lorna can't help pulling in for a tight shot of his mighty knot. She has been transfixed by this god since the moment he emerged on the dayworker scene.

Lorna can feel the hot breath spewing from her husband, Tom's, wiry lips, even through the shiny red bullhorn.

"Keep up! It's almost showtime!" he roars. "You think you can handle that?"

She nods, still preoccupied, disoriented, and horny. He turns around, his eyes following hers to the tall, striking figure across the street. He places a finger on her chin, guiding her eyes reluctantly back to him. She gathers herself, not even noticing that Tom continues to berate her to the amusement of their colleagues.

"Let's rock and roll, soldiers," calls Lorna's lookout. "The United States border needs us."

Before Lorna can pull back to a wider shot, focus, and press the red record button, the white van is almost totally encircled by the ambitious mob. Vigilante feet cross the street to the liquor store parking lot, anxiously approaching the first ambush of the week.

"Sir, did you know that hiring illegal immigrants is against the law? This is what you're here for, right? Prowling for illegal dayworkers?"

Spit splatters with the accusations intended for the van's driver. Angry, beet-red fingers claw at the windows, pressing down hard as the confused driver rushes to roll them back up.

Defeated brown faces sense what is happening. "*¡Hibridos!* Gringos!"

Lorna is a step behind the mêlée, capturing it all on the tape her group is desperate to sell to CNN. Her normally steady hands are suddenly wobbly, her vision unfocused, rattled, and hyperaware of the powerful presence she knows is hidden somewhere in the mix. She follows closely behind her husband, the creator and star of this spectacle, making sure he appears towering by her low angles, his voice heard clearly above all others.

"We demand that you leave the premises immediately, and if you select any workers from this illegal Mexican labor pool"—Tom shouts, briefly staring into Lorna's video camera—"we have captured time-stamped video images of you, your license plates and, essentially, your intentions, which we will not hesitate to share with federal law enforcement!"

Actually, Lorna hasn't yet managed to get a shot of the tags. She isn't even certain she got a clear shot of the driver, who is now covering his face with a newspaper. At the moment, all she can see is the sea of callused worker hands raised in protest, her own fingers shaking and clammy. She does manage to see the guy who throws the first punch, a matter of inches from her nose.

Her body is rocked from one end of the liquor store parking lot to the next, as fists and fury fly freely around the white van. The driver is pulled out, or perhaps he hops out, incensed. Either way, he finds his demise on the ground beside Lorna's husband, Tom, who caught a bad one from a stocky brown gardener in chalky work boots. Tom cradles his nose and his shiny bullhorn like a newborn, he himself folded in a fetal flop.

Panicked, Lorna takes two steps back before slamming into a brick wall, her camera plunging to the asphalt. She had no idea she was so close to the storefront that will serve as her refuge, but she quickly bends down to scoop up her camera and take cover before she ends up on the ground with a broken nose, too.

Her hands meet with his—pale against bronze—and she retracts, leaping to her feet, much in the way her heart also dives from her chest.

"You thieving wetback! That is American property and I will have your filthy ass back in the bush so fast, heads are gonna roll!" Her body is convulsing violently, undermining her feigned authority. She resents knowing that there is fear evident in her eyes, and avoids connecting with his. Her head is pounding wildly, and yet there is a curious pool gathering between her thighs.

He stands up slowly, and casually takes a step back. The camera's knowing red eye stares up at him, yet he is neither nervous nor self-conscious. He is amused, and insanely intuitive, fluently interpreting the implications of Lorna's unstable knees, shallow breaths, light perspiration, crimson complexion, and involuntary tremors. As the sun stretches in the east, there is a celestial erection stirring in the west. And Lorna Landry has it all on tape.

"Attack me again, *amigo,* and I will have your dirty Mexican mug on every news channel in America," Lorna warns, fumbling both her words and her camera.

She quickly turns to run inside and notices the building is another twenty feet away. Then she scans the brown-skinned tower standing before her, smells his clean, leafy scent on her skin, and realizes he is the brick house she slammed into, not the building. She is swiftly panicked, the mob assault around her is suddenly silent, and she does her best to escape it.

Not sure of whether to run back across the street or inside, her feet travel like a magnet toward the beautiful, dark statue, who is watching her think. She floats without breathing, and he subtly pushes out his chest, brushing against Lorna's flushed red face as she passes. This is the same shirtless torso she has spent the last two weeks watching glisten and bake in the California sun. She has always been content with the view from behind the camera, leaving no inch of the sculpted foreign beauty unnoticed. Until today.

She gasps. She is on fire in that split second of contact,

and she is finally behind the door of the liquor store, wishing she were a misty cloud disappearing into his sunrise.

There is a bell above the door that jingles upon her entry into the liquor store, signifying her presence to the worker behind the plate-glass counter and signaling Lorna's reemergence from her fantasy. She is out of breath and rattled, and her first instinct is to lock the door behind her. The stern eye of the brown man behind the plate-glass counter warns otherwise. Instead Lorna stalks past rows of tobacco and spirits, and finds refuge in the last aisle. Her eyes dart wildly around her until they settle on a short bottle of white rum. With her camera squeezed under her arm, she opens the bottle and swigs long, a trail of fire winding down past her heaving chest. She drinks until tears form at the corners of her eyes and her sinuses clear. She can still hear the fighting outside and is worried for her husband. Worried about their colleagues and their cause. But she is more concerned about satisfying the battle raging below her belt.

The deep desire pulsating throughout her body, coupled with the pressure rising in her ears, drowns out the sound of the jingle above the door.

This time Lorna is relaxed, oddly calmed by the anticipation. The sudden seizure between her thighs is like an instinct, a sordid gut feeling of sorts. She feels him before he ever appears.

And appear he does, in all his brazen glory. He approaches Lorna in the last aisle of the shady liquor store with the swaggering stride of a sexual savior. Lorna Landry's prayers are about to be answered.

She splashes the remains of the rum at him. Trying to buy time. Acting out. Resentful of the control he possesses without provocation. Rebelling against the sexual Svengali that she is desperate to follow. He is unfazed. He stops just inches from her, the insteps of his work boots flanking her sensible flats. He lifts the back of his hand to his nose, inhales the brutal poison, wipes it on the back of his fading tan pants. Takes the bottle from her hands and places it on the nearest shelf. Sets her camera, still recording, beside it.

Lorna Landry has never felt a harder body in all of her thirty-one years. She is not a small woman, and she has never been so easily handled. When he pulls her forcefully to him by the waistband of her skirt, her body floats, without her feet ever moving. Instead, it is her hands that are immediately in motion. Her eager caresses of his solid chest and arms quickly turn to insistent and urgent clutches under his T-shirt. Her fingers glide incredulously over ripples and waves of flesh that far surpass even her wildest imagination.

He stands motionless for one moment more, allowing Lorna a decent introduction to his physical supremacy. Then, without warning, he cuffs her pale wrists in one hand and holds them tight. Her breath is arrested, the unending stream of wet desire confessing a list of transgressions and guilt, all the way down her legs. His lips are hot and cold, satisfying the temperament of her barren nipples. Her bra is pulled down, an afterthought, his hands effectively replacing it. Then his tongue goes beyond the surface, tracing over the lines of deep-set yearning and deprivation developed over the years, effortlessly erasing them.

Lorna's free hands wander south of the border, first to the enticing round ass that fills out his fading tan pants, then to explore the emerging ethnic invasion behind his zipper.

She fumbles, either afraid to unearth his glory or terrified not to. He pushes her colorless, idle hands out of the way and pulls down the zipper and relieves the button with one flick of his hands—hands that now carefully clear a space right there on the wine shelf.

Without warning, and with Lorna's full breast firmly clamped in his teeth, he swoops her up by the waist and sets her down like a spirit on display. Cold, dusty, cheap table wine flanks one leg, a fine Northern California cabernet sauvignon the other. Lorna is keenly aware of the duality. She is at once an esteemed anthropology scholar of merit, and a split-legged slut in a flowery skirt with her pristine and patriotic panties pulled low.

He couldn't be bothered to take them off. He simply slides a hand inside, shifts them to the side of her drenched lips, and enters with a force so jarring that even he pauses. She welcomes his generous girth with tight but open arms. Yet he senses that he has many walls to knock down and he immediately sets about the task.

Lorna's legs attach themselves to his active waist. Her ankles hook like a bra behind him at the exact moment that he finally unlatches hers. Her heavy breasts weigh on his chest, her nipples screaming for attention. She lifts her shirt and he wastes no time answering them back.

Her arms slide down from his neck. The intensity of his deep thrusts cause her to mark his sprawling bronze back with bloody scratches, sanguine symbols of her primal pleading.

"Fuck me," she repeats in his ear. Over and over, each time a reincarnation of a new appeal.

"Fuck me."

Inquiry. "Fuck me?"

Command. "Fuck me, you bastard! Fuck me like Cinco de Mayo, you son of a bitch!"

Each time a step higher, an inch closer to her delicate borderline.

The deep desire increasing with every strong stroke coupled with the pressure of the tip of his manhood colliding with ease against her G-spot drowns out the sound of the jingle above the door. But not the voice that follows.

"Lorna!"

Before she becomes tense, before she can open her eyes and spy the tiny red spider crawling on the rusty shelf just beside her bare thigh, before another drop of sweat can drip from her bangs, before she spits another explicit curse . . . brawny, bronze hands lift her modest ass up off the shelf. He holds her up above the height of the highest bottles, his mighty erection pointed skyward, only a breath away from her raw lips, and slams her down hard back onto him. And holds her there for an extended stay.

Lorna has no words. Her mouth and eyes are as wide as her legs. Her inside walls leap uncontrollably around his exquisite dick and an involuntary tremor sends her foot flying, kicking a robust jug of Carlo Rossi Chablis to the cement floor.

"Lorna, are you in here?" calls Tom, limping into the last aisle of the liquor store. He is bruised, his clothes torn. He walks down the empty last aisle past aging bottles of Northern California cabernet sauvignon, in search of his wife, broken glass and a pool of white wine beneath his sensible loafers. Tom inhales a vaguely familiar scent, and follows it to the open door at the end of the back aisle.

• • •

It is clear that Lorna Landry can no longer focus on the job at hand. She can't seem to remember to press record on the MiniDV camera. She can barely drag herself out of bed for the eight A.M. vigilante call times. She hasn't eaten a full meal in weeks. Not since the Bronze Bomber filled her to capacity. The withdrawal is unbearable, and her husband, Tom, takes notice.

He knows Lorna better than anyone. He believes he knows her better than she knows herself. An arrogant and haughty asshole, yes, but Tom has reason. He plucked Lorna from relative graduate school obscurity and molded her into a scholar after his own heart. He intuitively pegged her for an insecure and self-conscious young woman in need of direction. He promptly assumed the role, under the guise of academic advisor and mentor, crafting a secret map for her future, then carefully pulling the strings as she traveled along.

It never occurred to Lorna that her success was prefabricated. It never occurred to her that Tom isn't the man of her dreams, despite being twice her age and physically unappealing. They both know their limits. The roles in their marriage are clearly defined. It was never about passion and attraction. Tom would never be able to satisfy her sexually, that much he always knew. Their arrangement is about success and accolades. And together they amassed many.

They are on the brink of national, perhaps international recognition. Their vigilante efforts and staunch stance on illegal immigration are catching on. Small news clippings are now turning into features and radio interviews. Any activity on Capitol Hill involving immigration translates into attention on their cause from local media. They know it is only a matter of time before the coveted elite media like CNN and the *New York Times* take notice.

So when Tom notices for the first time that his young wife is not responding to his prompts, that she is exhibiting signs of weakness, he takes action. He immediately removes her from photography duty and assigns her busywork. On this day, while Tom is out chasing down illegals, he sends her on an elaborate errand, which takes her to the outskirts of town, where a white woman driving solo in a luxury car is as conspicuous as a carcass to a vulture.

And there he is. Lorna sees his back first. Wide and sculpted. Then his ass. Rounded with muscles and draped in faded tan. He stands among a small group of white men this time. Employers, Lorna reasons. She sits in her car across the street, watching him, the task that sent her there suddenly a distant memory. Fear of her surroundings, gone. She has no way of knowing that Tom is her ubiquitous benefactor, even now. Her two fingers sinking deep inside her, bathed in her own sweet water before taking wide, lingering laps around her pulsing pleasure point, is her only urgent concern.

He is soon her full-time endeavor.

They fuck in her car, in dark theaters and well-lit parking lots, in Balboa Park, on the same countertop where Tom neatly cuts his morning bananas, in her two-car garage, in the shower of her guest bathroom, on the toilet seat of the master bath. But her favorite place is, by far, the bed she shares unceremoniously with her husband. That makes her feel like a woman, bound by strong hands and begging for mercy, her face buried in her own pillows. At night, when it's just her and Tom, she lies on her stomach and defiantly circles her own throbbing clit with her power hand draped in a tiny Mexican flag.

At first, Lorna's instinct is to inspect his brown back intently for bruises and bug bites. Migratory scars, outward signs of a hard, indigent life. But beyond the work gear, he is groomed meticulously. A cultural anomaly, she thinks. He is more frat boy than farm boy. And what is that fragrance? Her nose had been trained to expect a nauseous mingling of sweat, soil, and *sofrito*. But he smells oddly cosmopolitan. Manly.

She forbids him from speaking Spanish in her presence. It is like fingernails on a chalkboard to her ears. So she does all of the postcoital talking while he listens intently. She sits for hours, telling him secrets of an unfulfilling marriage, of waning interest in her academic career, of longing to retire early to the expanse of the Rocky Mountains, of the complex and corrupt underbelly of American immigration politics. He sits perched, staring a hole through her, and she can't help singing like a mariachi. It's all a joke to Lorna, and she laughs long and hard after every long and hard prompt from the mighty illegal pipe.

Lorna is content with these untranslated confessions. The release is what she has been craving. Before now she was sure that presenting research to a group of receptive scholars was her calling. Now she's certain she is at her absolute best perched on all fours with a tongue wagging, lathering her from top to bottom. She now straddles a big dick with pride and confidence, having never even seen one up close before then. She devours it at random intervals while riding, videotapes it from every sordid angle.

Instead of restoring focus and order to Tom's self-inter-
ests, the sex sends Lorna spiraling with disinterest. Again at
his wit's end, Tom takes action.

"Good afternoon. United States Customs and Border Pro-
tection. Pedro Hernández González speaking. How may I
help you?"

"Pete, how the heck are you? It's Tom Landry calling."

"Tom Landry, as in the legendary football coach? Or Tom
Landry, as in my old buddy, the prick who still owes me a
beer?"

"Well, Petey, my friend, I do believe that several beers
may be in order after you pull a few strings for me," Tom
responds with a chuckle.

"And I was hoping to get my kid a signed Cowboys jersey
or something." Pedro laughs. "Long time, Tom, my friend.
Good to hear from you. How are things on your end? I hear
you and the troops have been busy."

"You know better than anyone that keeping our borders
safe is a twenty-four-hour job, and one that all Americans
ought to take seriously. That's actually why I'm calling. I have
a tip for you. Can I stop by?"

Tom noticed the Bronze Bomber around the same time
Lorna did. He stood out, so tall and handsome. He had the
physical qualities of a leader, despite his observant, passive
presence. Tom sensed he might be a distraction. The mild, distant stirring in his own loins were all the proof he needed.

Tom slips a glossy 8-inch by 10-inch photo of him into a
large manila envelope and makes the half-hour drive over to
Pedro's office in fifteen minutes.

"What, were you calling me from downstairs, Tom?" Pedro says, welcoming his old buddy into his wood-paneled workspace. "That was quick, brother."

"Well, it's kind of important, Pete. And I have to be over at the university within the hour."

"Busy, busy, busy. Well, you have good timing, and I have good news. You just missed a guy from the *Times*."

"*New York Times*? Who? Why was he here?" Tom asks incredulously, standing up from his chair almost as soon as he sits.

"Doing a story or something. Heard all about you. I told him you'd be here, but he said he'd give you a call and set something up." Pedro slides a business card across the table to Tom. The raised black script is like a hypnotic swinging pendulum before him. This is it. The moment Tom Landry has been waiting for. The national spotlight. Attention that will catapult him to the steps of Capitol Hill along with the nation's elite advisors and scholars.

"David Rodríguez," Tom reads out loud. "General Assignment Reporter."

"I mean, he just left. I'm surprised you didn't run into him on your way up here."

"Jesus. No, I didn't see anyone," Tom says, folding down the window blind to look out into the parking lot.

"Well, he said he was gonna get in touch with you. I'd guess either today or tomorrow. He seemed urgent to wrap up his work here. Speaking of which, there's some work you need me to handle for you, Tommy?"

Still slightly preoccupied, Tom hands Pedro the photo. "Illegal. Pretty dangerous guy from what I can gather. An organizer. Possibly violent. Drugs, I'm guessing."

Pedro pauses to raise an eyebrow. Opens the envelope. "This isn't your guy."

"That's him, Pete. Looks like a goddamn movie star, doesn't he? Good news is, he hasn't been here long. A month maybe."

"Where did you get your info, Tom?"

"Very reliable source."

"Drop your source. They're not as reliable as you think."

"Okay, Pete. I admit, I hired the guy myself for a little landscaping in my front yard. Curb appeal, you know."

"No, Tom. Seriously. You have the wrong guy." Pedro slides the photo back across the table to Tom. "This guy in the photo is David Rodríguez, from the *Times*."

"What the hell are you saying, Pete?"

"I'm saying, you've got the wrong Mexican thug. This is the guy who was just sitting in the chair you're sitting in right now. Funniest thing, too, he's not even Mexican. He's Puerto Rican. From New York City. The Bronx. Doesn't speak a word of Spanish. Works with an interpreter, can you believe that?"

Tom and Lorna Landry finally make it into the *New York Times*. And CNN. And a host of other international media. Just as they had dreamed. Lorna's naked breasts even make their debut on several corners of the Internet. It is all she needs to finally cut the strings on her marriage and wander the expanse of the Rocky Mountains. A woman with her future in her own hands, and at this very moment, Lorna's own future is situated between her legs.

# An Even Swap Ain't No Swindle

Zane

## TAYE

I have never been a brother to freak out over women and be ready to fall down at their feet. On the contrary, women have always fallen down at my feet. From the day I realized that I had a larger dick than most men, I have used that to my advantage. It got me hired at many a job. I would only apply for positions with a female executive in charge. There was not a doubt in my mind that I could get them all in the sack, even the married ones. Hell, I even fucked a couple of devout lesbians. Yes, I brought them back to the dick, if only temporarily.

Then the shit went and happened. I met Alicia Coles when I was twenty-seven, got pussy whipped, and married her. Ten long years went by without me cheating or really even looking at another female in a sexual way. My wife was the shit and I knew it. Tall, with legs for days, smooth, ebony skin, perfect teeth, breasts that fit perfectly in the palms of my hands, and an ass that would make men cry. She was mine and I was proud as all hell to have her on my arm whenever we went out.

At one point, I got a bit possessive. She stopped being an animal in the bedroom and all kinds of shit started floating through my head. We had this contractor doing work in our basement at the time and I was convinced that Alicia was fucking him. We had met him when we were coming out of Home Depot one day and he handed us a flyer. I am not the type to be fixing shit around the house and was griping that day because we had to go get a new handle and lever for our master bathroom toilet. When he handed Alicia the flyer, I grabbed it, got excited, and immediately asked if he could come by and give us a quote on some drywall work we needed to have done.

I should have known something was up because he handed Alicia the flyer and not me. He was trying to mack and I never saw it coming. I called home one day and Alicia rushed me off the phone, stating that she was in the middle of making that fool a sandwich. I dropped everything that I was doing and sped home like a bat out of hell. When I got there, that maggot was sitting at the kitchen counter—on my favorite fucking barstool—and eating my bread, my ham, and my cheese. Alicia was bent over the counter in a skimpy pair of shorts and a baby-doll tee that had her nipples standing at attention. I busted in there like I was Five-O and confronted them. They both laughed in my face.

He left and it took Alicia all night to convince me that nothing was going on between them. She gave me head until I felt like I was dead. I had no idea my wife could suck a dick so damn well. Like the typical man, instead of being elated that she was going to town on me like that, I was upset and thinking that she had learned some new tricks from ole boy.

It took hiring a private investigator to follow her for two weeks before I believed that Alicia was faithful. It was around that same time that I started thinking about cheating for the first time during our marriage. My business partner, Michael, had met this chick—a Latina—at a business convention in Denver. They say it is cold in Denver but his hotel room must have been on fire because after a three-day week end, he was so sprung that he brought her back home with him to Maryland.

Her name was Marissa and she had it going on. There was just something about her that made my dick hard every time I laid eyes on her. She was petite, no more than five feet, with small tits and a round ass. The way she dressed was erotic; the way she spoke was erotic; the way she smiled was erotic. Shit, the way she did everything was erotic.

Now Michael and I had been friends for a long time. We rose through the ranks together at an investment banking firm and then ventured out on our own as partners. We had done extremely well for ourselves during the four years we had been in business. Michael changed women like he changed his drawers—until that weekend in Denver. She must have laid that pussy on him something fierce because he had sworn that hell would freeze over before he ever became serious about a woman. They had been shacking up ever since, but he was still holding out on the marriage thing. He was a child of divorce and he was determined to never do two things, get married or have kids.

Alicia and I tried to have children but she miscarried twice and we decided that the pain was not worth it. I could not stand to see the agony she was put through and I never wanted to face that again, so I had a vasectomy. Maybe one day we would adopt, but either way, she was the love of my life. Even though I loved Alicia more than life itself, I still had these intense fantasies about Marissa. I would have done anything to fuck her, just one time, to see if she could live up to my expectations.

## ALICIA

Taye was so naïve, or simply believed that he was so fine and so sexy that I would stay faithful. Do not get me wrong; I tried. His arrogance drove me into the arms of another man, not the sex, because that was on point. We met Brian at the same time, at the Home Depot, when he handed me a flyer about his contracting business. Taye thought he was too cute, or too good, to do anything around the house so I convinced him to hire Brian. One day I thought we were busted. Taye came home and found us in the kitchen. We played it off but Brian had been going to town on my pussy when we heard the garage door open and Taye's car pulling in. That man could eat the lining out of a pussy and my clit had never been so sore.

Taye hired a private investigator to follow me and had no clue that I was on to him. For a couple of weeks I led that detective on a wild goose chase, but made sure that I gave no appearance that something was out of sync. Men still do not realize that women are better cheaters. We are always con-sciously aware of what we are risking. I loved Taye but there was something missing and after my two miscarriages, we

did not have the same closeness that we'd always had before.

Truth be told, there was another issue. Taye's business
partner, Michael, brought this woman named Marissa back
with him from a business trip and they started living together. She was nice enough but she was also gorgeous and
Taye could not keep his eyes off her. I knew that he had always had a thing for Latin women. He had dated them ex-
clusively until he met me. Because we spent so much time
together as couples, I could tell that the attraction was mutual. I did not like it; I did not like it at all.

However, who was I to talk? Even though Taye had a
wandering eye, I definitely had a wandering pussy. Brian was
not my only affair; far from it. There was this dude named
Kenny whom I met at the grocery store. It is a shame that I
could not even go to a store like Home Depot or Safeway
without trolling for dick. Ladies, those are some of the best
places to find a good dick, while you are shopping for a
dozen eggs or some lightbulbs.

Now Kenny was serious about his shit. Since we had met
at the grocery store, I related to him that I had always wanted
to re-enact that scene from *Sea of Love* where Ellen Barkin
showed up at this grocery store to meet Al Pacino with nothing but a trench coat on. Kenny met me at the Safeway and I
waited for him in the produce section. While I squeezed some
melons, he squeezed mine and then fingered me while I was
putting collard greens in a plastic bag. When we got up to the
register, I couldn't resist being bad. I told the male cashier to
take a whiff and held Kenny's fingers up to his nose. He was a
young man, probably a college student, and his eyes lit up

when he recognized the scent. If I ever tried to do something like that with Taye, he would have a fucking fit.

Kenny and I left Safeway and went to Watkins Park. It was in November and they had already put up the Festival of Lights for Christmas. We paid our five dollars to drive through the breathtakingly beautiful display. All the cars were driving through there extremely slowly and while Kenny drove at a snail's pace, I sucked his dick. Up and down my head went, taking him into my throat like a bobblehead doll. I would sit up every now and again to see the displays, like Santa Claus playing basketball or tossing a ball with a reindeer. I love being naughty.

My affair with Kenny lasted a few months, until I tired of him as I had with Brian. I still fucked my husband, or fed him, as I liked to call it. My sex was his medicine. Part of me felt a tinge of guilt, but the other part figured that he was cheating as well, especially when he came up with some off-the-wall shit involving Michael and Marissa.


## TAYE

I came up with the idea one day while Michael and I were playing racquetball. I blurted it out while the ball was in the air halfway between us and he missed the next shot.

"How would you like to swap women for one night?" I asked nonchalantly.

Before the ball could even hit the floor, he said, "What did you just say?"

"Haven't you ever wanted to fuck Alicia?"

He paused. "Alicia's gorgeous, but she's also your wife. I would never disrespect you like that, man."

I looked him straight in the eyes. "What if I didn't think it was disrespectful? What if I was willing to let you fuck her?"

Michael chuckled. "And you expect me to let you fuck Marissa in exchange?"

"Yeah, something like that. After all, an even swap ain't no swindle."

"Listen to the two of us, talking about 'letting' someone fuck our women. They do have rights, you know?"

I shrugged. "True. They would definitely have to go along with it."

"Have you spoken to Alicia about this?" Michael asked, meaning that he was beginning to feel me on the prospect.

"Not yet. I wanted to discuss it with you first," I replied. "If you're not interested, there's no point in talking to Alicia."

"You do realize that Alicia might divorce you behind some shit like that?" Michael shook his head. "I'm not sure Marissa would do it. She's pretty caught up."

"She looks at me," I said. "I can tell that she's attracted to me."

Michael looked angry and then laughed. "We are two arrogant motherfuckers, you know that? We both think we're God's gift to women."

"Hey, whoever said God couldn't hand out two gifts?"

Michael and I both laughed and exchanged high fives. We decided to think about it for a few days and see where that left us. However, I knew what I wanted and thought that I might be able to convince Alicia to do it.

That night I brought Alicia dinner in bed—her favorite. From our first date, I had determined that she loved Spanish food. Her grandmother was from Spain, so that explained it. Even though she grew up in a household that served both soul food and Spanish food—her mother being African-American and her father being Hispanic—she leaned toward tapas and paella. That night I had stopped by her favorite restaurant and brought home some gazpacho *andaluz,* spinach with pine nuts, fish in salsa *verde,* and *churros con chocolate.*

She had been through a long day at the office so I gave her a foot massage while she ate. Then I sucked her toes one by one. I love Alicia's toes; they're beautiful and succulent. I enjoy doing anything that gives her pleasure. After she finished eating, she stared at me and asked, "You going to give me some of that Daddy Dick tonight?"

Damn, nothing could get my dick harder faster than Alicia talking dirty to me. In the beginning of our marriage, that was an obstacle for her to overcome. Over time, she had learned to talk nasty, but it was a rare occasion when she actually did it.

She sat up on the bed and pulled her cashmere sweater over her head, exposing the lovely white lace bra underneath. The way white looked on her chocolate skin was such a turn-on.

"My breasts have been sore all day," she said. "They need to be sucked. You going to suck them for me, Daddy?"

"I'll suck whatever you need sucked," I said. "I already did the toes."

She giggled. "And you did a great job. That's what made me so damn horny."

That's when I attacked her, on our bed. I pulled her pants off, along with her tights, and was sucking on her pussy in less than thirty seconds. She pulled my hands up to her breasts, where she had popped them out of the bra, and I caressed them. Alicia's moans are an art form in themselves. Her moans are the most erotic thing I have ever heard. While I was eating her, I thought about her moaning like that for Michael and it almost made me sick. Was I really prepared to share her just so I could get a shot at Marissa?

The entire time that Alicia was sucking my dick, then riding my dick that night, I kept imagining her doing those things to Michael and him licking and sucking all over my wife. It was not a visual that I wanted, but I realized that you only live once, and it had been years since I had touched another woman. I did not want to cheat behind her back, and besides, Marissa was the only woman I was attracted to, outside of Alicia. In order to get to her, it would have to be a trade. Michael was supposed to be discussing it with Marissa that same night, so I knew that I had to keep my word.

"Alicia," I whispered, right before she dozed off after getting her fulfillment from "Daddy Dick."

"Yes, baby," she replied.

"I need to ask you something."

"What, Taye?"

"Michael and I have been talking and . . ."

"And what?" Alicia lifted her head off my chest so she could look me in the eyes. "And what? What's wrong?"

"Promise me that you won't get upset."

"I promise," she said way too quickly, without having a clue about what I was about to say.

"We've been together for a long time, and you know I love you, right?"

"Yes, right down to my stanky drawers." She laughed. "You and Michael have been talking about how much you love me?"

"That, and some other things."

"Like what?"

"Like the possibility of us switching partners for one night."

"Are you out of your fucking mind?" Alicia lashed out at me. "No, you did not just ask me to fuck your friend. Aw, I get it. You want to fuck that bitch so you're willing to trade me off for her ass!"

"It's not like that, Alicia."

"Then what is it like, Taye? Explain this shit to me because from where I'm sitting, that's exactly what the deal is."

I sighed and tried to think of a way to keep my marriage together. I had a feeling that it might be over. Alicia confirmed that when she said, "If you want to fuck Marissa, why don't you just marry her ass? Michael's only shacking up with her, so she's available. Go trade up, motherfucker! You conceited bastard!"

Alicia punched me in the mouth and then kept on and on until we ended up grudge fucking to ward off disaster. After we had finished our second round of sex for the evening, Alicia shocked me.

She said, "If you really want to do as you mentioned, I'll do it." Then she did not speak another word. I fell asleep with a huge grin on my face.

## ALICIA

When Taye asked me if I would fuck Michael, I almost creamed in my pants. He had no idea what a huge favor he was doing for me. I had wanted to fuck Michael for a long time. If things had been different, I might have been married to Michael instead of Taye. Still, I had to make it look good, so I threw a minitantrum, seemed insulted, and then, after he fucked me real hard, I "reluctantly" agreed to lay bare my soul and fuck his best friend.

They decided that Michael would come over to our house and Taye would go over to theirs so that us women could feel more comfortable in our own beds. I broke out the champagne for Michael, put on some sexy Jamaican music, and waited for him on the sofa in the family room.

"Hello, Alicia."

His deep, sexy voice woke me up. I sat up on my elbows and stared at him. He looked scrumptious in a navy linen suit and leather sandals. He was tall, dark-skinned, and had a neatly groomed goatee that I had often imagined rubbing against the inside of my thighs while he ate me out.

"Hey, Michael."

He came closer to me, but hesitated. "Are you sure you want to do this? I can leave, if you want. It's not too late."

I patted the space beside me on the sofa. "Have a seat."

Once he sat down, I could smell his Burberry cologne, the same cologne that I had imagined licking off his body over and over again.

"Michael, I have to be honest with you. When Taye first approached me about this swap thing, I was not as upset as I pretended to be. If he is stupid enough to let me fuck you just so he can get some other woman's ass, then that's his problem. I don't mean to talk down about Marissa. You ob viously care about her, but they have been flirting in front of our faces from day one."

"I never noticed," he said with a grin.

"Well, trust me, they have. Now I am sure that the two of them are over your house trying to blow each other's backs out, thinking that they are pulling off some elaborate plan to cheat right in front of our faces. I also realize that we don't appear to be any better people than them because here we are. So, let me ask you, why are you here?"

Michael stared at me, but did not respond. I lay my hand on top of his.

"Michael, you're not the type of man to go for some shit like this so let me fill in the blanks for you. You're here, not to fuck me, but to make love to me."

He grasped my hand. "I love you, Alicia."

"I love you, too. I've always loved you, Michael."

"So what do we do now?" he asked.

"We take our time, do all the things that we should have been doing for the past ten years, and make up for lost time."

I leaned over and flicked the tip of my tongue in his ear.

"And then tomorrow," I added, "we'll do whatever we feel should be done."

## TAYE

When I rang the doorbell at Michael and Marissa's house, my dick was already standing at attention. Just the thought of fucking Marissa was all the stimulation it took. Then she opened the door and had on this smoking red teddy that was so sheer that I could see her pert, dark brown nipples playing peekaboo with me.

"Come on in," she said in that seductive accent of hers. "I've been waiting. What took you so long?"

"I got here as fast as I could."

"Just don't come too fast once you climb inside my sugary walls."

With that, she turned around and I followed her scrumptious ass into the living room. Her ass was bouncing up and down and her cheeks moved in perfect unision. It was a lovely vision and I made a mental note that I was definitely going to "hit it from the back."

"Taye, I want you to do me a favor," Marissa said.

I gazed into her light brown eyes. "Anything for you, baby."

"Michael's a great lover."

I hated it when she said that. Even though Michael was my best friend, I did not want to hear shit about him being a great lover. For a man, any man, to hear about another man's skills in the bedroom, was a letdown.

She bit her bottom lip. "But . . ."

I loved hearing that "but." It meant that something was lacking and I planned to make sure I filled in the blanks.

"But what?" I asked. "What do you need Big Daddy to do for you?"

Calling myself "Big Daddy" put her on notice that I had a big-ass dick. Truth be known, that was my only reservation. There was no question that I was slanging something major between my legs, but I had no clue how I measured up to Michael. All men have that "size factor" issue. No matter how mandigo they might be, someone else is always holding more meat. As much as women try to deny it, they love big dicks.

"I've always had this fantasy," Marissa said. "Ever since I was a little girl, back when I would watch my *abuela* baking cookies."

*"Abuela?"*

Marissa giggled. She had such a beautiful smile. "My grandmother."

"Oh, okay. So, what's your fantasy?"

"Come into the kitchen and I will show you."

She beckoned me with her index finger and I followed.

There was a bowl of flour on the table and a huge sack of additional flour beside it. There was also a bottle of vanilla flavoring and a bag of chocolate chips.

"What's all this?" I asked, excited. Alicia would never have gone for any freaky shit.

Marissa picked up the bottle of vanilla. "I want to get naked and cover our bodies with flour. Then I want to play find the wet spot. You ready for this?"

I grinned. "I was born ready."

Once Marissa and I were covered in flour, which was a strange-ass feeling, I had her lie on the table on top of a cookie sheet. I poured some of the vanilla flavoring on her clean-shaven pussy and sprinkled some chocolate chips on top. Then I commenced eating my homemade chocolate-chip cookie dough. It was better than any ice cream.

Speaking of ice, I went to the freezer and got a couple of ice cubes. I rubbed them over Marissa's nipples while I ate her out. She moaned and screamed out with delight. A couple of times she tried to pull away from me—I was giving her one hell of a tongue-lashing—but I was relentless with her pussy.

The ceiling fan was on high but I was giving the fast-moving blades a run for their money with my tongue. Marissa's pussy had a totally different taste than Alicia's, but they were both good. For a moment, I did feel a twinge of panic. If I was in Michael's kitchen eating his woman out with vanilla and chocolate chips, what the hell was he doing with my wife?

My panic vanished when Marissa propped herself up on her elbows, gazed into my eyes and whispered, "I want you to dick-feed me, *Papi!*"

Within ten seconds, I had switched places with her. She did not hesitate to wrap her succulent lips around me and it seemed like she was starving for dick. Damn, Michael was one lucky man if he was getting head like that every night. Alicia had never been one to suck my dick a lot. It was more like she would do me a favor, instead of her actually enjoying giving me pleasure. I would often have to beg for it.

"Oooh, you taste so good," Marissa said when she came up for air. "I love your big dick, your daddy dick!"

"And I love you for loving my daddy dick," I replied. "You can have all the daddy dick you want, baby. Wait till I get you on your back. You might go into shock."

"Umm, I've never had someone put me into shock before. You really think you can do that, *Papi?*"

"Shit, no doubt," I bragged, now confident that I would fuck her better than Michael or die trying. "I only hope you can handle all this dick up in you."

Then . . . it happened. I came when I wasn't ready to come. I shot a load that was unbelievable and damn near hit the blades of the ceiling fan.

"Damn, *Papi!*" Marissa said, then laughed. "I barely got started."

I got down off the table. "Don't worry, baby. I'm going to get hard again and then I'm going to blow your damn back out."

She pouted. "I sure hope so, because Michael can fuck me all night long."

The disappointment in her voice was ego-shattering. That was it. I had to rise to the top of my game.

## ALICIA

I was still wrapped in Michael's arms when Taye came home the next morning. We were awakened by the door slamming, not closing.

"Alicia! Alicia, where are you?" he yelled out from the bottom of the stairs.

Common sense should have told me to try to cover myself quickly, even though Taye was the one who had arranged the entire swap thing. But I did not want to cover up anything; I wanted him to see me with Michael.

He came storming into the room. "What the fuck is this?" Taye asked angrily as Michael and I sat up in the bed.

Michael stated groggily, "Hey, Taye. Back already? I thought we weren't due to see you until later this afternoon."

"Well, this is still my damn house." Taye came at him. "Don't the two of you look cozy?"

"Taye, don't start tripping," Michael said. "Did you have a good time with Marissa?"

"Yes, Taye," I said saracastically, jumping all in the mix. "Did you have a good time?"

Taye glared at me. "From the looks of it, you sure did."

I grinned mischieviously. "I damn sure did." I paused. "In fact, I had the time of my life."

Taye came closer to the bed and yanked my arm. "What the fuck do you mean by that?"

Michael reached over and grabbed his wrist. "Let her go, man. What's wrong with you?"

Taye glared at him. "Stay out of this. This is my business. Why don't you go home and handle yours?"

Michael continued to pull on his wrist. "I'm not going anywhere unless you let Alicia go and I'm convinced you're not going to do something foolish."

Taye released my arm. The pain in his eyes was evident. "I've already done something foolish. I'm not going to hurt my wife, but can you please leave?"

Michael looked at me. "Are you going to be okay?"

"Yes, I'll be fine. We'll talk later."

"What do you mean? You'll talk later?!" Taye yelled. "You don't need to talk to him about a fucking thing!"

I surpressed a smile. Fucking was exactly what I intended to talk to Michael about, among other things.

Both Taye and I watched Michael get dressed. It never ceases to amaze me how comfortable men are with their nudity. Women might take two years before they feel at ease about walking around the house naked in front of their man, but men will walk around in the buff the day they meet you.

I could tell that Taye was trying to figure out whose dick was bigger. Since Michael was soft, he had no idea . . . but I did. Michael was definitely holding more.

Before he walked out of the bedroom, Michael turned to me. I could tell he was searching for the right words and was concerned about how Taye would react if he said what he wanted to say. We both knew the truth about our feelings so I made it clear that he did not have to even go there.

"Michael, we'll talk later," I whispered. "Just go, please!"

With that, the love of my life was gone. But not for long.

Taye stood there, staring.

"Don't you dare," I said once I heard the front door close. "Don't you dare pull some self-righteous shit on me, Taye. All of this was your doing."

"Go take a shower. You reek of him," Taye said. "And then you need to change the sheets."

I got up and headed for the bathroom, not because he told me to. I did want to bathe so I could get the hell out of there.

Before I climbed into the shower, I yelled out to Taye. "You change the damn sheets!"

*Three months later*

## TAYE

I could not believe that Alicia left me for my best friend. Michael, that rat bastard, was lucky that I did not kill his ass. I found out that when she went out the next day, while I was remaking the bed from their tryst, she ran directly back to his arms. They met at a motel and fucked all day. They tried to tell me, later on, that they had always been in love but had kept away from each other since Alicia and I were already hooked up. Alicia said that she had wanted to be with Michael from day one, but I had approached her first. What the fuck?!

I was so mad when they told me they planned to make a life together that I went over to claim my prize, Marissa. She did not want to be bothered. In fact, she laughed in my face.

After I had shot that first load the night of the swap, I could not get another erection to save my life. I think it was because I had built up so much anticipation, or it could have been subconscious guilt about cheating on my wife.

I made the biggest mistake of my life when I suggested swapping mates with Michael. Never, in a million years, would I have foreseen what would happen. It is going to take a long time for me to get over Alicia. I would do anything to get her back. Take a lesson from me. An even swap might not be a swindle but make damn sure that it is an even swap before you make the deal. Mine sure as hell wasn't!

# About the Contributors

**Anna Black** resides in the Midwest, where she finds that reading and writing erotica helps to make the winters somewhat bearable. She has previously published in *The MILF Anthology*. Although she enjoys writing short stories, she's finally settling down to write a novel.

**BlissDulce** is a former exotic dancer who now lives in your neighborhood. At least once a month she sneaks a peek into the black satin chest that holds her diamond-encrusted keepsake G-string, sighs, and wonders if she will ever dare to work a pole again.

**Gwyneth Bolton** is the author of three romance novels, one erotic romance novel, and an erotic romance novella. She loves hearing from readers and can be reached at gwynethbolton@syr.edu. To find out more about Gwyneth and her novels, visit her website at www.gwynethbolton .com.

**Kathleen Bradean**'s stories can be found in *The Best Women's Erotica 2007*, *The Mammoth Book of Best New Erotica 6*, and *She's On Top*. Visit her blog at: www.KathleenBradean .blogspot.com.

**Kaia Danielle** would like to thank Kimberly, Nathasha, and Steven for their encouragement and support on this project. She dedicates this story to everyone who's ever lived with "The Ache." Check out Kaia's website at www .kaiawrites.com for updates on her future projects and information on the real-life Afro-Brazilian hero Zumbi.

**Leni Davidson** is formerly from North Carolina but now lives in Woodbridge, Virginia. "Picture Perfect" is her first published story.

**Penelope Flynn,** a South Florida native, now makes her home in the Southwestern United States, where she produces literary works of erotica, horror, science fiction, and fantasy. Updates regarding her current and planned works can be found at www.PenelopeFlynn.com.

**Jordan Grace** is the pen name of a writer lucky enough to call the beautiful islands of the Bahamas home. Her first novel, *Loving Gabriel,* was published by Whiskey Creek Press in 2007. For more info visit her at www.myspace.com/ blackbutterfly74.

**Kimberly King,** a Chicago native and Atlanta resident, has written several confessions stories and articles published by

Dorchester Media. She and her alter ego, KD King, are hard at work on several paranormal erotic series. Check her, and the infamous No Sex and the City blog, out by visiting www.myspace.com/pornwriter. Or go to www.kimberly king.net.

A native New Yorker, **Gracie C. McKeever** has authored several novels, among them the Siren Bestsellers, *Emilia's Emancipation, Once Upon a Time—Fairy Tale Collection, Eternal Designs,* and *The Wolf in the Mansion* (www.sirenpub.com). She has been writing since the ripe old age of seven, when two younger brothers were among her earliest, captive audience for various short-story readings and performances. It wasn't until 2001, however, that Gracie caught the erotica bug that produced an instant affinity for the genre and spawned her first erotic romance, *Beneath the Surface,* published in 2006 by Siren Publishing, Inc. Visit Gracie at www.graciecmckeever.com.

**Patt Mihailoff** is the author of *Two Fantasy Novels, Over 100 True Confessions Stories.* She lives with her husband in New Jersey.

**Mitch** is a retired university professor who researched and wrote on one of the social sciences for a major Southern institution. He has an extensive professional bibliography, has presented research papers on five of the seven continents, and has served on the editorial boards of a number of leading interdisciplinary journals. Writing fiction and erotica was only discovered after retirement. This story is his first published erotica.

**CB Potts** is a full-time writer who makes her living tucked away in the Adirondack Mountains, not far from where "Alibi" takes place. She splits her time between ghostwriting books for business professionals and penning romantic tales for lovers of every persuasion. You can find out more at www.cbpotts.net.

**Kim Rose** is a writer from New York.

**E. Charles Smith** lives in Detroit, Michigan, with his wife and their five children. By day, he works as an engineering technician with a Detroit-based geotechnical engineering firm. By night, he moonlights as an aspiring author of erotica fiction.

As a child, **Hugh Smith** was privy to a rich Jamaican storytelling tradition, which he credits as his inspiration. He enjoys writing and reading across all genres and is a contributor to www.oystersandchocolate.com. Hugh is currently hard at work on other writing projects, among them a novel, a book of short stories, and several children's picture books. Hugh lives with his family in New Jersey. He loves to hear from readers and may be reached at hugh.smith05@gmail.com.

Growing up, **Amie Stuart** wanted to be a lawyer and psychologist. Obviously, she's seen the error in her ways, though she's never settled down into any one profession until she took up writing. She's a native Texan who divides her time between three crazy cats, two hilarious kids, and one demanding muse.

**Zane** is the publisher of Strebor Books, an imprint of Atria Books/Simon & Schuster. She is the *New York Times* bestselling author of more than ten titles, as well as a television and film producer. You can join her mailing list by sending a blank email to eroticanoir-subscribe@topica.com or visit her MySpace page at www.myspace.com/zaneland.